PRAISE FOR
ALWAYS THE FIRST TO DIE

"R. J. Jacobs's *Always the First to Die* is an utterly unique thriller that combines horror movies, hurricanes, and deadly secrets from the past. It's also an intense ride about a mother who will do anything to save her daughter. Fast-paced, suspenseful, stormy, and definitely not to be missed."

—David Bell, *USA Today* bestselling author of *The Finalists*

"A storm is coming, and its name is *Always the First to Die*. It's a breathtaking thriller filled with jaw-dropping twists and lump-in-the-throat emotion—a love letter to cinema and family. R. J. Jacobs is a masterful storyteller. A must read."

—Alex Finlay, author of *The Night Shift* and *Every Last Fear*

"In *Always the First to Die*, fans of horror movie tropes will fly through this fast-paced thriller. A deliciously wicked read."

—Rea Frey, award-winning author of *Not Her Daughter* and *Secrets of Our House*

D0043264

ALWAYS THE FIRST TO DIE

ALWAYS THE FIRST TO DIE

R. J. JACOBS

Published by Sourcebooks Landmark, an imprint of Sourcebooks
P.O. Box 4410, Naperville, Illinois 60567-4410
(630) 961-3900
sourcebooks.com

Library of Congress Cataloging-in-Publication Data

Names: Jacobs, R. J., author.
Title: Always the first to die / R.J. Jacobs.
Description: Naperville, Illinois : Sourcebooks Landmark, 2022.
Identifiers: LCCN 2022006651 (print) | LCCN 2022006652
(ebook) | (trade paperback) | (epub)
Subjects: LCGFT: Novels.
Classification: LCC PS3610.A356486 A79 2022 (print) | LCC PS3610.A356486
   (ebook) | DDC 813/.6--dc23/eng/20220225
LC record available at https://lccn.loc.gov/2022006651
LC ebook record available at https://lccn.loc.gov/2022006652

Printed and bound in Canada.
MBP 10 9 8 7 6 5 4 3

This book is dedicated to you, the reader. To quote Carl Jung, "The debt we owe to the play of imagination is incalculable."

"Every love story is a ghost story."

—DAVID FOSTER WALLACE

"The fundamental truth of existence is fear, nothing else compares. To experience terror is to live with no illusions. Try it sometime."

—RICK PLUMMER

PROLOGUE

The air buzzes with silence while I listen at your door. Soon, faint sounds emerge within the silence: the groan of truck tires on US 1, a woman laughing hysterically in the distance, the hush of waves rolling onto the beach. But nothing from inside your room.

Part of me hates that you'll never know what I'm about to do. It's a plot too intricate for you to have dreamed it up yourself, one so brilliant you'd be proud. Waiting for it to begin has been agonizing.

And I know better than to rush. I've waited long enough for it to begin.

Are you afraid? Like the others? Of the legend of the ghost haunting your estate?

You give fans of your films "a promise of fear."

"The fundamental truth of existence is fear."

That's your famous quote, right? You're so proud of it all. The irony makes me smile.

Once, I caught your eyes on me, your gaze lingering just a second too long. I wondered if you understood the truth. But suspecting is different than knowing, right? If you really knew what I am, your expression would have betrayed you. I would have seen something in your eyes besides the foggy confusion that washes over you all too often now. For a supposed genius, you can be painfully dense.

But you'll be happy you know me soon enough, I'm sure of it. You'll cling to me when this is all over.

Desperately.

You'll have to.

Now my sunburnt skin tingles as an eerie calm comes over me. The faint light from the hallway enters your room before I do, and I wonder: Should I be more nervous than I am? I close the door behind me as I quietly slip inside, listening for movement as the latch falls, and I let go of the knob. The rich scent of the aftershave you used earlier hits my nose—part leather, part citrus. It smells like wealth. It smells like exclusion.

No, it smells like vanity.

It makes me want to slit your throat, right this second, as my face warms with rage. I grind my teeth and swallow to choke it down.

Now I face you. I shake my head and clench my fists, and I step closer. Moonlight pours in through the window on my right, turning everything pale blue. The light shimmers, just slightly, from being reflected off the bay.

My shadow falls across your bed. I reach into my back pocket for the metal scissors, warm and heavy in my palm, their blades so sharp they threaten my thumb's skin each time I test them. The blanket covering you rises gently then falls. Your eyeglasses rest on the nightstand beside your glass of water. In the washed-out light, I study the curve of your cheek, the angle of your jaw, the three wrinkle lines gashed across your forehead while you rest in almost heartbreaking peacefulness.

You are seventy-two years old, and your life is nearing its end.

But your legacy, the films you made, are immortal. Your legions of fans, still strong even after all these years (guys in black T-shirts, film students, midnight moviegoers), made you a star.

And your box office sales made you incredibly wealthy.

None of it would have been possible without the terror you stoked in your actors.

None of it possible without the ghost haunting your estate.

You encouraged people to believe in it, and they did!

And the money was fun, wasn't it?

You said in an interview once money gave you incalculable convenience. That phrase stuck in my mind, like a vague sense of nostalgia for things that never happened.

I lean over you now, so close I can hear you breathe. I could count your eyelashes from this distance. I open the scissors and cut, here and there. You barely twitch when the blades scrape, then take what I need and tuck it safely away.

Now, that wasn't so bad, was it? I should have been a surgeon, not a specter, I think, smirking as I move toward the door, just as silently now as on the way in. The doorknob is cool against my palm when I grasp it. But now, I hear the rustling of your sheets and your bed creak as you sit up behind me.

I stop, hold still. The ceiling fan casts a faint, slowly rotating shadow on the floor. I watch it as I carefully pivot toward you, holding my breath as my hand finds the blade again. I don't want to kill you now, but I will. Oh, how the things I should say to you fly through my brain.

You rub your hand over your face then fumble for your glasses, knocking over the water glass beside you.

My heart pounds as you curse at the shattered glass and watch the spill spread, mirroring the moonlight farther and farther as it creeps outward.

I open the door, and a sliver of lights cuts across the room.

"Who's there?" you call out.

But I am already gone, running down the hallway, my pulse jackhammering in my neck and chest.

I'm laughing.

I'm a monster now, like the ones you created.

I'm here, a real ghost, my steps echoing in the stairwell, then disappearing as I rush into the night and the hush of sand.

I heard genuine fear in your voice a moment ago.

Fear like you've promised everyone, like the fear that made you.

You'll reassure yourself by thinking I'm imaginary, that there are no such things as ghosts. You'll tell yourself I'm something you made up.

But that's just vanity.

You're about to learn, Rick Plummer, just how real I am.

Chapter ONE

OCTOBER 31ST

Go.

I toss my suitcase in the backseat of my Volvo and drive. The tires splash through puddles while the radio blares the music I listened to yesterday, late Beatles, a song meant to cheer everyone up. The knob clicks as I quickly switch it off. I glance at the fuel gauge—I have just enough to get me halfway into the Keys and back to Miami, where there may still be a radio station functioning.

I hope.

But I don't want to stop for gas. Stopping will only let worry in. Even *more* worry and fear than I already have coursing through me.

I squint at the sun rising in the direction of my seventeen-year-old daughter, Quinn, who I need to get to as quickly as possible.

What Quinn did is what teenagers do. She fibbed, I tell myself. It doesn't make her a terrible person. It makes her human.

Except this time, it's more than a simple fib, more than a neglected homework assignment or having "forgotten" to mention that a friend's parents wouldn't be home to supervise during a party.

What Quinn did was *lie*.

Boldly and cunningly, and with chilling ease, if I'm being honest with myself, which I'm not sure I'm ready to do. Honesty would mean recalibrating how I think of her (still somewhat innocent, too close to me to do something so hurtful). I need to make sure she's safe first, and *then* I can question how she's capable of creating such a deceptive story about where she went.

I play our last conversation over and over in my head as I drive. I hadn't heard from her at all yesterday, nor had I seen anything of hers on social media. Quinn had told me she would be on a school trip for dates that were slightly too specific—the *exact* dates of the visit with her grandfather I'd forbidden her to take. How could I have been so utterly, stupidly naive? I tried her phone two times yesterday afternoon, and the call went to voicemail.

Then, she called me, and the second she answered, I knew what had happened. The nagging intuition I'd been ignoring evaporated, and the vagueness of her cover story sharpened. Is that how a lie is recognized? Gradually, then all at once? I heard the ripping wind in the background, and my gut told me exactly where she was. Suddenly, all I needed was confirmation.

Her voice, hoarse and afraid. "Mom?"

"Quinn, tell me where you are."

But inside, I already knew. In the background, there was a crashing sound, like a vase hitting a floor. She screamed, and my stomach knotted. "You're with your grandfather right now, right? In the *Keys*?"

"Mom, I'm *sorry*." She didn't have to say "yes."

I realized the screen of my phone hadn't turned blurry. It just looked that way because of how my hand shook. I pictured Quinn tucked into the enormous living room, probably beneath his shadow-box-framed dive knife from his movie *Red Sky*, and could hear the thump of the wind batting against the wooden sides of the estate.

My mind had been a sluggish detective, but it became a whirlwind, assessing Quinn's safety and the sequence of events that put her in the Keys with google-like speed. All the facts were clicking.

She started to deliver some explanation, but I cut her off abruptly. "Put your grandfather on the phone," I said.

A second later, Rick came on the line, out of breath. "I'm sorry, Lexi. We got caught off guard by this."

I could have screamed a million questions at Rick about how Quinn got down there in the first place, but I forced them all aside for the time being. The exasperated words that did escape my mouth were, "How did you not see the news?"

Rick explained they'd been deep in the mangroves when the sky began to turn.

Of course, I thought, *they had no idea.* The weather had probably been perfect, the way it is just before and after a major storm. I know how time melts away on the water, just like I remember the sinking, emptying feeling of a plummeting barometer. Rick's excuse was believable, reasonable, and extremely unlucky. He mumbled something like, "...your permission to come." The line cut in and out. At least he sounded sober, I thought, which was a relief. "I'm not sure we can leave now," Rick continued, eventually.

"Can't leave?" I asked.

But I knew he was right. Evacuations have windows. Once one closes, it's better to stay where you are than risk driving to the mainland. Rick was getting his news from the same meteorologists I'd been watching for three hours, except now it was too late.

"The eye is going to pass over us in a few hours," Rick said.

There was another crashing sound in the background, louder than the first. I scurried around collecting my things into a bag, even as I heard the TV announcer say that no one would be going in or out of the Keys until morning.

Period.

I could hear the same broadcast echo distantly in the call's background.

I knew boats and channels and weather as well as anyone. Even now. And I knew this storm was going to be dangerous.

Even deadly.

I pictured the darkening horizon and imagined the delicate sound of thunder in the distance. Unrealistically, I thought I would have known when to evacuate. I would have triple-checked the storm track, or would not have gone far from shore, or would have returned a faster way. I wouldn't have allowed Quinn to come to the Keys in the first place—the last place on earth I wanted her to be.

If I'd been there, I would have gotten her out.

"Here's Quinn," Rick said before passing the phone off to her.

"Everything's going to be okay, Mom." Her optimism terrified me. Of course, she thought the storm would turn out okay. She was seventeen and felt invincible. To her, a hurricane seemed like an adventure, something she could tell stories about later to her friends or maybe post about on Instagram. I wanted to scream that she had no idea how *not okay* Hurricane Stephen was about to make everything. She'd never lived through a Category 4 storm. But I had, and Rick had, too. That's why he sounded scared. She'd never seen a building blown to bits or seen someone die at the Pinecrest Estate like I had.

The sun was going down.

Stop. Think.

I asked Quinn, "Are you in the main house?"

"Yeah, on the first floor."

Despite everything I'd seen happen there, I felt a tiny flutter of relief. The Pinecrest was more than a century old and had withstood hurricanes that had blown away more modern buildings. I closed my eyes and tried to picture the estate's layout, estimating the safest space within the interior. The estate spread over fifteen acres, with the main building facing westward toward the Gulf. It was three stories tall, the top two consisting of mainly guest rooms with multiple windows. Rick had always maintained what looked like a lobby on the first floor, including the original front desk. A large, ornate staircase with a carved wooden banister led upward. Beneath it was the center of the house and the most protected place. "Quinn, listen, I want you to find the door below the staircase, the storage area. That's where I want you to ride out the storm. Do you hear me?"

"Yes, okay."

"I want you to find some empty containers and start filling them up with water."

"Granddad's already doing that. There's more water than we'll..."

"Then go to the pantry and find some food—things you may need to eat for the next twelve hours. Then candles and matches. Are there oil lamps?"

"Oil lamps?" She asked as if I'd just asked the dumbest question in history. I heard the echo of Rick's voice in the background. Behind her came the shrieking howl of one of the estate's shutters being blown off by the increasing winds. That caught Quinn's attention. She paused before saying, "Yes, Granddad is holding up a lamp right now. He says we're going to the interior storage room like you said. No windows."

"Good. Stay on the phone with me."

"Mom, we'll be fine, I promise."

I wanted to believe her.

"But there's something else, Mom. I need to tell you something..."

The broadcaster talking on my TV said, "It's going to be a long night for residents. Let's just hope and pray for whoever didn't make it out."

I heard another violent gust of wind, then something heavy slamming down. Terror squeezed my insides as I glimpsed the possibility of losing her, a feeling almost as strong as love itself. The world, I saw just then, would be unrecoverable if she was gone.

The call was breaking up, but I heard her voice say, "Mom, I found something here. Something *strange*."

The wind gusted again. "What? Quinn?"

"...Dad's. I found...*something* is happening here."

Then came a sound like a car crash.

Quinn screamed, and then the line went dead.

⤳

I'd tried to stop her from going.

Two months ago, when Quinn walked into the kitchen holding her phone ready to make a "proposal," I was semi-prepared for the conversation. I'd read online Rick was going forward with developing a sequel to *Breathless*, but I probably would have guessed what Quinn wanted anyway from the mischievous smile on her lips. She sharply inhaled as she sat across from me, the way she did before asking for favors. "Mom, you know how you said I should take some risks and put myself out there? You know how you've said before that no dream was too big if I worked at it?"

Teenage manipulation skills can be predatory. "I think I was talking about taking AP Lit at the time," I said.

"Right, but there's more to life than just school? Right? There's being book smart, and then there's real-world experience."

Your father was a writer, and I'm a librarian. Stick to book smart.

I bent to pet Phoebe, her soft fur brushing against my calf as I looked over the bridge of my glasses at Quinn. "What are you asking?"

She cleared her throat, tucking her hair behind her ears. "You know the room in the estate where Dad was working still has all of his things in it. I have to get them, Mom, especially his typewriter. But it's more than that—I want to learn how films *get made*. I always have. And now's my *chance*. I just finished FaceTiming with Grandad, and he offered to let me help with the movie he's about to start making. He said production *starts* during my fall break and that I could help with other parts over some weekends and maybe during Thanksgiving break. And *maybe* a filmmaking story might look good on college application essays. He said there could be a small part for me. It's a tremendous opportunity."

Tremendous, I thought. Rick's word, surely. Imagining the faux kindliness of his pitch to her made my blood boil. And now here I was, positioned as the bad guy, the killer of fun, the dreaded responsible parent. Quinn pressed her elbows into the tabletop as the morning light paled her skin. Her blue eyes seemed so incredibly young.

"No," I said simply.

She pushed away from the table as if I'd slapped her. "What?! *Are you serious?* You can't stand in the way of this chance! Mom, it could make me..."

Famous, she was thinking, clearly.

Like the fame that destroyed *Breathless's* star, Marla Moretti. Or the fame that made Rick so very rich.

Or fame I'd tasted years ago, however briefly.

No, I knew better than to let her admire fame. I'd watched it literally set lives on fire.

I could, and I *would* stand in the way. The Pinecrest Estate's creepy relics and leftover props alone could have been enough for me to nix Quinn's trip. I could easily picture the estate decked out with Rick at the helm of a new production, new sets constructed, and the crew striding purposefully around. The scaffolding raised against the south side of the main building where the light rigs could shine down through the palms at night, and the bathrooms would all be covered with tarps to protect the grout from being stained red with fake blood. The props lined up in the trailers would look prepped for a serial killer convention. And Rick Plummer would be standing with his arms folded over his chest, leaning back on his heels while he scared the shit out of everyone, relishing every cry, every scream coming from the cast and crew.

No, I would never let my daughter set foot near that place.

"You just don't want me to spend time with Grandad. Do you?"

She had me there. She looked in my eyes and could see she'd hit the mark.

"You promised not to be a helicopter parent, remember?"

"This one's actually a pretty easy call," I said, willing myself to stay calm. "No way you're taking part, sorry."

"Oh, I get it, *you* got to star in a movie, but now are threatened that I might get the chance, too?" She coughed.

"Hey!" I said, feeling the sting of a verbal slap, myself. "I know this isn't a 'cool' decision, but I have to protect you."

"Yeah, right. Well, you're doing a great job, that's for sure. I'm completely and totally protected. I'll just tell Grandad, no, I'm not allowed."

"Fine with me."

"Or maybe *you* can explain. Oh, never mind, you're too scared to even have a conversation with him."

It was a low blow, and she knew it.

Even if "scared" was probably the right word. I hadn't spoken to

Rick since Cam—his son, my husband—disappeared more than a year earlier. Rick had reached out several times, but I'd angrily ignored his calls, blaming him for the senseless loss—blame that only made sense in the twisted logic of grief, but that I'd stubbornly held on to anyway. I deleted all of his voicemails, but I listened to one twice. He'd had too much to drink and was rambling. "You and Quinn are all I have left. I want to make sure you're were taken care of in the future," he'd stammered. Maybe it was his sincerity that caught my attention, tugging at my heartstrings. I nearly called back but wasn't ready to have a conversation with him. Either way, Quinn and I were busy moving and moving on, and the pace of life then was so incredibly fast. I had other things to think about.

And now Rick and I were estranged. I'd allowed, I suppose, or didn't disrupt his continuing relationship with Quinn, except that it led her and me to this moment—one that I could've navigated better because it was so predictable.

I rubbed the back of my neck.

I might have let her comment go if I'd been *less* upset and let Quinn go be "in her feelings," stewing over not having my permission to go back to the Pinecrest. But I knew that sharp barbs covered proportionate hurt when it came to teenagers. If she'd walked away right then, we'd have ended up resenting each other over the exchange.

And I knew she wanted to go to the Keys for other reasons but didn't want to say them.

I put my hand on her forearm before she could leave the table. "I know...what that place means to you, but you have to trust me. I'd let you go if I thought it was at all safe, believe me."

Her eyes brimmed with tears when she looked up. "Would you? You *never* did let me go, even when they searched. I wanted to see for myself because how could Dad have just..." She made a motion with her hands of air dispersing. *Vanish*, was what she meant. "Maybe they missed something he left there."

"I wish they had."

"How do you *know*, Mom? You don't."

Did I? *Know* he was gone? Or was I so tired of us both hurting last year that I'd needed her to move on?

My head dropped. It has been a conflict between us from the moment we got the call that Cam was missing: she wanted to go to the Keys to look for him. I'd said no way. I grew up in the Keys. I'd seen enough boating accidents to know how search and rescue efforts went and how often well-meaning would-be rescuers usually got in the way. It was heartbreaking to watch, but it happened again and again: family members flew in. They wanted to head right out onto the water to comb the area, unaware that the best way to search was looking down from a Cessna and that the chances of surviving in open water decreased exponentially by the hour. When the Coast Guard found the boat Cam took out, they estimated it had been adrift for twelve hours.

I had no idea how the accident happened, but it was apparent he was already gone. My chest ached for wanting to be wrong, but I knew the odds. If I'd been alone, I probably would have gone to look, too, if only just to go through the motions of searching. Maybe it would have been better, psychologically. And maybe in retrospect, staying away was the wrong call, but my protective instincts kicked in, and I anchored Quinn in our home where we could keep in contact with the Coast Guard just as easily.

Search parties established a perimeter and scoured the area. I helped them figure out how the tide and currents would have carried his boat from where he put in, and they went over that space tirelessly. I never let the word "suicide" be spoken around Quinn, and there was no note, but I always wondered. He could get so depressed.

"If we had gone down to look, you would have been—"

She interrupted. "In danger? Right?"

I swallowed and squeezed her forearm before sitting back. "Yeah. It's impossible to see much on the water, and you wouldn't have wanted to stop looking. The search planes were the best chance." I'd helped look for lost boaters four separate times when I was in high school, and none of the searches turned up anything at all. They all went on until the families collapsed, desperate and reckless with exhaustion. I wouldn't let Quinn go through the same thing.

"Quinn, do you think there's a *single day* I don't wish your dad was here? Every day that goes by, I wake up and put my hand where he slept."

The cracks in my heart were starting to show again. I took a breath and reeled them in.

"Grandad looked," she said quietly.

I actually bit my tongue. "Only because he wouldn't listen," I said.

"Mom, *talk to him*. Please. About me helping make this movie. Maybe there's something he could do that would make you feel safe about it. It's not as if I'd be down there alone. There'll be, like, tons and tons of grown-ups on that crew. If I were going to some beach house on break, it would be way more sketch."

I'd seen the kind of grown-ups that worked on Rick's movie sets and had to disagree.

"Maybe there's *some* way," she'd pleaded.

I'd folded my hands. "There isn't."

～

Now, I wring my hands around the steering wheel while the Everglades spreads out around me for four thousand square miles. Reeds and cypress swamps fly by my windows, the southern mainland a river of grass, feeding into the Ten Thousand Islands that reach mistily into Florida Bay. I glimpse a bolt of lightning in my rearview mirror, the rolling thunderclap catching up a few seconds later from the outer band of the storm. Fires in the Everglades sometimes start from a single strike, blazes so enormous they can cloud Miami with impenetrable smoke before a downpour sweeps them away.

Rain dots the windshield as I step on the accelerator and watch the Volvo's speedometer sluggishly rise. When I bought this car, I imagined it would be the one I would teach Quinn to drive in. I pictured it parked in the tiny covered parking spot in front of our new apartment, not weaving around hurricane debris. But does anyone anticipate emergencies before they actually happen? My late husband, Cam, had flashes, odd premonitions here and there. Once, in college, he found a set of keys I'd lost in the middle of a field following a concert. It seemed miraculously intuitive. Another time, a few years ago, Cam woke up one Saturday morning saying he'd had a dream our house had caught fire. I tried to brush it off, but his seriousness shook me. He went to the hardware store and bought a fire extinguisher and smoke detectors for the hallway and bedrooms. The next night, the shrill scream of one going off awakened us. Quinn was crying, and there was a haze of smoke—some lint in the dryer had caught fire. Cam rushed to the cabinet beneath the sink, found the extinguisher he'd bought earlier that day, and put out the flames.

None of us slept the rest of the night.

"That was some *Final Destination* stuff," he'd said, sipping a bottle of beer.

"No kidding," I'd tentatively agreed, my heart racing.

He and I used to smile and call them "The Shining," but he hadn't had one in years before he passed. Not that he told me, at least.

Whatever those were, I wish I'd had that gift.

Two days ago, I'd ignorantly looked into Quinn's undilated pupils as I helped her pack, talking through the details of what she might want to wear during her school-sponsored fall-break trip to Disney World. We estimated whether she'd be warm enough in just a sweatshirt (some of the indoor rides like Pirates of the Caribbean can get chilly) and how much spending money she should allot for meals—with her knowing the trip itself was pure fiction, all the while. She'd gone so far as to register, then canceled her reservation so none of the chaperones would realize she was missing from the roster and call me. She'd told me she'd paid for the park tickets with money saved from babysitting.

Now I began to wonder if the babysitting had even happened.

The deception burns behind my eyes, a feeling that might push me to cry, but there's also the sinking of deep hurt, a recognition of being slightly more alone in life than I realized. I thought I knew my daughter better. And I'd wanted...no, I'd *needed* her to go on that Disney trip too. I needed some time to reflect. Not just because single parenting turned out to be harder than I'd imagined, but because two weeks earlier, I'd discovered something I'd never expected.

Something I've told no one.

So even though I'd said no to Quinn going to the Keys, I then compromised, allowing her to go on the trip to Disney World instead.

And she lied as she packed her clothes, then ran to work on the horror film with Rick.

Only to get trapped in a hurricane.

I try Quinn's phone again, and the call goes straight to voicemail.

I try Rick's and get the same result.

Knowing the two of them must have colluded makes me grit my teeth. She's a teenager. At least she has an excuse. But how irresponsible, how absolutely reckless can one man be? The answer is pretty damn reckless. The same kind of recklessness that prompts a man to produce a sequel to a movie that became a curse. *Breathless*—Rick's most famous film premiered in 1999—was set on the Pinecrest Estate, which he bought before filming. And even after everything that had happened, he was arrogant enough to make a second.

It was big news in the summer of '98 that Rick planned to film parts of his magnum opus in the Keys. The Pinecrest was less than two miles from the modest house where I lived with my stepfather, Don, and at the time, there was no one *like* Rick on the island, who seemed to *enjoy* standing out or else didn't get that he did. Before Mom married Don and moved us to the Keys, I'd never heard of Islamorada, an incorporated village of five islands situated between Key West and Miami. Most people know it as "The Sportfishing Capital of the World" because it sits in migratory routes between the Gulf of Mexico and the Atlantic. Still, only a few of the residents actually fished for leisure. Mostly, the 6,100 or so people living there made their money facilitating tourist fishing or tending to one of the local hotels. Growing up, our neighbors were charter guides, bartenders, maids, shopkeepers.

On the other hand, Rick special-ordered his groceries (there were rumors about what they contained). He wore mostly black, paraded his mistresses around local restaurants, and drove a Maserati with a specialty tag that said: DZE 185.

Locals' eyes rolled.

He made seven films altogether, beginning with *Ax Handle* in 1998 and concluding with *Gone but Not Forgotten* in 2004. *Breathless* is the one I remember best—not because it was Rick's most critically acclaimed film, or because it was by far his most commercially successful. I remember *Breathless* best because it was the backdrop of meeting Cam, his son, who worked as a second assistant director while a bunch of us theater kids volunteered to be extras. And because of the tragedy on the set that scarred us all but made the movie famous.

Cam was the one who asked our high school drama club, "Would any of you guys want to be part of a horror movie?"

What teenager wouldn't?

After I left the Keys to go to college, I intended to never return, partly because I never got over what I saw—what *everyone* on the set witnessed—on the last day of filming.

Could I have guessed three days ago that Rick and Quinn might later cook up a scheme?

Yes. I could have, and I *should* have.

Rick's capable of anything, I remind myself.

My cheek registers pain when I bit it after hanging up with Quinn. I pass another car and glance at the high, heavy clouds, reaching upward like smoke from an explosion, then adjust the windshield wipers as I slow at the toll booth, where I-75 hits Naples. I hand two dollars to the toll collector, who clearly wonders why I'm headed east. Who drives into a devastated area besides first responders or the National Guard? I'm obviously neither.

My phone rings, and I hastily flip it over. It's Don: not who I need to hear from right now. I picture him in his cargo shorts and white socks, the faded Navy tattoo on his forearm flexing a little as he grips his old flip phone impatiently.

I can't believe I lived with this man for fifteen years.

Whenever I talk to Don, part of me forgets I'm a thirty-eight-year-old librarian and feels instead like I'm eight years old again, the age I was when Mom died, when Don became, oddly enough, my only parent. He moved to central Florida to live among other retirees years ago, but he's surely seen the same images on television that I have and wants to make sure Quinn and I are safe and sound on the west coast of Florida.

I hydroplane for a second and reset my grip on the steering wheel, then answer. "Don, hi, quite a storm, right?"

"Bet you're glad not to still be living in the Keys this morning." Practical Don gets to the point right away. After my mom died, he was a taskmaster and nearly worked me to death at his marina but revealed himself as a loving grandparent to Quinn. "Have to wonder if the famous director got out in time and found a way to be reached by agents, fans, or whoever. I read he's making a sequel to the...original movie." Don had been mistrustful of Rick Plummer since I first mentioned him in 1998. It's because he probably viewed the movies Rick made—about serial killers and haunted houses and zombies—as completely unacceptable forms of entertainment. He never forgave me for starring in one.

"I wouldn't know much about it," I say.

Don's thoughtful in his own way, but I have no capacity to converse with him.

We talk for another minute about the weather before he says something that sounds like "okay," and we hang up. Growing up in the Keys, I'd learned to go about daily life while watching forecasts out of the corner of my eye, but this was no usual storm. It was late, for one thing. Hurricane season was nearly over. By the time Hurricane Stephen spun to life, eighteen other storms had already come and gone. So far, all had tracked right along their predicted paths. Everyone had gotten used to trusting the computer models and letting their guard down. Keys residents take pride in their toughness. Tossing aside concerns about storms, dismissing alarmist forecasts were practically a local pastime when I was a kid. And I could see why—even a Category 1 storm might only knock down a few loose tree limbs or tear into unsecured awnings. Sometimes it flooded the streets a few inches if it moved slowly enough. But that was what I missed: Stephen's speed. He was twitchy, edgy—an angry late-season storm that refused predictability. Floridians might have been over hurricane season, but that didn't mean hurricane season was over.

For a week, Stephen had been headed directly toward Galveston, Texas, following a nearly straight line across the Gulf of Mexico. I'd felt bad for Texans since Harvey's flooding devastated Houston in 2017, and I'd envisioned sending positive energy westward. It's a little too woo for some people, but in my mind, protective energy was pink, like the stripe in my hair.

Each time I glanced at a screen, Stephen strengthened. First, from a tropical depression to a tropical storm, and then to a Category 1 hurricane.

On the day Quinn left, warnings began to post from New Orleans to Corpus Christi, only to see Stephen's eye veer north toward Pensacola. From Southwest Florida, that still sounded safe, easily a ten-hour drive from us. And I'd assumed she would be far enough inland in Orlando that she might only see some rain and an occasional downed tree limb.

If everyone canceled plans in Florida every time it rained, nothing would ever happen. Forecasters assured us that neither Southwest Florida nor the Keys would take a direct hit. Stephen, they said, would be nothing but an occasional rainmaker. I hardly paid attention when Stephen strengthened again to a Category 2 storm and pictured newscasters rushing around the northern Gulf Coast, trying to plant themselves as close to the projected path as possible to capture the most dramatic footage. I radiated positive energy toward the journalists, too. I missed the headlines saying Stephen had again been upgraded to a Category 3. It had been a hot summer, the news had said, and the Gulf's waters were especially warm and nourishing to a storm that year.

By Saturday afternoon, I needed to check in with Quinn. After half a dozen unanswered texts, I began to panic.

That's when I finally got a hold of her and learned the truth. After the call with Quinn dropped, I was glued to the news all night. I read news stories, scoured every Facebook and Twitter post that went up. The Keys had no power. The streets were underwater. Some neighborhoods were being completely destroyed.

I'd slept for a few minutes. Maybe. And then it was daylight. I shook my head to dislodge the bits of my dream about Cam. I miss him, I don't hesitate to admit that to myself, but I don't miss his angst, that Plummer family trait. Or Cam's depression over his writing career, fueled by wanting to measure up to his father, the most famous horror film director in American history.

Now, driving toward the place I never wanted Quinn to go, I wonder: Could the storm have blown the Pinecrest apart?

The Pinecrest Estate. The place has loomed in my memory for so long. It's hard to picture it in disarray, even if I know it's vulnerable to hundred-mile-per-hour winds. I try to imagine the shutters blown off, the wide-plank wood floors flooded, the steep, imposing roof in tatters.

I think ahead to what I'll soon pass: the memorial beside mile-marker eighty-two. I didn't pay much attention to it as a kid, but the remembrance is suddenly startlingly relevant. The marker went up after the Labor Day Hurricane in 1935. Four hundred and twenty-three people were killed that day. I couldn't wrap my head around that number when I was growing up, but now I realize what that must have meant: the complete devastation of a community. Whole families must have been lost.

Some victims, surely, never found.

Now, the sameness of the road hypnotizes me. The tall reeds on either side sweep like curtains against the screen in my mind. I turn the radio on to distract myself but find only static or fading signals. Last night, Quinn had meant to sound brave, to reassure *me*, even while the wind howled behind her—that baritone, train-like growl that took me back to my own childhood in the Keys, where I thought I had left it. It cried out in the dream that woke me this morning before there was enough light to let me start driving east, then south, to begin searching for them.

Of course, I realize, the radio towers have been damaged or downed, just like the cell towers.

I didn't know she'd lied, I tell myself.

But there's no time to lament, now.

Now, I have to get to the Pinecrest, a place I know is cursed.

Quinn's words from the call replay in my mind: *"I found something here. Something strange."*

What could it be this time?

Chapter TWO

I'm about to watch a woman die.

I begin watching, as always, between thin wooden slats.

Her name is Casey Lloyd, and she is stranded after a storm at the inn where she works. She's just taken her first shower in two days and tilts her head as she faces a mirror, brushing her still-wet chestnut brown hair by lamplight. Her facial expression is somehow both blank and preoccupied, as if she means to conceal what worries her, even from her reflection. She stands and sets the brush on her vanity, then moves silently into her bedroom, her footsteps muffled by the fuzzy rug in her suite. The dampness from her hair darkens little spots on her emerald-green nightgown—one that used to belong to me.

She's about to be choked and then stabbed, and I can't look away.

I want to watch this.

I am Casey. Casey is me.

It's always startling to see how young I was.

In the background, the audience hears the heaving sound of breathing, bass deep, as if it's rising from the floor. It quickens as Casey moves closer. In horror films, that's a theme, the male gaze—the power of watching and observing. Weirdly the audience, and me, lying in bed, complicit as any other viewer. I can practically smell the sweetness of her shampoo and the traces of the shopping mall perfume that clings to the fabric of her clothes, hanging there in the dark.

There's a slash-cut to Casey's friends standing at the shore, their conversation muted by waves crashing before she opens the closet door and takes a quick step back. She half hides her mouth with her hands as her eyes widen, terrified. Her scream is loud and siren-shrill.

A man has been waiting, watching her undress and shower to prepare for bed. The horror of having been unknowingly observed all this time washes across her face just as she recognizes him. She falls backward, turning over her bedside table in an attempt to block him. She's feared he would come for her, and he has.

He steps forward roughly—his point of view is also the audience's—as he kicks the table out of his way. When Casey looks up again, her eyes gleam with the reflection of the knife the man holds beside his leg.

It's a hunting knife visible in silhouette, long and jagged down one side. She grasps for the phone so she can—what? Call for help? She seems urgent but unsure.

The man slaps the phone from her hand, and it lands against the bed. Her eyes snap up, show her surprise at his force, and with the soles of her bare feet, she pushes herself back across the carpet.

The man—an actor named Doug Johnson—picks up the plastic telephone receiver and pulls the cord taut. It's the shade of beige not seen since the 1990s. I remember Doug clearly, partly because he was Marla Moretti's boyfriend. The film's lead actress and actor, the slasher and final girl, dating. But also because the day he died started a wave of hysteria that still ripples through the film's legacy.

I *also* remember Doug being a particularly lovely person, even after he murdered me.

Casey shakes her head back and forth, mouthing the word "no." Her shadow is cast on the wall behind her, distorted and wavering in the amber-colored lamplight. "Oh God, no," she cries, pleading. The receiver calls out in sharp-toned, off-the-hook beeping while the man wraps the cord around Casey's neck. The camera zooms in as she gasps loudly, and her eyes widen. She struggles to slip her fingers underneath the cord, but the man pulls it tight—so tight, the slight bulge of her skin is visible around the plastic edge. She makes a choking, gurgling sound while her feet beat primally against the carpet as her hair whips around, strands of it clinging to her forehead.

The muscles in his hands flex; the tendons and veins are prominent.

It's so real that even now, I clench my hands into fists.

Now Casey has the ferocity of a startled animal. I root for her even though I know she has less than a minute to live. Her eyes, *my* eyes, flash rage as she squares her shoulders to face the man who murdered her best friend earlier that morning. She swings her fist, connecting firmly with the man's cheek, and screams a little, a kind of karate-like sound that always makes me pump my fist.

A pain-filled bellow rises from the man's throat, and Casey looks over her shoulder then sits up, raising her hands as if to protect herself, even though blocking the knife will obviously be of no use.

The blade rises, reflecting just a hint of the suite's rosy bathroom light.

"Don't!" Casey yells. "You don't have to!"

But the man evidently *does* have to because soon, the lilac wall splatters with her blood.

Well, not her actual *blood.*

It was a mixture of corn syrup, food coloring, and water. I watched Rick Plummer's assistant, Ann, make it, but it sure looked a lot like blood, even at the time. I had to wash my hair three times after the scene to get it out.

On the screen, the telephone receiver's beeping grows louder. It sounds more insistent and plaintive, as if making clear the fact that Casey will never hang it up again.

The camera pans to Casey's face, zooming in for a close-up of her eye that's a clear homage to *Psycho*. A water droplet from her wet hair, which may or may not be a tear, even rolls down her cheek.

Now my TV screen flashes as the Southwest Florida sunset fades through my window, the royal palms languid as if they've surrendered to darkness. I'm surprised I can watch the scene at all, having done my best to avoid seeing clips of *Breathless* since it came out. As far as I'm concerned, the only good things to come out of that production that summer were spending time with my friends and meeting Cam; I'm happy to leave the rest of my memories of it completely in the past. I snuggle deeper in the tangle of my bedsheets, find my phone, and text Cam.

Breathless is on TV, I tell him, before adding: Don't the networks usually save it for October?

Cam has been staying at the Pinecrest Estate, where the movie was shot, but I was happy to never go near the place again. The estate had become fairly dilapidated over the past several years—the relentless Floridian sun and salt air have taken their toll—and Cam planned to help Rick with repairs prior to putting it on the market, while at the same time finishing the last edits of his new book: a manual on how to survive a horror film. He'd struggled for several turns with the soul-crushing pursuit of a career as a novelist, publishing two in four years that I liked a lot but had only sold "fine," according to his agent.

So, Cam decided to finally capitalize on his last name. And in truth, the horror survival manual sounds like fun. He's a true expert, after all. I knew he just needed the time and space to write it.

My phone vibrates, and his picture flashes on the screen. He and I haven't spoken all day, and the first sound that comes across the line is him laughing, which I take as a sign of his good writing progress. I hear the clip-clap of his shoes and notice he's slightly out of breath from trotting up the stairs. "You usually turn the channel when that movie comes on. You're watching it?"

"I guess knowing you're down there made me want to take another look. All of us look so young. Especially Marla." I feel my toes curl up from embarrassment like I'd been caught looking at something I meant to keep to myself, something shameful or taboo. The bigger *Breathless* became, the more tragic it seemed, but being on the set when we were kids felt so *alive*. Aside from watching murder being acted out over and over, hanging out with Cam and my friends that summer was almost like being at camp, except no one monitored our intake of questionable material. I remember the transgressive, almost sexual thrill of seeing the lights going down, then hearing the shuffle of play violence, then later, the screams.

"I had the same thought about Marla the last time I watched it. She seemed so worldly at the time but was only, like, twenty-four. How far along are you in the movie?"

"I'm sorry to say you just missed my famous scene. Poor Casey hardly got to brush her hair."

"*Your* hair, you mean?" I can hear him smile.

The television channel's commercials stop, and I hear the faint click of buttons before the movie's audio comes across the line, doubled as an echo of the broadcast coming from my television. Cam then evidently mutes the sound because it stops on his end. We watch together in silence. I don't say anything for a moment, and neither does he. "You're right about the networks usually saving this for Halloween," Cam says. "Maybe news of the sequel broke."

For a second, I think he's joking before I realize his tone is completely even. I feel my head jerk back into my pillow. "What sequel? What are you talking about?"

Cam hesitates. "He's making a sequel to *Breathless*, and he's going to film it here. He's already got a crew scheduled and is starting to cast for parts. He told me he doesn't need a producer to green light anything because he's financing it all himself."

I don't know how to respond.

"Lexi, I didn't mean to keep it a secret. I just found out a few days ago. I guess I've been putting off telling you. I knew it would upset you to hear, which is stupid because it's not like you wouldn't hear about it. The idea is insane, but he's being stubborn. He wouldn't listen when I tried talking him out of it."

I take a deep breath. "Stubborn is one word for how he's being. Psychopathic is another. Hasn't he hasn't had enough? After everything that happened?! He needs more, what? Fame? Money? At whose expense this time?" My tongue presses against my teeth as if holding back more of the tirade swirling in my mind. I know Cam is just the messenger, but my blood feels like it's boiling. Part of me is irked that Cam mentioned plans for the sequel so offhandedly, but I understand him not wanting to tell me. His relationship with Rick has been heartbreakingly complicated for years. Rick could have helped Cam in so many ways but instead seemed to stand in Cam's way. He would disparage Cam's creative efforts, often publicly. Cam and I had twice left dinner parties after Rick had too much to drink and told jokes about the quality of Cam's writing. The last time, with Cam fuming, Rick called out that Cam needed to grow up in front of everyone. Maybe the prospect of his son succeeding in another field threatened Rick, but the source of his behavior was anyone's guess.

It left me feeling protective of Cam and Quinn and wanting to put distance between Rick and us. I already resented Rick for exploiting the tragedy on the *Breathless* set and Marla's eventual mental instability to promote the film, but it was how he treated Cam that I found unforgivable. I watched Cam practically go crazy trying to measure up to his father—growing distant from Quinn as he became obsessed with his writing, then later drinking to self-medicate his discouragement over tepid reviews of his novels.

Which was how the *Horror Film Survival Manual* came to be.

It would be the last thing he wrote.

I switch the phone to my other hand and wipe sweat from my palm on my sheets. "Just when I think I understand your dad's capacity to be outrageous, he moves the line farther. He's going to call the movie, what? *Breathless 2*?"

"That's the working title, according to him."

Cam's steadiness gives the news a surreal feeling, and a laugh escapes me.

"The idea's legit enough that Dad's scrapped plans to put the Pinecrest on the market for the time being. He loses money on it year after year now. An old building down here is really too much to maintain, and he's hardly here, anyway. Mostly, he stays in his little cottage at the far end of the property. And ready for this? Dad told me this morning Marla is interested in a part. Apparently, she's flying down in a few weeks to go over the script."

"That's not possible," I say.

Marla was a massive star when *Breathless* was filmed. But after Doug died, her life fell apart spectacularly. She gave slurry interviews expressing frustration about the lackluster investigation into Doug's death. She claimed to have seen a ghost on the set, which the media blew up into a sensational story about how Marla was "losing it." She sobbed and yelled at reporters who acted "patronizing" or seemed not to believe what she was saying, or worse, actually laughed in her face.

"*I know what I saw,*" she once screamed during an interview that quickly became infamous. The consensus was that she had lost her mind. Around that time, Marla started dating the guitarist of an eighties metal band she vacationed with in Mexico. Very often. According to the tabloids, they tattooed each other's names on parts of their bodies. After a party in Beverly Hills, Marla tripped down a flight of stairs, then was seen wearing an orthopedic boot in a grocery store parking lot the next week. There may or may not have been a sex tape, depending on whether the person visible in the hotel mirror was her.

The spiral continued further and further down. Marla cursed out a photographer at an airport, then later that week, shaved half her head. She absorbed one DUI, then a month later, another. Her desperate-eyed mugshot graced the cover of the lesser grocery store magazines.

She was "troubled," articles said, difficult to work with. She quit a major movie, then was fired from another. Her temper caused her to storm off sets, throw objects against walls.

She seemed so alone.

Rick told Cam he had reached out to her numerous times with no response. But even if that was true, I hardly blamed her. If anything, he used her breakdown for his own gain. I remember one interview where Rick was asked about Marla—his smirk was so telling it became a meme years later. "Maybe it's part of the curse," he'd said mysteriously.

"Poor Marla," I say. "Twenty-five *years* since *Breathless* came out? Really?" The number is hard to believe, somehow.

"Twenty-five years. *Breathless 2* hasn't even started production, and already the diehards are speculating on the return of the curse."

The curse. The words make me shift restlessly. Two cast members quit, another lost their mind. Another died. Rick had set out to terrify the actors in his film to get our true and authentic reactions. Still, the curse itself was mysterious. Even Rick seemed surprised at some of what went wrong that summer—the broken riggings, the frayed cord that sparked and nearly started a fire, the malfunctioning special effects—he couldn't have engineered every mishap even if he'd been trying to. Some events clearly happened while Rick was on set in another part of the estate. No, he couldn't have been solely responsible for *the curse*, even if he was who benefited most.

Yet *the curse* became iconic to *Breathless*—they became one and the same—and the film would have never been such a wild success without it. Doug was buried. Marla spiraled. And Rick campily played up the ghosts in his haunted production in every press release, every interview, using the tragedies to promote his film.

And it worked, stunningly well.

Disgusted, I kept my distance from Rick going forward, knowing what lengths he would go to for fame. And I wanted Cam and Quinn to keep that same distance.

I run my hand over my hair and shift in bed. "Did you ever think, all those years ago, that we would end up married?" I ask, eager to change the subject.

I don't know what I want Cam to say. We've known each other since we were teenagers; he was only my second boyfriend. It's hard to imagine a different life.

"Of course," he answers a beat too late, but with a hint of teasing to cover the lapse. "I knew from the moment I saw you everything would turn out like it has."

He was two years older than me when we met. I assumed he would always be. How often had I thought back to this conversation—if he sensed, even then, what would happen? The accident that caused his death would occur the following day, nine months before his book published. The irony seemed too cruel. The curse of the Pinecrest so tauntingly real.

By the following afternoon, he would be gone.

I hear the clink of a bottle cap landing on a hard surface. I picture the bay and the bottle of beer on the nightstand, sweating from the humidity.

Doug stalks his final potential victim on the screen, played by Marla. She looks focused, almost angry, as she presses a finger to her lips and squints, deep in thought. Marla wears a red flannel shirt and rubs her arms, her expression shaded with worry. The volume muted, I obviously can't hear what she's saying, but I know what it is exactly—she's worried she should have heard from my character, Casey, by then. She bends to examine a footprint contemplatively, holding up a blade of grass and dropping it to see which direction the wind carries it.

"Speaking of the creative process, how's the book coming? Getting close?" I tread delicately—if I show no interest, I'm indifferent. Too much, and I'm pestering. Writers, so temperamental.

"Actually, I mailed the manuscript to you a little while ago from the little post office here. I'm just fussing over a few citations now and some other details."

"You might beat it home? I hope? Depending on how you sent it."

"Very possible. I interviewed a few horror fans this week and what they all seem to like is the idea of a meta-narrative in a horror movie, with the characters realizing elements of the story as it goes along. Like they know they're *in* a story."

"Like *Scream?*"

Cam begins taking another sip of his beer but stops, his voice echoing just slightly off the inside of the bottle. "Sort of, but in *Scream*, the murderers are acting out scenes from *other* horror films. There's no real explanation for why the killers go after anyone aside from just them being crazy. This will be more like how to survive by mastering the genre's themes. Did you know horror is the only genre named for the feeling it aims to elicit," he says.

"I...had never thought of that."

"It's true. And there's something archetypal about it. Kids can describe the villains in scary movies they've never seen. The monsters become urban legends, probably because we're all afraid of the same stuff."

When we were teenagers watching a movie *about* teenagers being stalked, it added a charged undercurrent to the air. Fascinating but edgy, making us jump when someone entered a room, prone to yelping when a voice sounded behind us.

My eyes refocus on the TV screen, where a truck's headlights switch off. "Like being isolated," I say.

"Exactly. *I* like movies where the place looks normal enough, but you can tell something is off. Like the neighborhood in *Poltergeist* being on an ancient burial ground. Or how the suburbs in *Halloween* look creepy because they *seem* deserted. Usually, characters have to retreat to somewhere remote, then get cut off from anyone who could help. Marooned in the arctic in *The Thing*. Stuck in outer space in *Alien*."

I know what he means—a place appearing off in a way that's hard to put your finger on. Those places trigger a kind of unnameable fear, maybe one waiting deep in the collective unconscious, ready to be woken.

"In space, no one can hear you scream," he mutters.

"Stop!" I say. I'm half laughing, but my voice breaks.

"It's not like that *here*," he says.

Maybe not now, I think.

"And I didn't ignore some blatant, creepy warning on the way down because I wanted to make the best of this vacation or start minimizing strange stuff I can't explain." The levity in his voice is a relief, but a second later, his tone settles back into seriousness. "You know what happened after the shoot was an accident, right? And Marla blaming everyone and seeing things...she was not in her right mind."

I want to change the subject so strongly, realizing I'm gripping the comforter. I release my fingers and adjust my position in bed, summoning the enthusiasm to say, "There's probably no place better to work on a book about horror than on a haunted estate, right? Like the Overlook in *The Shining*?" My thoughts flash back to Jack Nicholson's character interviewing for the position as the innkeeper at the beginning of the film, saying the same things Cam did before he went down: *I'll enjoy the solitude. It sounds relaxing. I'll work on my book.* Then, I picture the look in Jack Nicholson's eyes the moment his wife finds the manuscript repeating the one famous sentence over and over—when she realizes he's been going crazy—and I close my fingers again.

Cam laughs. "Sliiiiightly better circumstances here. There's plenty of sunshine, and it's not like I'm actually cut off from civilization. *And* there's no hedge maze, which is unfortunate. That could help pass the time."

The Pinecrest may give me the creeps now, but Cam's right—it's no Overlook Hotel. It's the opposite, in fact. Strip away my fears and the stories I've heard, and I know Cam is essentially in paradise. There's a hammock strung between two palm trees where a person could look out onto the gently rippling waves of Florida Bay.

Who wouldn't want to write there? You enter in what used to be the lobby of an old hotel, the front desk made of carved wood. A bell still sits on top—the edges bear flecks of rust from the salt air. The flooring is made of broad pine planks, cupped slightly from the humidity. Everything smells like what you'd expect from a historic home in the Keys: like sea salt and fresh air and lemon furniture polish. Upstairs are the bedrooms. Half face west and take in views of the sapphire bay over the tree line. At sunset, the sky goes vermillion and looks like a postcard of heaven through the window frames.

Cam clears his throat. "Actually, the movie I keep thinking of is *Key Largo*, with Humphrey Bogart and Lauren Bacall in that old hotel during the hurricane. Now that I'm down here, I keep wanting to re-watch it. The part I've been thinking about is when Johnny Rocco forces his girlfriend to sing. The second she starts, the story breaks—like, where is this headed—a minute earlier, they were watching a movie about a gangster, and now a woman is singing. When Rocco denies her the drinks, and she's devastated, you realize the point of the scene is to reveal what an awful, merciless human being he is. She breaks the fourth wall. Sort of."

On the screen, Marla runs through the woods. Shadows from the pine branches fall over her face as her lips tremble, the movement creating a momentary illusion that she's underwater.

"Yeah," I say, still distracted. "Plus, I'm sure your dad is happy to have you there. What is he up to? Still driving all the local women crazy?"

Rick never lived down his reputation as a ladies' man.

Cam's voice drops with a hint of sadness. "Seriously, Dad mostly stays at his cottage. I can't quite figure it out. It's like, we agreed that I'd come down, but now he seems so distant as if he's ready for me to go. He asks about you constantly. Getting ready to sell reminded Dad that you have a set of keys to everything—the estate, the boat.

You even know how to get into the safe. He said you're one of the only people he's ever fully trusted."

I shake my head. The trust between Rick and I extends in one direction.

We talked a little more about the business of the house, Quinn's grades, and when my school year is scheduled to start back up. I hear him yawn. Then he groans a little.

"What?" I ask.

"Oh, nothing. Just some indigestion, probably from all the take-out I've been eating."

"Get some sleep," I say.

"I'll turn in soon. I...guess in a minute. It looks like I left a light on downstairs."

"Leave it," I say. The words escape me. There's fear in my voice that's instinctual, and I can't help it. I want him to close the suite's door. And lock it. Leave whatever is downstairs for tomorrow. "Seriously," I say.

"Oh, Lexi, you've watched too many movies. I *have* the survival manual, remember? I'll run down and turn it off. It'll take two seconds."

"I'll stay on the phone," I volunteer.

"Just a few days till I'm back," he says as a way of declining my offer. "I've gotten a ton of editing done. Believe me. I'm looking forward to being home."

After we hang up, I tuck the covers under my chin, my eyes settling again on the movie. The teenagers find a set of train tracks, choose a direction, and stride purposefully into the mist. The fog grows thick around them while Marla focuses her eyes forward. The brilliance of her acting, I realize, is that trying to appear unafraid makes her seem truly terrified.

She had no idea what was about to happen in real life.

And that night, neither did I.

Marla wasn't the only one to see things she couldn't explain the summer *Breathless* was filmed.

I saw them, too.

⌐

The next morning, I didn't hear from Cam at all.

The first call came midday from Rick while I was at school. He left a message asking if I'd heard from Cam, which shouldn't have alarmed me on the surface. Even from opposite sides of the estate grounds, they communicated so poorly it was completely believable they would fall out of touch. His message *shouldn't* have troubled me, but it made my insides tighten, my breathing speed up. The phone rang again just as I stepped outside to return his call.

He sounded panicked. "They've found the boat, Lexi," Rick said. "Capsized, carried a mile offshore by the current."

A mile.

I covered my mouth with my hand. "He was on it? Are you *sure*?" Already, hot tears were filling my eyes.

"No one's sure about anything right now. That's just what the Coast Guard called in. The boat was gone this morning. He takes it out sometimes. I didn't worry until he wasn't back by noon."

I started estimating the trajectories: you could trace the boat's progress back to earlier that day to figure out when it went over, maybe look for him in the water along its path. Conclusions the Coast Guard would've already drawn.

"They're searching."

That was how it began: the incessant questions, the worry, the doubt. Then ultimately, the horrific lack of closure.

My husband had disappeared.

The search lasted forty-eight hours, then scaled back and continued another forty-eight before being called off. No one knew how long to wait before giving up hope. Quinn never believed he was gone, and there were words for her disbelief: non-acceptance, denial. I didn't know what to say.

There was an investigation that yielded absolutely no answers.

It was as if the ocean had swallowed him up.

One detective started explaining how dangerous boating could be before I stopped him. I'd seen too much when working at the marina to not understand.

There are guys who make their living scraping barnacles off of ships while they're in the water. Once, I saw one get hit by a passing ski boat. When I was sixteen, I helped pull a man out of the water who got wasted the night before and fell asleep below deck on his cutter. A storm blew in, and between the rain and waves, the boat sank with him stuck in the cabin. The only thing that saved him was that the boat was secured to a floating dock and that the ropes he tied onto were strong enough not to break.

I'd seen props cut off people's limbs, even at very low speeds.

The worst, which always stuck in my mind, was the crew of fraternity brothers visiting on spring break who rented a boat without understanding the tides or channel markers and hit a sandbar at forty knots. It stopped the vessel but threw them all forward a hundred feet. At least. One was paralyzed from the waist down.

Another didn't survive.

I didn't need to hear how dangerous open water could be from a detective.

I knew exactly.

Chapter
THREE

OCTOBER 31ST

After Cam's memorial service, I read in one of the dozen books friends gave me about the grieving process that after a loved one dies, the relationship can live on, even if their physical presence is gone. In one, there was a whole chapter on communicating with the person who had died. At first, I found myself smirking as if I was being given some cheesy, new-age permission to have my own private séance, but as I kept reading, I remember my whole body starting to relax. The truth was that until then, part of me was worried I was losing it. The book said if you ask people, really candidly, if they communicate with someone who they've lost, some of them will look at you curiously.

But others will show recognition in their eyes before calmly nodding to acknowledge it, even if they can't admit it out loud. The book said some people "see" a presence in particular objects—rainbows and butterflies were the examples—that tie them to their person. Others hear a specific song and feel the person who's passed on. Not quite their ghost, the book said, more of a transmission from the other side. And sometimes, the grieving continue the conversation. The idea made perfect sense, except I don't have something conventional like seeing a sparrow or hearing the song "Imagine" to help me recall my relationship with my husband. I have memories of a book he wrote that happens to be a *slightly* tongue-in-cheek manual on surviving horror films. After his death, I helped edit the manuscript before sending it off to his publisher. Cam mailed the draft the morning before he disappeared, but it didn't arrive for a week after Rick told me he was missing. When I opened it and started reading, it felt like I was reading some sacred communication from beyond this world. Those first weeks—the hardest time—those pages were the closest I could get to him.

"You don't think people will buy this as an actual survival manual?" I'd asked one afternoon after he'd just started the project. Sunlight streamed in the windows of our Southwest Florida home. I could hear Quinn in the next room, her voice in perfect sync with a song from the soundtrack to a musical she'd listened to a hundred times, "...but just you wait. Just you wait," she sang.

Cam smiled coyly. "What do you mean? It *is* an actual survival manual."

I remember laughing out loud. "Cam, if anyone pulls this book for advice on how to stay alive, they're in trouble."

He leaned back in his desk chair, the one that had always squeaked. That day he wore the soft, old T-shirt he went running in. He folded his arms behind his head. "Lex," he told me, "There are probably worse sources of information."

Now, the sunrise reflects off a CD on my dashboard, blending into a rainbow along the edge. Around it are Quinn's fingerprints in the dust, which I should wipe down but won't until I find her. I blink my eyes and wish.

Just drive.

It'll be hours till you can help her.

Right now, there's no one to call.

I know I'm not the only widow who talks to their late husband in their head. Sometimes, like now, it feels as if he's right there.

"This, what you're doing right now, is essentially the plot of *Aliens*," he'd say.

I'd take the bait and ask, of course. His smile would crease the place between his eyebrows, making him look deep in thought. He always saw things differently, imaginatively. The summer we met, we would lie in his bed and try to read each other's thoughts. I haven't met anyone so magical since.

"*Aliens*," he'd explain, "starts as Ripley is found years later by a salvage ship, the only survivor of the first expedition. She learns a human colony has been established on the very planet she'd escaped. Earth has lost contact. Sleepless at night, she returns to the planet for a search and rescue mission. And what choice did she have? Since so much time has passed, many people she knew are already gone."

"Okay?"

"I mean, she'd left the past behind her, escaped it. But then she responds to a distress signal, going where exactly she knows she shouldn't. Ripley *knows* waiting would be impossible. She knows she couldn't live with herself if she didn't go."

"Except I don't have a platoon of space marines to help keep me safe," I'd point out.

"They didn't help Ripley much. The end came down to her mothering instinct and her ability to innovate to save that girl."

"Pretty deep," I'd say, now grinding my teeth, a part of me still irrationally angry at him for leaving. For dying. For disappearing.

His loss transformed Quinn completely. At seventeen, how could it not? Her sense of humor receded, leaving snark in its place. Her skin paled, and her posture slumped. One day I came home from work to discover she dyed her hair jet black. The light inside, the essence that made Quinn *Quinn*, flashed with terrifying infrequency, just long enough to be recognized and stuffed away again.

But then, like a seasonal change, the cloud over her seemed to lift. Her voice emerged over meals, curious and thoughtful. One clear winter morning, I heard singing from her room and opened the door to find her head bopping, two white earbuds in place. She squealed and tossed a pillow at me.

Maybe we'll make it, after all, I thought.

Maybe we can survive what happened.

That was before she told a lie I thought she was incapable of.

I wipe my eyes and return my focus to the road. I reach for my phone to check for new messages. Of course, there are none. The ringer is switched on with the volume turned up as loud as it will go. As I lay the phone on the passenger seat, I realize I don't know whether I packed a charger while throwing things into my bag. I tell myself Quinn will have hers, then remember it will do me no good because she has a different type of phone. I press the button on the side of mine. My battery still has fifty-two percent life, probably more than enough, I reason. I won't be in the Keys long. The tires rumble as they catch the road's edge. I straighten the wheel, startled.

Focus. If you crash this car, you won't help anyone.

The windshield dots with Stephen's final whisper as I drive across I-75. When I lean forward, I see what I'd expected: clouds breaking apart, edges of a sunrise the color of cherry blossoms. A ribbon of blue sky appears on the horizon, high above the weather. The paradox of a high category hurricane is that after the outer rain bands pass, the weather that follows is often stunning. All the clearer to see everything that has been demolished.

My phone rings again, and again I check whether Quinn is calling.

No such luck.

This call comes from Luke, my... I don't know what to call him. The man with whom I've been having an undefined relationship for the past five months. I silence the ringer then bite my lip as the phone vibrates in the passenger seat. It dings a second later, signaling he's left a message, which I decide to listen to later.

Then, the phone rings again. "Oh, God, *Luke*," I say aloud.

His persistence is a double-edged sword—it's why we have any relationship at all but also why I keep backing away. I picture him in his white T-shirt and the blue ball cap he always wears, his fishing sunglasses probably dinging around his neck or else folded and hung in his collar. He's so deeply tanned from his hours on the water that I've wondered about the long-term health of his skin, but at forty-one, he's holding up better than most of the men his age. He's nothing like someone I should be attracted to. I hadn't meant to date him, but he wore me down with his calm smile more easily than I'd expected.

Could he possibly have some information about Quinn? Maybe she's come home, and he's standing there beside her?

"Hi?" he asks as I answer. "Everything okay?"

"Honestly, no. But hopefully, it will be soon." It comes out more clipped than I mean, probably because I feel guilty not speaking to him for two weeks.

The phone is warm against my palm. *Does he know?*

We met while having a coffee table delivered to the apartment Quinn and I were moving into. Luke, who lived three units over, appeared just in time to help the delivery driver navigate it inside. I tried not to feel like I was betraying Cam or Quinn.

"Okay. I don't mean to be nosy, really, but I noticed your car pulling out super early. Do...you need anything?"

Why does his thoughtfulness make me feel upset? "No, it'll be okay. Listen, I'm on the way to find Quinn. Have you heard from her?"

A pause. "Have *I* heard from Quinn?"

"Sorry, I can't explain right now. Just... Listen, will you be home this morning?"

"What's happening with Quinn?" he asks. "You sound upset."

"Luke, will you be *home*?"

He pauses, his answer paced with the maddening slowness of someone uninvolved in the emergency. "I'm planning to be here. What's..."

It occurs to me that, even though I haven't been able to reach Quinn or Rick this morning, there's a chance they did evacuate, and they might pass me going the other way. I cut Luke off. "Can you keep an eye out for her, please? And call me if she shows up there? She's in the Keys."

"In *the* Keys? Right *now*? I thought you said she was on her school trip to..."

"We should be home by tonight. Just, Luke, please call if she shows up?"

"Sure," he says, more distantly now.

We hang up, and I focus again on the road.

No, he doesn't know.

～

It's not like it was with Cam. I have to explain things to Luke.

One night, a month earlier, he confessed, "I have never watched *Breathless*. What was it about? I don't go for horror. I get too scared."

The room was pitch black, but he could feel my head turn against his shoulder as I looked toward him in disbelief. *He doesn't go for horror,* I thought. Even though I stifled a laugh, I admired his honesty. It was easy to take for granted that famous horror movies were common knowledge. I was immersed in them as part of the Plummer family. But Luke not ever having seen *Breathless* meant he didn't know me from my role. I couldn't tell if I was disappointed or relieved.

"That's okay, really," I said before explaining the plot.

"That actually is really creepy," he said. I couldn't see Luke's eyes in the dark. My gut told me he was safe, but getting close can be so dangerous. He knew nothing about Doug's death and vaguely about Marla's life on and off the screen. "Creepy, yes, but the script is fun because it's chock-full of horror film tropes. One character is a bumbling cop. Another is an aspiring actress who's also a nerd, in this case, obsessed with the weather. Essentially on an island, there is nowhere to run. One by one, they all get picked off, slasher-film style. Marla's character, the virtuous heroine, is the last one alive."

"And you?"

"I played a party girl. She's always the first to die."

⌒

Forty minutes later, the encounter I've anticipated happens. This one, much less numinous. The National Guard. I'd seen their photos on the news last night before I left—which feels like an eternity ago. I slow to a stop at the stark white barricades blocking no fewer than four Army trucks idling on the asphalt. A wisp of exhaust rises from the Jeep waiting in front of me at the makeshift gate. Aside from it, I see no other civilian vehicles. No one is leaving the islands, which means everyone there stayed to wait out the storm.

One of the soldiers nods to two others who scramble to lift and then swing the barricade, allowing the Jeep in front of me to proceed.

Its engine is a low growl as it chugs ahead. They set the barrier back in place, and the soldier raises his palm as I idle to the checkpoint. He hardly looks older than some of the twelfth graders at the high school where I work. His posture is formal, even stiff, as I crank down the old window, but the tremor in his voice gives him away—he's exhausted and probably as disoriented as everyone trying to pass, still making sense of what's happened, just like me.

And *he* conveys more confidence than the soldiers behind him.

He swallows before delivering the lines he's probably gone through a hundred times that morning. "Good morning, ma'am. You've reached a checkpoint before this bridge into the Keys. We're just letting homeowners and essential medical personnel pass at this point." He smells like the kind of baby shampoo I washed Quinn with years ago. He tugs at his tight collar.

I wonder if his home is behind him, on the islands. I wonder if his family is okay.

"I'm from here, yes," I say, trying to skirt around the technicalities of homeownership, of any of the circumstances. The less I say, the better. I try to smile when I add, "I'm going down to help my family. My daughter is caught down on Islamorada."

"So, you're *not* medical?"

I shake my head. "No, I'll be helping my family. My father-in-law technically owns the property. He's staying there with my daughter but—" I'm straying into the weeds. The soldier squints even more deeply while he processes what I'm saying. A bit of white powder from a donut he'd just eaten clings to the lower corner of his bottom lip.

"Please," I say. "I lost contact with my daughter last night."

He glances at the others, one of whom makes a questioning face. "Can I see your license?" he asks.

I reach into my purse, open my wallet, and show it to him. I suddenly feel like I'm nineteen again, trying to talk my way into a college bar.

"We're not supposed to allow visitors on the island, ma'am—just essential personnel at this point. I mean, the whole area has been evacuated. You understand, keeping out looters." He shakes my license like it's a drying Polaroid.

Looters. I hear Don's voice in my memory, his upper lip curled with disgust, and the words of a newscaster covering a previous hurricane's recovery, who'd said, "When gas and supplies run short, society crumbles quickly." I think back to a sign I saw after Hurricane Andrew that read, "Looters will be shot on sight." The image brought to mind postapocalyptic movies I'd seen on late-night TV, but I realize now those featured slow-moving zombies, far less scary than well-armed thieves.

A white pickup truck rolls up behind me. A metal ladder rests in the bed, the top jutting at a forward angle against the cab. Two men sit inside. I squint as their headlights shine directly into my rearview mirror.

The soldier motions to them with his index finger, saying, "One second," before leaning down my window.

"Your father knows you're coming?"

Don't correct him.

"Absolutely," I say.

I catch the driver behind me raising his hands like he's asking, "what gives?"

The soldier acknowledges him again before turning back to me. "Just so you know what you're getting into here: most of the islands have no electricity. They're saying two or three more days before the power comes back on. So, after the sun goes down later tonight..." He points to the pink-gray horizon. "There will be zero light. As in, zero.

The main cell towers were knocked down by the wind, so cell service is spotty, at best."

Like I hadn't noticed, I think, gripping my hands on my jeans to keep from tapping them impatiently.

"It could be another day or so because—"

"Because everything is down," I finish. "And they're using generator power to fix the towers."

"Exactly," he nods, evidently impressed. "How far down did you say you're planning to go?"

I point. "The Key where they are is eighty minutes from the end of this bridge."

"Double that because of the sand and debris. Police and first responders are focusing only on emergencies, and even there, communication is severely limited. I'm not trying to scare you, but you'll be on your own for the next forty-eight hours, at the very least, just saying."

I grew up here in the time before cell phones, and hardly any services existed, I want to say. "I'll be alright," I say. "Promise."

He motions to the other guards, who pick up the barricade and walk it back, like a gate opening inward, then he leans closer to my window. "Ma'am, four bodies have been found already this morning. You'd think the locals would be the first ones to leave. You'd think they'd sprint out, knowing what's coming. But it's the tourists who flee. The residents are the ones who are stubborn. Structures collapse. Cars get trapped between trees. People try to walk, debris hurling in at more than a hundred miles an hour."

The way his tone changes makes the hair on the back of my neck stand up, and for the first time, I take the warning seriously.

A look passes over his face that I can't describe. His eyes are wide with fear, but there's something else: maybe it's curiosity. "When people take their lives in their own hands like that...there's nothing any of us can do to help."

Like in any good horror movie, I believe this is my warning. The exchange when the audience starts to think, *Stop! No! Turn around!*

But me? I'm going forward despite it.

How could I not?

Cam would have pushed the wave of brown hair out of his eyes. "But those characters have a choice," he'd have said. "To turn back. *The Amityville Horror, An American Werewolf in London.* None of them knew what they were getting into. They didn't understand the risks ahead of them. You do. That's your advantage."

Let's hope so.

"I'll be careful," I say, waving to them both as I drive on. I'm running on minimal sleep. I can say and think whatever I like.

"Let's hope so," Cam would have agreed. "But it *is* starting to look like the perfect setting of a horror movie. Granted, this isn't the creepy backwoods or Gothic suburbia, but this would definitely count as cutoff—isolated. It's not much different in some ways than being in outer space. Remember how in space, no one can hear you scream?"

I roll my eyes.

"Another favorite location is a haunted house with a mystery," he'd add.

"Stop."

"With evil burned into the walls."

"Really, stop."

I turn the radio knob, trying to find a new station. It's all yacht rock halfway through the dial, Steely Dan singing "Dirty Work" as I chug up the first bridge. The sun has risen a few degrees over the water, burning away the morning mist.

Islamorada, under normal circumstances, is objectively one of the most beautiful places on earth, a truth I completely took for granted when I left at eighteen. The fishing and birdwatching are some of the best. Everyone is tan. Crystal clear water surrounds tangles of mangroves, perfect for fishing. The sandbars are lined with boats, laughter carrying to the beach on Saturdays. Growing up here distorts your sense of the world. For starters, there's no winter, so all images of snow, of people wearing coats, all holiday carols require imagination. That, and most people around on a day-to-day basis are visiting. They're beyond enamored with the place—they're ecstatic about it. Locals often see no reason to travel anywhere else. They can be protective of the islands they treasure to the point of suspiciousness and treat anyone who hasn't lived in the Keys for a decade like an outsider.

Now, the first thing I see on the back end of the bridge is a forty-foot sailboat resting on its side in a grocery store parking lot. The sail itself lies unfurled across the blacktop. Its mast has snapped, the end resting against the hood of a maroon van. The van's windows are all shattered, shards held in place by a loose film of gray tint. I touch the brakes because I can't look away, and the Volvo skids in the loose sand at the bottom of the bridge.

The bravado I'd felt as a native evaporates. The tremor I heard in the guard's voice a moment earlier was completely appropriate. I cut the wheel and start forward again, dodging a shopping cart in what seems to be the road, though it's hard to tell. It stands upright, somehow, its wheels mostly buried. My tires sound like shush, shush, shush through patches of sand blanketing the road. Each registers the crunch of debris and small branches.

Buildings on either side of the road look as though they've been dynamited, cinder blocks scattered at odd angles across wet gravel parking lots, their former functions indiscernible. I wonder as I look: Was that a church? A small business? A school? It doesn't matter now.

I'd been concerned about flooding, but I can see the real problem is not being able to see the edges of the roadway at all.

The soldier was right. The drive is arduous.

A never-ending strand of power lines running down one side of the road, a series of sandy parking lots on the other, limbs and leaves everywhere. On my left, three beach cruiser bicycles tilt languidly across the gravel, a chain still running through the frames.

There really was no warning when this storm hit.

Rick had been right. There may have been time for nearly everyone to drive out of the Keys, but not to secure anything the wind might turn into a missile. His comment from just before the phone cut out yesterday echoes in my head, or maybe it's just now that I can hear it: "—your permission to come."

Had he been saying that he thought Quinn had my permission to come? Or that he knew Quinn didn't?

An hour later, I push the brakes as I come down the last bridge before the Pinecrest. At the bottom, a light pole lies on its side, and the streets are half covered in sand. Someone runs into the road and waves frantically as I approach.

She looks wild-eyed as she wrings her hands and looks around, her clothes stained and disheveled.

I know who it is.

I recognize her immediately.

Marla.

She's so thin her collarbones are visible from this distance beneath the tangle of her dark hair. I roll down the window then cut the engine, the rushing tide audible in the distance. "Lexi?" she asks, backing away from my Volvo warily as if I might lurch into her. The sunlight hits her eyes. She blinks and tries to shield them with her hand. "Oh my God, it really is you, isn't it? What are you..."

Clearly, she didn't make it off the islands, but why is she out here? The urgency in her eyes makes my heart accelerate. "Marla, what's going on? Are you okay?"

"Are you here with *him*?"

I don't answer, but my expression must show confusion because Marla's features turn dark and terrified. She presses her hands to her face. "Lexi, Rick tried to kill me."

Chapter
FOUR

SUMMER 1998

The weekend filming started, the marina's side door creaked, its hinges rusted by years of salt air. A gust of warm air followed Don into the office as he turned on the television that sat on the marina's office counter. He'd quietly become obsessed with President Clinton's protracted legal drama, concerning himself with details about who might testify before Ken Starr's grand jury next. "Some friend," he muttered about the witness as he picked at the masking tape holding the remote's AAA batteries in place. "Recording conversations with your friend. What's that show you like? *The World*?"

"*Liked*," I said. "*The Real World*. And that was years ago."

Don nodded at the screen. "*Real* world right there." He mused about patriotism and loyalty for a few minutes before bursting back outside to help a family of tourists lug a cooler the size of my bedroom onto a pontoon boat. I read once that people sometimes fantasize about having a different family, imagining they were switched at birth, somehow, and that their real family was out *there*. A family with whom they could be themselves, who understood them, and who could help develop their ideas and talents. Creatives often feel this way. Painters. Poets. Actors. I managed a few ensemble parts in high school theater productions when I could sneak away long enough to make rehearsal. Some part of me was hoping that when I got in front of the production crew for *Breathless*, I'd meet my kind of people.

I clicked off the TV and glanced at the wall clock. I had three hours left to do a full day's work; politics was a distraction; what I needed was a beat to help me focus. I slipped *The Miseducation of Lauryn Hill* into my Discman, put on my headphones, and pushed play.

If social media had existed then, I would have seen the poolside photos, trim bathing suits, and vermillion sunsets of my classmates' weekends. But the version of the Keys I saw was from behind a splintery desk, between the aisles of Sunshine Hardware or the bait and tackle shop. My paradise was lying on the musty sofa in the tiny break room, daydreaming about the world north of where I was. My Saturdays started at five thirty with a blur of reservation slips and lists of equipment to prep. I watched graying skies swallow stars at sunrise. A faint mist would cloud the horizon until colors exploded, all at once, yellowing the peaks of waves before settling above an endless landscape of heedless indigo.

I usually met with customers while Don pulled the boats and helped load the gear. If his hip injury from the Navy acted up, we reversed roles. By the time I was twelve years old, I could operate the fuel pumps. By thirteen, I could take out the whaler unaccompanied to tow stranded boaters off sandbars—people too drunk to navigate channel markers or who thought nautical rules didn't apply to them. I saw plenty of both, learned to carry my own with red-faced, middle-aged men, usually elbowing each other, sipping beer from koozies as I pulled up.

"Aren't you a little young to be doing this?" they'd ask.

I'd be direct about what I wanted, saying things like, "Throw me that bowline," or simply pointing my intent.

I'd hear, "You know what you're doing?" and knew rather than ask, "Do you?" how to shoot stern looks with barely a glance at their overturned hulls, ruined props, or burned-out engines.

By fourteen, my fingertips were calloused from handling rope, the back of my neck was permanently tan, and I scrubbed my hands daily to wash away the scent of gasoline. By fifteen, I could secure a rig faster than Don could, not that he was ever impressed. Just another day at the office, while my school friends were busy living their normal teenage lives. How strange their dramas seemed to me at the time, and how enviable.

Don was never bad to me, but he couldn't appreciate the value of daydreaming. And I was a daydreamer: a black-T-shirt-wearing, nose-ring-donning, aspiring actor in the unlikeliest of places. His was a world of checklists, invoices, lumberyard hauls, accounting. His lack of imagination didn't bother me as much as his inability to recognize mine.

What let me toil at the marina so dutifully throughout high school was the knowledge that my days there would eventually end. The day-to-day operations were enough work for three people. But Don and I managed passably, sometimes working ten-hour days and still underperforming for foot-tapping tourists, impatient with delays. I never hid my plan to leave Islamorada and the marina, but aggressively patient Don would dismiss my reminders that I planned to go to college. I cared about him, truly, and had a sense of kinship with the place's creaky boards and peeling paint, but I didn't know how he was going to keep it going with me not there.

And by the summer of my junior year, my runway was shortening.

Don burst back into the office. "Six, six fifteen slips are ready," he said, as much to himself as to me. I marveled at how my mother ever fell for this man, decided she wanted the life he offered. "Two more ready to come down," Don said, sipping his coffee. "That third pylon on the right dock is leaning now, bad." He liked updating me on the marina's physical structures: the boards he replaced, pylons of questionable integrity.

I glanced again at the wall clock. "I need to be gone by two thirty today, don't forget."

"Remind me for what?"

"It's a theater production," I fibbed, implying it was a school function. I hated dishonesty, but there was no choice. Don would have seen being an extra in a movie as self-indulgent. He would never have let me go if I had told him what we were really doing.

He set down his coffee cup. "Over the summer?"

"Yeah, most of the theater department is doing it," I said, again skirting the truth. "Someone" involved with the production looking for beach scene extras had contacted the department.

"Hmm," he said. He raised his ball cap, scratching the back of his head before retreating onto the dock.

Don didn't pay me. I wasn't an employee. I rationalized that I was more of a volunteer, and volunteers don't have to beg for time off. At two fifteen, I straightened the day's receipts into a neat stack beside the cash register, grabbed the bag full of clothes I'd packed in the pre-dawn dark, and ran out the side door to meet the friends I'd asked to pick me up. Behind me, the screen door clapped shut as loud as a firecracker. I prayed Don wouldn't hear, wouldn't change his mind and try to make me stay.

I waited beside the road in the shade of the gumbo limbo tree, the shadows of its moon-shaped leaves shadows waving across the gravel around my black Converse.

I heard my friend Jessica's car before it appeared: a black Ford Probe with dark tinted windows she named "Dracula." I wasn't a mechanic, but I knew an engine's death rattle when I heard one and just hoped Dracula had enough life left in it to get us to the Pinecrest Estate. When the door flew open, I glanced over my shoulder at the marina's gray shingle roof, baking in the afternoon heat, pushed the seat forward, and climbed inside. Jessica stomped the gas so hard I knocked into the passenger seat, the spray of shell gravel behind us. The red cloth seats smelled like sea salt, cigarette smoke, and hairspray.

"Watch it," our friend Cassie said, all of us laughing. The windows were halfway down so Cassie could smoke, and at the end of her Marlboro Light was a plum kiss. Hair blew around like a riot.

Cassie was the coolest of the three of us and got the most attention from boys, even if there was something vaguely needy about her confidence. She'd talked so often about her one foray onto South Beach with a twenty-three-year-old from Canada that Jess and I had begun to doubt it ever happened. "Spencer," after all, was the perfect name for a fake boyfriend. But Cassie had pushed us to attend the open call, so we had her attitude to thank for that.

I unzipped my bag and took off my paint-stained white T-shirt and khaki shorts.

"Are you getting naked back there, or what? There's going to be a wardrobe coordinator," Jessica said in her overly cautious way. A few months earlier, she still listened to the Backstreet Boys and had a Leonardo DiCaprio poster on her closet door.

"I'm not showing up to a real-life movie set in work clothes," I said, pulling a black T-shirt over my head. Since middle school, the three of us had been a trio, but neither of them still completely understood my job at the marina. Jessica's family owned a resort and had money, a rarity among locals, and Cassie's mom was a single parent but somehow avoided work. With calluses on my palms and sunburnt forearms, I was definitely the most working-class among the three of us, the one who changed Jessica's flat tire one night the previous summer so we wouldn't get home late.

I wiped away the sweat beading at my temples, unrolled my best pair of black jeans, and yanked them several times up my legs. "What time is it now? We're supposed to get there before three if we want to get in."

Cassie exhaled a puff of smoke and flicked away her cigarette, then mercifully rolled up her window and blasted the air conditioner. "Relax, they probably want us to be early. Supposedly, the scene they need extras for is at sunset."

"Can you believe we get to do this?" I asked.

"You're so *excited*," they both teased. It didn't hurt my feelings. I *was* excited. I smiled from ear to ear while I looked over Jessica's shoulder to brush and fix my hair in Dracula's rearview mirror.

It was Jessica's car, but Cassie controlled the stereo. She slipped in a Sisters of Mercy CD and skipped ahead to her favorite song, then turned the volume up so loud the backseat speakers rattled.

"Guys, what do we even know about the movie?" I asked over the music.

"How much do we *need* to know?" Cassie shot back. I could see her thick, black eyeliner in her profile. She wore her hair in a red butterfly clip I suspected she took from my bathroom, bleached white and flat-ironed straight. "It's not like we're not doing it."

"I just mean do we know what it's even *about*? It is a horror movie, right?"

"Who *cares* what the plot is," Cassie groaned with weapon-grade indifference.

"*Horror* was the word whoever called the department used," Jessica chimed in, glancing over her shoulder. I could hear a faint tremor in her voice.

Cassie rolled her eyes. "Take away the scary music and darkness, and what they're doing is going to look pretty silly between takes."

Jess gave her a look like, "you promise?"

"Stop with being such a wuss. Those fog machines? They're the same ones the high school used for *Into the Woods*, the same as the Stone Temple Pilots concert my mom took us to in Fort Lauderdale. Or the club I went to on South Beach."

"Boy, you loved that trip to South Beach," I said.

Cassie frowned at me as Jess reassured herself. "But they said we wouldn't necessarily *see* any blood or stuff if you're worried about that. We're just extras."

"Maybe not *just* extras," Cassie said. "Maybe they only *think* they need extras. You never know what'll happen once we get on the set. People get discovered all the time."

Maybe they do, I thought.

I caught Cassie inspecting her reflection. Through the window tint, the sky behind her was flat gray, like a blank TV screen. The ocean looked teal.

Jessica turned the music down slightly and met my eyes in the mirror. "Do you think I should wear my hair up in a scrunchie or down like it is?"

"Down, I think," I said.

Cassie rolled her eyes and turned the music back up, this time even louder. I could feel the bass rumble against the bottoms of my legs. "Down," she said. "It's not even a question."

I smoothed out the wrinkles in my shirt. "He directs only horror movies, right? Mr. Plummer?"

"Whatever you do, don't call him 'Mr. Plummer,'" Cassie scolded. "It makes us sound like we're in fourth grade. When we meet with the casting director, call him 'Rick' or 'The Director,' okay?"

"Okay," I said. My eyes could roll, too, and I didn't care if she saw.

"But *yes*, he strictly directs horror films. One haunted house movie, one about someone who's back from the dead. One sort of vampire kind of thing, and now this. It's a serial killer, slasher-type movie. It's called *Breathless*, I heard."

"It's supposed to be his biggest so far," Jessica added.

We crossed a bridge, and the car wheels went thump-thump, thump-thump over the pavement sections. Cassie wanted to be discovered, and she wanted to be a movie star. I wanted to be an actress, too but knew I'd settle on being a part of the production just to see how one was made. Movies were magic. They arrived at our local Island Cinema as if beamed in from another world. I wanted a peek behind the curtain.

"I heard that when they were filming the last movie, Rick Plummer had a séance and that all the lights on the set flickered and the clocks in the room started turning backward," Cassie said.

"I don't believe it," I said.

"Creepy!" Jessica waved her hands in front of her face as if she needed air. "A kid in my art class told me Rick Plummer works only at night and that, like, he hasn't seen the sun in twenty years or something."

"Eww," Cassie said.

"It's just what I heard."

"Guys, he's shooting his movie in the Keys. I'm sure he's okay seeing the sun."

"Fine." Cassie smirked. "But I heard he made a snuff film," she said quietly.

I leaned forward, gripping each of their seats. Close up, I realized the fabric smelled like Captain Morgan Spiced Rum.

It was quiet for a second.

"What's that?" Jessica asked.

"*That's* a dumb rumor," I said.

"*But what's a snuff film?*" Jess repeated.

"It's a movie where someone really dies," I said. "Anyway, that rumor's not true, Jess."

"What I heard." Cassie shrugged.

"It's going to freak me out just to be in the Pinecrest," Jessica said, looking at us both. "In a good way, I mean. You guys haven't ever actually been inside, have you?"

Cassie and I shook our heads. We'd grown up hearing the locals murmur and narrow their eyes at the mention of the place. Muttering of "strange folks" and "stranger goings-on" before it was a hotel and then left abandoned. Even now, it had the feel of an urban legend, a haunting. Locals always said it was cursed.

"My mom told me the director bought it," Cassie said evenly.

"*Bought* the Pinecrest?" Jessica asked. "Is it even still considered a hotel? By the way, the person who called the department and asked about extras was actually the director's son. He's an assistant, but he's like twenty years old and in college or something."

"Assistant *director*," Cassie adds. "And Cam is his name."

Cam, I thought, fleetingly, as Cassie raised her eyebrows. I could tell from her expression that she was already plotting to meet him, and based on her confidence when it came to striking up conversations with boys, I didn't doubt she would. At least I would have Jess to hang out with while Cassie flirted. Not that I blamed Cassie. There weren't very many interesting boys living in our stretch of the Keys. Visitors inspired imagination, telling stories that made faraway places sound exotic, like Toronto or New York. They made you feel like you could leave Florida and go anywhere.

"Almost there," Jessica whispered before the volume of her voice rose. "Wait, what's up with all these *people*? They're *all* here for the shoot?"

A line of parked cars stretched along the side of the side street that led to the estate, the rear of the last one nearly touching US 1. On the other side of the road, a group of kids hopped out of the back of an old Toyota parked facing the other way.

"You didn't think we'd just pull in the main driveway, did you?" Cassie asked. She pulled down the visor for one last look at her makeup. "Come on. Cam, or whatever his name is, probably called a few high schools. Who wouldn't want to be in a movie? Nothing else is going on down here."

My heart sped up. Jessica parallel parked, and we got out and started toward the estate, the back of my neck warm in the sun. Above the treetops, I could see the peaks of the Pinecrest's green shingled roof. I adjusted my T-shirt and jeans, tugging at where they had bunched from me changing in the car. Already, it felt like I'd left the marina ages ago. The group of kids in front of us turned off the road and started up the front steps, the concrete still shiny from a passing storm that morning. None of us spoke for a moment until Cassie reached behind Jessica and grabbed her leg, making her jump. "Boo!"

"Not funny. At all," Jessica said, smoothing down her hair.

I couldn't hide my smirk when she glanced at me. "It was a little funny," I admitted.

As we neared the steps, we saw the signs that had guided the kids in front of us: black with yellow letters and an arrow stapled to a palm tree. EXTRAS. We ascended the steps and followed the path around the side of the estate, where two of the shutters rested on the ground, another hanging precariously by a single rivet. The landscaping had seemed tidy from outside the gate—neatly trimmed hedges along the front steps—but began to look disheveled as we approached the estate itself. Fronds were strewn everywhere, and one of the windows had a spiderweb crack in the center.

"I've never been this close to the main building," Jessica said. None of us had. We'd taken enough of the rumors to heart to keep some distance. Being this close felt like touring some historical site we'd read about in school. Jessica frowned. "I knew the place wasn't being used as a hotel anymore, but I didn't picture it being *this* run down."

"It's part of the movie, genius," Cassie said, sounding slightly unsure. "I mean, it must be. They're trying to set a tone."

But were they?

After a few more steps, something landed in front of us with a bang. Jessica yelped as all three of us jumped back. I leaned forward to take a look, sweat forming across my hairline. At my feet was what looked like a broken rigging for a microphone—black, metal, and bent where it stuck into the ground—something we might have seen in the chorus room at our high school. A shadow fell across it, and we all looked up. A man's voice called out, "Sorry! You guys okay down there?" I visored my eyes but could only see his silhouette in the sun. "It slipped off the side. Everyone all right?"

"We're okay," I called back.

A second figure appeared beside the first silhouette. "Sorry," called a different voice.

"Totally fine," Cassie called, giving the men a confident wave. "No worries."

"That thing could have killed us," Jessica whispered.

"Be cool," Cassie answered under her breath as she stepped around the destroyed rigging.

I followed, then Jessica followed, too, across the sun-striped ground. Lined up at a gate were a group of people all dressed for a party, except no music was playing ahead. It was like a line for a club we were all trying to get into. I could hear the rumbles of muted conversations and see cigarette smoke rise in puffs. I saw a woman with straight red hair pulled back with a white visor between two people. Her eyes were invisible behind her tortoiseshell-framed sunglasses, but I could see streaks of white sunblock on her cheeks.

"What's going on?" I whispered.

"Shhh," Cassie warned, then lowered her voice as she told me, "I think the casting director is deciding which people to let in."

"Next," the woman said. Then, "Okay, you and you. Not you. Sorry." Then, a few seconds later, "You two are free to go."

Two guys and a girl strode past us in the opposite direction. Jessica and I shared a glance as the line advanced. When the kids in front of us were also turned away, we finally stepped forward. The lady in the white visor, who I would later know as Ann, looked the three of us up and down. She tapped a pen against her chin as if she was counting. "You kids will have to change. You're okay with that?"

"Absolutely," Cassie said.

Ann nodded as her gaze became evaluative. "One of the scenes is a beach shoot. You're okay with wearing bathing suits, I'm assuming?"

"Of course," Cassie immediately agreed. I touched the lump in my bag where I knew my bikini was, verifying I'd brought it. Jessica nodded less comfortably. She was less sure of herself in a suit, but I knew she wouldn't let that cost her the part.

"Okay. You three go in," Ann said with a slight glance to her left. "Check in with wardrobe. It's straight through there."

It felt like we had gotten away with something. We hugged each other once past the garden gate and followed another sign with the same black background and yellow letters as the one at the estate's front. This one read: WARDROBE. We checked in, met with a wardrobe supervisor, who explained we'd be waiting a while. "They want to shoot the beach scene between seven and eight fifteen when the light is right." She helped Cassie find a sundress, and Jessica locate a pair of linen shorts. She looked me up and down and suggested I change into a tank top. Then, we went out and waited by the pool with the other twenty-five or so extras, the water the same bright blue as the sky.

At three, Ann appeared and cleared her throat. "Sorry, I know everyone's been waiting for a while. There's a small technical issue they're working on that's paused filming until it's fixed. Anyone want the five-cent tour while we're waiting?" The three of us looked at each other. Jessica bugged out her eyes, her eagerness seeming to rise from her in waves. I thought of our conversation on the drive over, the mythology and rumors about the place.

"Definitely," Cassie said, speaking up for the entire group.

I saw two other girls exchange glances. Cassie could grate.

We followed Ann to the door. One of the guys behind me whispered, "Not to make an obvious *Thriller* reference, but this place smells like the funk of forty thousand years."

Laughter followed as Ann cleared her throat. "A few rules to go over. First, don't touch anything. Walking from one side of the set to the other, we pretend we're all on a ride at Disney: keep your hands down at all times. And please keep your voices down, even between takes. Random noise can be distracting. Did you see the props as you came in? Our team has wizards that make normal household items look pretty menacing."

I felt my muscles loosen a bit, reassured that I wasn't about to be startled.

Nothing to be afraid of, I told myself.

Ann looked at her watch, then led us into the lobby. "Some of you know the original Pinecrest was a hotel and speakeasy. The first floor was a restaurant, and the second was for gambling and socializing." Ann added air quotes around the last word. "A shipping executive built it in nineteen twenty-one. After watching repairs to nearby wooden structures following a tropical storm, he built his estate out of brick. You may have noticed the turret. He wanted a Victorian with steep, gabled roofs, bay windows, and stained glass. There are six bedrooms total, with six bathrooms, all upstairs, all with sash windows that open by sliding up."

Of course, the windows slide up and not down, I thought. Around the other side of the lobby, I spied three crew members crouching over a camera, evidently addressing the technical issue. All three wore baseball hats turned backward.

Ann's speech began to accelerate, like a tape being played slightly too fast. She caught the eye of one of the cameramen, who gave her a thumbs-up, then looked again at her watch before continuing, "It has open-water views, two large public rooms downstairs, two second-story balconies, and large stained-glass windows. The floors are made of Dade County Pine, a hardwood impervious to termites but is actually extinct now. The exterior doors are cypress, and the staircase is mahogany."

I looked up at the largest, most ornate staircase I'd ever seen. I thought of the iron railings outside, nearly saying it all looked like something from a movie.

"Whoa," Jessica said while Cassie gaped at one of the designs in the woodwork. Even she was impressed.

"Celebrities and gangsters stopped for a visit on their way to Havana. Hemingway, Tennessee Williams, Truman Capote all stayed here, probably because it was the first hotel on the island with electricity." She name-dropped without breaking stride.

I knew most of this history already, but I hadn't caught a glimpse of the inside. And I hadn't known about the Pinecrest having the first electricity—I tried imagining the utter darkness of nights down here without it. Ann turned on her heel and gestured with her index finger for the group to head back out to the pool deck.

Around six forty-five, she came back around passing out contracts and blue Bic pens. After everyone signed, she collected them into a folder and stepped onto one of the chairs. "Okay, you guys, listen up. We're ready in about ten minutes. The producers obviously don't want the details of the movie to get out, hence the nondisclosure agreements you just signed. I can tell you guys the basic plot if anyone's interested."

Under the shadows of the eaves, a slight breeze blew through the fronds. All of our eyes were focused on her.

Ann smirked. "Okay, then. Here are the basic elements: There's been a hurricane. There is no power and no phone in a creepy hotel. An unexpected visitor arrives, and of course, it wouldn't be a horror movie without a skeptical police officer and a few murders, twists, and turns, right?"

I glanced at Cassie, who smiled.

Ann went on, reading from a page attached to a clipboard. "A skeleton crew of caretakers, mostly local teenagers, stay to tend to a hotel during a hurricane and are without power on the island. On the night after the storm, they're eating dinner by lamplight when they hear a loud knock at the door. It's a young woman, alone and panicked. She was caught on a sailboat in the storm, and everyone but her drowned. So, the crew takes mercy on her, welcomes her in, and gives her something to eat. Pretty soon, though, they start noticing inconsistencies in her story. When a police officer stops by to check on them, he takes her statement and says he will call in a report. But one of the crew noticed the story she told the cop doesn't fit what she said earlier. He suspects there may not have been any sailboat or drowned crew. In a lightning flash, a crew member sees the body of the police officer in the yard. The crew is super freaked out and plans to confront the young woman. But they arrive just in time to witness... Well, that's all you get for now."

A few groans rose from the group, mixed with smiles.

"Essentially, what we're creating today is a beach scene that's a flashback to just before the storm hit. It's supposed to look idyllic, almost dreamy. There will be a small bonfire on the near side, and a few guys will be fishing back toward those trees." She motioned toward some fishing poles leaning against the fence.

"You'll be arranged in place as we're getting ready for a shot. Stay as still as possible until Mr. Plummer says, 'Action.'"

Jess shoots me a look as she smirks and tenses up her muscles.

"Any questions? No? Great."

Glancing at the fishing rods, I raised my hand. "Ma'am?"

Cassie hissed at me through a nervous smile. She reached to pull my arm down, but it was too late. I'd already caught Ann's eye. She pivoted on her foot and smiled with her mouth but not her eyes, sighing in a short huff. "Yes?"

"It's nothing," Cassie volunteered eagerly.

But I shook my head and spoke up. "Ma'am, I don't know much about the setting for the movie, but if it's set in the Keys, you'll want different lures attached to those rods."

Ann was chewing gum but stopped, glanced over her shoulder, then looked back at me. "And why's that?"

I paused before answering. I could feel the eyes of the other extras on me. "Because those are for saltwater fishing. Most saltwater fishermen don't use them anyway, but they especially wouldn't if they were casting on the island's west side. It's too shallow, and the water's more brackish."

She narrowed her eyes and nodded slowly, then the pace of her chewing resumed.

"Unless you mean for the characters to not know what they're doing," I said.

Ann issued a quick nod, then pointed at the rods. Already, a production assistant was scrambling over. "You're...from around here, I'm guessing?"

"I am, yeah."

"And what's your name, miss?"

"Lexi."

"Well, thanks for the tip, Lexi," she said before turning away, her folder tight against her chest. "I'm going to remember you."

Chapter FIVE

Marla's years of hard living are plain in the lines on her face, and there's a vacancy in her eyes like she's perpetually searching and exhausted by it. Yet even in her frantic state, Marla Moretti is unmistakable. When she glances over her shoulder, I see the same ethereal profile that's graced a dozen movie posters.

Her white summer dress is shredded around the hem and is missing a shoulder strap. Mud is streaked over her arms, and her brown hair—longer than I've seen it in recent photos—hangs over her shoulders in tangles. But it's her eyes that strike me—they seem to quiver as she looks me over, reminding me of how suspicious she's always been of me.

"Rick saw his chance to kill me, and he *took it*," she said.

I step onto the washed-out road and face her, the two of us engulfed by the postapocalyptic quiet. "Rick tried to kill you?" I repeat slowly, sounding incredulous. I can't help it. Marla has a track record of being dramatic, and part of me is still caught in my race to find Quinn.

She steps back, the mistrust plain and her tone demanding, *"Did he send you to find me? I know you two are family."*

I raise my palms. "What? No! I'm here to find Quinn, my daughter. I lost touch with her during the storm." I'm not sure whether to tell her that Rick and I don't speak—that I don't trust him, either.

"Oh, that's a very *convenient* excuse for you to be in the Keys. Little Lexi, always showing up at the last minute to save the day. Always helping her father-in-law with anything he asks. Always skating by, by the skin of her teeth."

I rest my hand on the car door. "I don't know what's going on here, but I stopped to help you. If you don't want it, I'm gone."

"Wait!" she cries. She wrings her hands, looking around as if verifying no cameras are rolling.

I take a deep breath. She's clearly not in her right mind, but my patience is wearing thin. "Marla, why are you here—why didn't you evacuate? And why would Rick want you dead?"

Marla runs her hands through her hair, letting out a bitter laugh. "Oh, didn't you hear, I'm shutting down his movie? I'm about to cost him a *lot* of money, not to mention eons of time in court."

I blink. "Why would you want to do that?"

"He wanted me on this cast—begged me. And I signed on as the final girl. The key word is *signed*. So when he found out he couldn't kill me on screen, he decided to do it in real life instead. He nearly ran me off the road during the storm."

I think: *He ran you off the road?* This sounds like the kind of lashing out Marla did so publicly years before. But even as I doubt her, I realize the hair on the back of my neck is standing up. Her story might sound ridiculous if she talked about anyone but Rick. But I know Rick. And Rick always does whatever it takes to get the shot.

We're less than a mile from the Pinecrest, and I can't stop the panic surging through my chest.

She squints like she can see the recognition in my eyes.

I open the car door and start the engine. "Tell me the rest on the way," I say.

She looks at the car, then over her shoulder again. "Oh no, I'm not going back *there.*"

I understand her reluctance, but there's no time to waste. "Marla, you can stay here or come with me. I have to find Quinn."

"You can't just leave me out here *alone.*"

I shift into drive, then hit the brakes as the car lurches forward. "Marla, *get in.*"

She makes the sign of the cross as she opens the passenger side door and drops into her seat. I don't want to believe Rick's capable of this, but I know better than most what can happen to people in his world. They end up dead.

And now he's alone with Quinn.

It's odd having anyone beside me after being alone and focused, and Marla wrings her hands in her lap and leans against the door as if I might reach over and attack her. I catch the rich, floral scent of whatever perfume she had on the day before as she fastens her seatbelt. I don't know what to make of her story, but I don't *have* to—she believes it enough for the both of us. Whether or not her account is accurate, her fear is real.

Chillingly so.

"We find your daughter, then I'm going to the police," she says in a shaky voice.

"Fine by me," I say.

"She was getting on a boat with him as I left."

My heart thumps as I take in her words; it was impossible not to think about Cam's disappearance last year. But her story fits what Quinn and Rick told me on the phone—it was how they missed the evacuation window when the storm shifted course.

"What happened last night before you left?" I ask.

"Aside from complete pandemonium? Rick and I fought, and everyone told me I needed to calm down, but I would *not* calm down. He walked out and took your daughter with him. I started packing and couldn't find my phone, but pretty soon, *everyone* started packing, saying the storm had turned. A few people offered me a ride, but I waved them off. I wasn't in the state of mind to just jump in someone's car." She rubs at her temples. "I started to drive, but there was a ton of traffic headed north, all the stores and motels were closing, and the sky started to get dark. I made it a little bit farther before I pulled over a few blocks from there." She points at a small building on the left side of the road, with a sign reading "Sea Shell Café." It's white with turquoise trim, and its roof looks miraculously intact. A silhouette is visible in the window.

"A woman came out, young, friendly. She offered to let me ride out the storm inside, and I was so frazzled I took her up on it. She found some rum, and we drank as the storm passed over us, but I guess I drank too much because I woke up around dawn in the rental car. I tried driving, but the tires were slashed."

"Maybe it was from debris, or you ran over something in the road."

"No, they were cut along the sides, like with a blade. I went back to look for Audrey, that was the woman's name, but the door was locked, and she was gone. That was when I heard the truck coming up behind me, *accelerating*. I jumped out of the way at the last second, but it clipped my elbow. It was Rick's truck, I'm sure of it. When I saw it turn around, I ran. I ducked behind a building, cut through a yard when I heard a loud bang. It was a gunshot."

I look over when I hear her voice break. Marla's eyes are red and brimming with tears, which have begun to streak down her cheeks. She looks at me expectantly, like she's trying to gauge whether or not I believe her. I'm wondering that myself when I notice her elbow—a plum-colored bruise has begun to bloom right where she said she'd been clipped by the rearview mirror on Rick's truck. She rubs at it with her opposite hand.

Something hit her.

I shift my eyes back onto the road, anger suddenly spinning in my head.

And fear.

"I know it sounds crazy, but it's what I heard. Rick was shooting at me. I went through some bushes and hid under a bridge, and then after a while, I heard some cars passing and ran out here to look for help."

I should be skeptical, but the way her hands shake makes my stomach tighten. I force myself to breathe. Could Rick really have done this?

When I see the Pinecrest's roof, I swallow and rub my eyes. I'd been running on a kind of grief-fueled adrenaline up to this point, but now that I'm here, I hesitate. It's both paradise and the worst place I know. I think of how my stepfather avoided it. I picture him folding down the newspaper he was holding. The summer *Breathless* was made.

I come around the corner, onto the side road leading to the Pinecrest, when I see Quinn, standing in the middle of the drive beside Rick's old white and red pickup truck.

"That's the truck," Marla shouts, pointing.

But I don't respond, and my eyes suddenly sting with tears. Quinn wears a T-shirt and a pair of green khaki shorts I could have sworn I donated before moving to the apartment. She looks somehow taller and tanner than just a few days earlier. The road beside her is submerged in water, rippling from stray droplets that fall from the trees. Closer toward the estate, palm fronds and shingles lie scattered around on the sand.

I park and rush out of the car, then wrap my arms around my daughter, not bothering to close the door before I breathe in the miracle of her. Time slows down, and for a few seconds, everything— all the destruction around us, the mystery of what she said she'd found—feels fixable. She smells the same as when she was a child. Rising in my chest is the same mix of exasperation and relief as when I searched through a Publix supermarket when she was three and when I combed every dusty inch of a country fairground when she was seven. She's older now, but my protectiveness never subsided.

Don't ever do that again. I'm sure I said back then. *Don't you know how worried I was?*

"Mom, I'm okay," she says quietly, now. *"Mom."*

I hear her, but I need to hold her for a second.

"I'm *okay,*" she says, more impatiently, returning my embrace with a quick squeeze before releasing. There's a word stuck in her mouth. "I…"

"You *lied,*" I say.

Tears fill her eyes. "I know it's bad. I'm sorry. I'm so sorry."

I glance over my shoulder at my parked car, where Marla looks on. "Why would you do that?" I ask.

Quinn's hands clench as her voice rises. "I didn't think a *hurricane* would hit! They were starting production on the sequel, and I just really wanted…" Her voice trails off. "Mom, I found something you need to see. It's Dad's."

I don't have the capacity to look at whatever she found. "Later," I say. We'll be back in the car momentarily, with four hours to process what happened. And I *know* why she came. It wasn't just the chance to be in Rick's movie.

She never believed Cam died. That was why she healed so fast, shifting back from being moody and abrasive to being her old self. She came down here looking for proof he's alive, but whatever she found, I'm not strong enough to handle.

Quinn looks past me. "Is that Marla?"

It occurs to me that she hasn't seen her since before the storm.

"I just found her five minutes ago. She said she was attacked."

"After she left?"

"We don't need to sort out what's happened. I just want to help get her to a safe place and get out of here. Where is your granddad?"

"Inside." She motions.

Great.

"He and I found the center of the old house last night, just like you said. Around sunrise, he made me stay inside where it was safe, then came out to look at all the damage. But, Mom, I need to show you..."

I brush my fingers through her hair, already sticky from the salty air. For the first time, I look up. I catch my breath and feel my eyes widen, a bead of sweat running down the inside of my arm.

"I found..." Quinn starts before seeing my reaction. "Mom, what is it?"

I can hardly believe my eyes. Behind Quinn, the windows along the estate's front are cracked in jagged angles, the sun reflected on the fragments. Most of the trees in sight are snapped in at their bases or turned over, their roots helpless looking, baking in the late morning heat. The landscaping is upturned, limbs and rocks were strewn about, and shutters lie on the ground. One, I swear, the *exact* same one as twenty-five years ago hangs on by one rivet. A piece of metal sticks up from the bottom, right where the microphone fell from the roof—the one that startled Jessica, Cassie, and me that day. "It's... nothing. It's just that the estate looks just like the set did for *Breathless*. Almost exactly."

Above us, branches are creaking in the gentle breeze. What's the psychological term for numbness from anxiety? The one my grief counselor taught me? *Derealization*. When things are too much at once, you float above.

"Just taking this in for a second," I say. Suddenly, part of me wants to see Rick. I want to read his expression for clues about whether he's messing with us. His reputation has always been taking actors to the edge, capturing their true, authentic *fear*. Raw, unfiltered terror. Other directors tried the same process with varied results, *The Blair Witch Project* being the most notable, but Rick was the first director to do it in horror. He said in an interview once, "Remember Alan Rickman's expression when he fell at the end of *Die Hard*? It looked real because it *was*. He didn't know when he was going to drop."

Audiences loved Rick's results, but actors hated his process, and the list of cast members who refused to work with him again was long, but then, wouldn't you have to be a little crazy in the first place to agree to let Rick scare the hell out of you whenever he saw fit?

I know it's impossible, but somehow, everything about this situation feels engineered. I know, of course, that Rick can't arrange a hurricane. He may *think* he can do anything, but even he can't accomplish that. What I'm seeing right now is just a coincidence. But still, my unease grows.

Quinn's eyes brim with tears as she steps beside me. "Do you think they'll tear it down? It's damaged beyond repair now, isn't it?" This is how teenagers break. They're tough until the instant they're not. She opens her mouth to say more, but it's a voice over her shoulder that speaks.

"It's all my fault."

I turn my head.

Rick Plummer emerges from around the corner of what remains of a wrought iron fence, a branch snapping beneath his boot. He wears blue jeans and the same leather vest he's had for years. He's more weathered than the last time I got a good look at him, my mind whirling to remember when. Was it really Cam's funeral? His hair was even whiter, and he's let his beard grow in, which makes him look even more like Donald Sutherland, a comparison I know he enjoys. "Hello, Lexi," he says, his tone cool.

"Hello, Rick," I answer, my tone matching his.

The sun streams around him on the porch like it was a light he'd put in place. He's already grinning, his smile somewhere between playful and wolfish. This is the way of charming people: they act like everything is easy, including forgiveness. "I'd have called you if I knew the storm would change course. I didn't think there was anything dangerous about being here. No one did until yesterday afternoon. Of course, *I* wanted Quinn here. I was glad you changed your mind about her coming."

He's not my father or even my stepfather, but I know he's referred to me as his daughter in conversations. I've called him "Dad" before, too, because it seemed like an appropriate way to address him at the time.

Not anymore.

"I'm not ready to talk to you," I say.

Quinn steps right in. "Don't blame him, Mom. Me being here is my fault. Grandad didn't know the full story until last night. By then, there was no way I couldn't explain."

"The *full* story," I say. "Quinn, let's just get your things. We have a long drive in front of us."

Rick squints at my car. "*Marla's* with you?" he asks.

"Don't worry about it," I say, raising my hand. "Let's just all keep our distance, okay? Give me a second to talk to Quinn. And stay away from my car."

As Quinn turns around, I see something sticking out of her back pocket.

A box cutter, perfect for cutting a tire.

That's when I remember a critical fact that I've learned all too powerfully in the last day.

Quinn lies.

Chapter SIX

SUMMER 1998

"Well, there's *Beetlejuice*, but that's pretty obvious."

"The 'Banana Boat Song.' Not exactly horror."

"...has horror elements."

"Please."

"Fine."

It was day two of shooting *Breathless*. We extras were waiting in one of the old estate suites to be called. Over time, the humidity had discolored some of the wallpaper, and cobwebs adorned the crown molding. The furniture was wooden and heavy looking, the sort of ornate curls on the ends that were perfect for a dilapidated hotel setting. And to add to the vibe, the space smelled musty. We hadn't seen the casting director, Ann, for over two hours. She told us on day one that movie production involved "a lot of hurry up and wait," but me, Cassie, and Jessica weren't completely ready for this much downtime. Beside the window, a group of kids from another school sat in a circle, engaging in a heated debate.

I leaned toward Jessica, who was blatantly eavesdropping, and whispered, "What are they talking about here?"

"They're ranking the top dinner scenes in horror movies because everyone's hungry."

Cassie groaned behind me. "God, I'm starving. I know the producers or whoever don't have a huge budget, but there's no catering at all? Can no one make a Publix run? Subs?"

"I guess not," I said with a shrug. I'd seen one of the leads eating a sandwich from a brown paper bag earlier that afternoon as if he'd packed it himself. We were all there by invitation, of course, but in some ways, the production seemed like one wildly extended home invasion, long enough for a movie to be made. The furnishings were incomplete like the previous owners had just left, abandoning what they didn't need as if fleeing during an evacuation. The room we were in had a bed but was missing bedside tables, which made the space it took up in the room seem odd. A phone jack dangled from the wall as if someone had attempted to rip it out.

"Am I going to be the one to just say it?" The oldest looking boy in the conversation asked as he threw his head back, his hair raven black dipping over his right eye. "*Alien*? One of the most famous dinner scenes in film *history*? Probably one of the most famous *scenes*, period?"

"The lighthearted conversation right before the creature pops out is what makes that scene."

"Agreed."

"No, the looks on the crew's faces—iconic."

It was late afternoon, the kind of light before sunset that gave everything a golden glow. The room was so hot my T-shirt stuck to the center of my back. I rested my hand on my stomach, which had been growling for an hour, and tried not to think about the work hours I was missing, or how Don was managing at the dock, or how he would dry-dock boats while getting customers away at the same time, or how... I pressed my fingers to my forehead, telling myself to stop.

"What about the pub scene in *American Werewolf in London?*" one of the girls asked. She had on fishnet stockings I envied and wore eyeliner so thick it made Cassie's look discreet.

"Did they order food, though?" someone answered.

"True. I don't know if they even sat down."

"Oooh, the Jiffy Pop Drew Barrymore makes at the beginning of *Scream!*"

"Not a meal. Plus, it burns."

"Wait, wait. We're forgetting the Chinese food scene in *The Lost Boys.*"

"I'm leaving," Cassie turned and told me. "We've been here all day and may literally die. And I can't take this conversation. I'm waiting two more minutes, and then I'm out of here. Seriously."

There was a knock at the door, and the casting director, Ann, stepped through. Her presence alone commanded a sense of purpose, and the boys jutted out their chins and straightened up. One stood up off the floor. Everyone was quiet.

Ann pushed her glasses up her nose and scanned the group until her eyes rested on me.

"You're Lexi Kennedy, correct?"

I drew in a breath, then looked at the others, Cassie's palm pushing on my back. "Yes?"

"Would you come with me, please?"

I shrugged at my friends. *I've done something wrong,* I thought. Or Don found out I was working on a horror movie and called to tell me to come back to the marina. Ann held open the gate as I shuffled behind her, the anguish of being singled out for anything at seventeen weighing me down like cement. "We wanted to have a word with you, please."

"Is everything okay?"

Her sandals clicked on the floor. "Quite," she said.

I followed her past a cluster of potted palms into the dark and cool lobby, then down a half-lit hallway to a door she knocked on twice.

From inside, "Yes."

The first time I saw Rick Plummer, he dangled from a chandelier. He'd grasped ahold of the curled base and was balancing on his tip-toes on a chair, squinting into the light as he called out, "Can someone tell Jodi to take it easy with the cobwebs? Please? It's supposed to be a functioning resort, not the fucking temple of doom." He picked away a handful of the loose, white strings and shoved them into the pocket of his black jeans. The crystals' jostling sounded like coins being shaken inside a jar as flecks of light scattered like frightened birds.

On the other side of the room, a woman I didn't recognize walked in holding two nightgowns on hangers, then stopped and extended them toward Rick. "Well, here they are."

From the way Rick glared at her, I guessed she was Jodi. "Get a little carried away with the spiderwebs, did we?"

"Those are, uh, real, Rick. They were already there."

He looked at her for a few seconds, then burst into laughter, a sound that made everyone else in the room loosen up, including me. "Oh, for fuck's sake, *of course*, they're real. They told me the place was haunted. Why shouldn't there be actual cobwebs?"

Ann cleared her throat. "Rick?"

Rick glanced at us and held up his index finger as he turned his attention back to Jodi. "These are the dress options?"

She nodded.

He leaned back on his heels, steepling his fingers beneath his chin. "Here's the problem: the lace is going to absorb way, *way* more blood, but it looks too...I don't know what, Victorian? Or something? The silk will catch the blue moonlight, but blood will run off and go everywhere. It has to *stick*."

Jodi nodded pensively.

"*Stick*. Am I right?" Rick asked the room rhetorically before turning to Ann and me. "What do *you* think?"

I shifted my weight from one foot to the other, reluctant to make direct eye contact. "You could make the silk tacky with resin," I suggested.

Everyone's heads turned, and I felt the pressure of a dozen sets of eyes on me.

Ann shook her head like she was prepared to endure the moment until it passed.

Rick's eyebrow raised, prompting me forward.

I cleared my throat. "Where I work, we use a kind of clear resin to repair punctures in boat hulls. A few dabs of that before it fully dried would make anything stick, even liquid."

Rick looked at me, then at Ann, his eyes narrowing with a kind of academic curiosity as he asked, "And this maritime scholar is..."

"Rick, this is the person I've been waiting to *introduce*. Meet Lexi. She's possibly the new Casey."

A smile crept across Rick's face as Ann stepped away. "Ah, perfect timing, in that case. Well, *new Casey*, which of these nightgowns would you like to die in?"

I must have given him an incredulous stare for being so completely caught off guard, part of me wanting to run back to the room where we'd been waiting. What was Ann talking about?

Rick's brow furrowed. "Too soon for nightgown decisions? Let's back up." He hung the nightgowns over the back of a chair, asking, "Will you come with me?" then started down a dark hallway before I could answer. I looked at Ann, who nodded. The hallway was cooler than the main room, and I rubbed my upper arms as I followed him. There was cardboard taped over the windows in the room on either side. It had formerly been the mail room and the pantry. I heard murmurs of practiced lines through the wall to my left, as if they were shooting a scene in the next room. But how was that possible if the director wasn't there? *Maybe the actors are just rehearsing,* I thought.

Rick turned and entered the hotel manager's office, which he had turned into his own. On the walls were taped pieces of scripts, maps of the island, and stapled Polaroid photos of actors, arranged like the collection of a serial killer. Rick checked his watch as he sat behind an ornate desk. "Lexi, right?"

I nodded.

He motioned toward a metal folding chair, the kind that sat in my high school's cafeteria. "Sit, please. Apparently, you've shown *exceptional* poise." He spoke with an odd familiarity that made me unsure how to address him.

"Mr. Plummer, I..."

"Rick, please." He waved his hand. "I'll cut right to the chase. You're an extra in this film, but Ann recommended you for an opportunity."

The sorts of apprehensions Don might have had flooded my mind. Had I been naive to think I was safe here? I folded my hands in my lap and set my jaw. "What kind of opportunity?"

"I'm offering you a different part, a much larger role than you're currently in." He paused. "An actor who had previously been cast in the film cannot fulfill her contract. There's an opening."

The word "opening" sounded ominously vague. Had the actor quit? I rubbed my hands together, picturing my friends passing the time in the tiny waiting room. "Is everything okay? With the other actor?" I felt the need to clarify.

Rick smiled mysteriously and leaned back in his chair. "Some people have very vivid imaginations, I suppose, but yes, she's quite well. On her way back home as we speak."

"Oh, okay."

"Lexi, I don't have long to fill this spot. For about two days' work, you'd take a starring role in this film. Your name would go on the poster. You'd be famous. People would kill to have this chance." His right eyebrow rose.

I had the out-of-body sense that this meeting wasn't happening, that there was no way I was being offered a starring role in *Breathless*. My friends and I had just walked onto the set the day before. But everything around me was vividly real: the musty office, the creak of Rick's chair, the worn wooden floor under my sandals. Cassie was going to be so *pissed*. Through the wall, I heard more conversation followed by nervous laughter.

"Well?" Rick asked.

"I... What's the role?"

"You know how I work—I can't tell you too much. But, well, you saw those two nightgowns? One of them..."

"...Eventually gets covered in blood?"

Rick shrugged, then rested his elbows on the desktop. "Precisely. Is that a yes?"

I hesitated.

The murmurs through the wall continued, more loudly than before, people engaged in a heated conversation. What were they talking about? Rick caught me glancing in that direction and cocked his head, prompting an answer.

"Okay," I agreed.

"Good." He clapped his hands together and stood. "Your scene will shoot tomorrow, probably, so let's get you into hair and makeup right away. We'll need some test shots so you can try on both of those nightgowns for wardrobe, and I'll send a grip out for...what was that sticky stuff called?"

"Resin."

"Resin, right. Your character's name is *Casey*, by the way." Darkness swallowed his voice as he disappeared back into the hall. "Lexi, you're the *new Casey*."

I followed Rick back toward the room we'd been in earlier, where everyone else was going about their business. Jodi walked past carrying what cobwebs she'd cleaned from the chandelier, and Ann studied a clipboard with a penlight. Rick passed her and said, "It's a yes," to which Ann nodded. Jodi sidled up beside me. "Congratulations on getting the part, and don't worry about any of the other actors' egos. You're going to do *great*."

Which egos? I wanted to ask. Who could be upset? I only agreed to take the role a minute earlier. "Thanks," I said, mustering a smile.

"Rick said for you to go ahead and get ready, so if you don't mind, could you try on both nightgowns in case we can't get that blood to stick?" She extended both on hangers.

"Sure." I took them from her and stepped into the bathroom to change. The tiny room had authentic horror movie lighting from a flickering overhead bulb and smelled like furniture polish and soap. I could hear the crew laughing through the door as someone told a story about the lights suddenly going out during a shot the day before. I couldn't catch every word, but the laughter was slightly mischievous and contagious. "That blood went *everywhere*."

I found myself smiling as I took off my clothes and slipped on the nightgown, and straightened my shoulders to have a look at myself in the mirror. My whole life, I'd wanted to go to summer camp, and the feeling I had in my chest, right then, was how I hoped I'd have felt there.

Why was this, of all places, somewhere I felt I fit in?

I came out of the bathroom with my clothes in my arms to find several people waiting for me. A woman with pink hair and a green flannel shirt with rolled-up sleeves asked me, "You're Lexi?"

"Yes?"

She pulled out a small chair in front of a vanity mirror and patted it. "Madeleine. Have a seat." She took the clothes I'd been wearing and hung them in the closet. Little did I know that the sleeve of my white T-shirt would eventually make it into a few of the shots.

Soon, Madeleine was applying something to my face and shoulders, telling me what she was about to do before each step. "Now, I'm going to spread some of this here. Now, I'm going to brush this across your forehead." Some of it felt cold on my skin, some I could hardly feel at all. My eyes were closed, but I could hear the sound of metal adjusting against metal, like tent poles extending. I could see the light growing brighter, then softer, through my eyelids. I could hear a male voice asking, "How's that? Getting any glare off the mirror? Better? How about now?"

"Keep your eyes closed for just one more minute?"

"Mhmm," I said.

I felt a cool mist and then a brush through my hair. "I'm adding this dampness because the character you're playing has just come out of the shower. It's just for the test, but we'll get it perfect for your actual scene tomorrow." I heard the shushing sound of a spray bottle a few more times, then felt a chill settle on my neck and shoulders. I felt like I did during trips to the dentist as a kid, not quite understanding what was happening but knowing instinctually it would be over soon.

"Still okay?"

I nodded.

"Okay, Lexi, you can open your eyes."

I nearly gasped. I looked five years older, the way some girls do when they get dressed for prom.

"What do you think?"

I'd opened my mouth to answer when across the room, I heard a door open and slam shut, and then quick footsteps march disruptively across the floor. Everything was still until a woman's voice cut the quiet like breaking glass. "So that's it, Rick? You just decided?"

I could hear Rick mutter a response behind me.

"A *new girl* is playing Casey? *Done?* No one wanted to mention anything to me?"

I heard someone sigh, then a hushed reply to the woman. I turned my head.

"Speak up! That's her?"

She was visible only in silhouette, but I immediately knew who I was looking at. I'd seen her in half a dozen films. In front of me was Marla Moretti, the star of the film. And I was in her movie now. She stepped forward and stood in front of Rick, arms folded over her chest. She wore no makeup, yet her features seemed pronounced, ideal, and angelic. Her chestnut hair was shoulder-length, and freckles dotted her creamy skin. She looked like she belonged on a screen and as if the ground she stood on belonged to her. In person, she was smaller than I'd imagined but even more striking. Since we arrived on set, I'd wondered if I would even see her, and now here she was. I caught my breath.

Jodi stepped back into the room, her expression curious. "Ms. Moretti, can I help?" she asked.

Marla shot Jodi a withering look, and she stepped back.

Rick took a step toward her, hand extended, a smirk on his lips. "Lexi, let me introduce you to Marla Moretti. She's just learning about your new role in the film." I had just met Rick three minutes earlier, and already I realized he was unafraid to ruffle feathers.

Marla looked me up and down, then rolled her eyes. "If I'm being honest? You won't fill out that nightgown nearly as well as the other girl," she said. "Just saying."

My expression contorted like I'd been slapped. Everyone standing in the darkness around the edge of the room pretended not to watch, but I was sure they'd heard every word. I took a half step back, my calf knocking against a chair.

Rick came and stood beside me. The room's silence was a soft buzz in my ears.

"Marla," he said, delicately but firmly, "aren't we better than that?"

There was a pause before Marla's expression melted. Her chest rose and fell with a quick heave, and she shook her head like she was disgusted by the ten-second-earlier version of her. She grabbed my limp hand and shook it—her mouth twisted like she'd gritted her teeth. "Oh, God, sorry. I'm Marla Moretti. I haven't slept in a while, so don't mind me. And you look just fine." She squinted. "Actually, better than fine. You look...nice."

Nice. I wanted so eagerly to take in her compliment, even as another part of me was dizzied by how abruptly she'd changed character. She certainly was an incredible actress.

It was then that a loud, horrific scream sounded through the wall. I jumped, and my heart leaped into my throat. Rumbles of conversation carried from the next room. As they grew louder, I could make out the exact words. "...have mixed feelings about it a bit—jumping out to scare someone out of their wits doesn't seem like a kind thing to do," the man who I'd later know as Doug said, as he appeared, rubbing at his temples. "But it's all in good fun, I suppose. It's not like they didn't know what they were getting into, working with Rick."

"Someone mention my name?" Rick asked, smiling.

Ann shook her head, clicking off her penlight. I could feel the energy change for the third time in as many minutes. Was this what movie sets were like?

A young man, blond, maybe twenty-five, pushed his way into the room. He wore board shorts, flip-flops, and a T-shirt bearing a hotel logo I didn't recognize. I realized later he was playing one of the innkeepers.

Marla turned and looked him up and down.

The man stormed over to Rick, his voice loud and shrill, "You didn't want to say anything before that...that guy..."

Marla made a circular movement with her hand, saying, *speed up*. "...Doug?"

The guy looked back and forth. Was he complaining to Rick? In front of Marla Moretti? He coughed. "Sure, yeah, *Doug*, the dude who jumped out of the curtains. You didn't want to say that was an actual take, or to look out, or something? I didn't know we were rolling."

"We're always rolling," Rick said.

"Well, he fucking freaked me out."

"That's the idea, genius," Marla said.

"You realize the film is about a murderer?" Rick asked with patronizing calm.

Snickering came from the dark.

"Just *scaring* us like that? It's...it's *cruel*. I mean, if it was some other genre, maybe, but this one?"

Rick stroked his beard. "My boy, I can't think of another genre where authenticity matters more."

A look of disgust washed over the actor's face, his color

draining slightly. "This is sick," he said as he turned and stormed out of the room.

"The world is sick, love. I'm just holding up a mirror."

A door slammed.

"Too many rookies on this set, Rick," Marla said, then cut her eyes toward me. "No offense."

"None taken."

Marla rested her hand on my shoulder. "Good luck, New Casey." She turned to Rick before sauntering away. "Have my assistant fetch me when it's time?"

Rick turned to me in a way that felt suddenly fatherly. "Of course, I don't tell the actors what's *about to happen*—I'd be robbing them. No audience wants to see fake feelings. Anyone can tell when someone's just *acting* scared. Do you think the cast of *Alien* knew that creature was going to pop out of a chest?"

I shrugged, remembering the conversation the extras were having ten minutes earlier.

"I promise you, *New Casey*, they did not. The truth was in the actors' eyes."

Chapter
SEVEN

OCTOBER 31ST

I grab the box cutter from Quinn's pocket and toss it into the pitch apple bushes.

Quinn turns as she feels what I've done. "Hey, what was..."

She and I are halfway between Rick and my car, where Marla waits. I've stepped far enough into the brush that I don't think either could have seen what I've done. I have no reason to believe Quinn would've had anything to do with Marla's tires being slashed, but I want nothing that *could* be evidence anywhere near my daughter. Protective instincts come automatically, overriding my sense of logic. And my conscience.

I pinion Quinn's shoulders and turn her toward the car. "I'm reminding you, Marla was attacked last night. She said her tires were cut. We're taking her, now, to file a police report, then we're getting out of the Keys."

I try reading Quinn's expression but detect no flash of guilt there. Her tone becomes skeptical immediately. "But by *who*? Like some looter or something?"

"Lexi?" Rick calls as he follows us.

I ignore him. "Marla doesn't know. The police are going to have to sort that out."

Quinn chews on this for a second. "But everyone mad at her is gone now, evacuated. Maybe someone just took it out on her car?"

"In any case, time to get going."

A breeze pushes through the branches overhead, and in the quiet, I hear the clink of wind chimes somewhere in the distance.

"Lexi?" Rick calls again. I'm about to tell him again to stay away from Quinn, me, and my car when Marla emerges, charging toward him as if looking for a fistfight. "Just tell me *why*. *Why'd you do it?*" She screams, her hands balled into fists. "You're getting sloppy. You know that? Even if I hadn't seen your truck, it wouldn't take a genius to figure out what happened. The person who benefits most from me being dead is *you*! Breach of contract, anyone? *Attempted murder*, anyone?"

Rick draws a deep, comically patient breath. "Marla, what an unexpected pleasure. I assume you're talking about your abrupt resignation? Quinn and I were out on the water when everyone left, so I didn't have the pleasure of seeing you off."

I'm reminded of the feeling I had years ago—Marla is *always* acting, whether she means to or not. She's fascinating in the way an accidental house fire is fascinating. You wonder how high the flames will rise and how far they've already spread inside. She wrings her hands, then puts her hands on her hips. "I'm only this close to you because there are other people around, and I'm *only here* until we can get the police. Maybe you didn't like that my lawyer said I have a case to do it, so you thought maybe you'd run me off the road then take a few shots for good measure. Well...you missed."

He looks around, gauging my and Quinn's expressions for some grounding in reality, and catches my eye, his lips curling ever so slightly with his impish smile. I know what he's thinking: whatever lawsuit she's referring to, he was sure he could talk her out of filing.

That's Rick.

"Ah, there were *gunshots* as well," he says, before adding with patronizing calm, "Marla, none of that happened. If you think I want you dead, let me remind you I'm the one who asked you to be in the movie."

"Then who *did* try to hit me, just as the storm picked up?"

"I...can't guess."

"It was *your* truck. Pretty *damn* recognizable. You're just terrified you'll lose all your money once I get the movie stopped." She looks at me. "Did he tell you? He financed all of *Breathless 2* himself."

Could that be right? My heart accelerates. Movies are so incredibly expensive to make. Would Rick have gambled so much?

Of course, he would have.

Rick coughs into his hand, clearing his throat. "I know this is a line from a horror movie, but *don't be ridiculous*. No one tried to kill you."

"Stop smiling," she says. "This isn't a joke."

But he can't stop smiling. Everything for him is both serious and not. Even fear.

He turns to me. "Marla is no longer happy with her role and has been asked to leave the production. How do magazines put it when there's a break-up? We've amicably decided to part ways and wish each other the best going forward?"

"Fuck off," Marla says before turning to me. "He cut my part down to nothing. I'm in what, *two* real scenes? The role is barely a cameo at this point. I'm suing to stop the whole production. Without me in the lead, it's shit anyway."

You're lucky to be working at all, I think, *after everything you've gotten into*.

Rick folds his hands on his chest. "I've said this a hundred times, but the part would have been great for you. A fitting role, considering your extracurricular activity. It's different than you're used to, but fans would have loved it."

"The *party girl*? That's for debut actresses, and they're always the first to die." Marla says, then mutters something I can't quite hear.

"What?" Rick asks.

"I said you deserve to lose your movie after the way you treated me when the first film came out!"

"Ah," Rick leans back on his heels. "So that's really what this is about? Not just vanity but revenge. It was a nice attempt."

"*It's not over*," Marla says before looking directly at me. "And what about *you*? You return—the prodigal daughter? You just *happened* to find me there?"

I'm taken aback after having driven Marla here, but she has the sensibility of a cornered animal. Slowly, I say, "As I said, I arrived this morning. I promise I didn't mess with your tires or run you off the road." *But I did see someone with a box cutter.*

She shoots a look at Quinn, then uses the back of her hand to wipe at her lips. Her fingers tremble. "And *you. You* remember when I left," she says, taking a step toward Quinn that's aggressive enough for my arm to rise, blocking her.

Rick speaks up, answering for her. "Marla, I think *everyone on the set* remembers when you left. You made quite an exit."

My stomach tightens into a knot as I picture Quinn with the box cutter I wonder: could she be capable of having some part in this? And what reason would she have? I wouldn't have questioned it a week ago, but she's full of surprises. Quinn steps closer behind me and leans her chin against my shoulder.

"I suppose you'll be taking over the lead now? I'm sure you wouldn't have minded too much if I'd just vanished last night."

"Wait a second," I say, jolted. I turn to Quinn. "You were going to take the lead role?"

Quinn looks at her grandfather. I can't turn my head fast enough to catch the look that passes between them. "It was just an idea," Quinn says softly.

"What?!" I ask. There's no way.

"I was intrigued, I guess."

"Oh, I bet you *were* intrigued. *I'm* the *final girl, Rick*," Marla says. "I *made Breathless*. The lead part is mine, no question."

I catch an unreadable glance from Quinn.

"Lexi..." Rick begins.

"No. Just *no*."

"Think of the stories she can tell at college. The part can be tailored specifically for her. Although it's your call, I suppose, letting her miss a once-in-a-lifetime opportunity."

Suddenly, I'm so angry that my skin burns despite everything going on. I don't raise my voice when I get upset. I lower it. I step toward him now like I mean to poke him in the chest. Quietly and calmly, I say, "You don't get it, *do you*? I don't want Quinn to experience being stabbed to death, even if it's on film. Do you know what that does to a person's dreams? To their sense of what's safe? Of what's real and what's not? I don't want that for *her*, and I don't want to watch my child die, even if it's on screen. You of all people should under..."

I'd stopped, but not soon enough. There are tears in my eyes, some because of my losing Cam—my husband, Rick's son—and some because I know I've strode carelessly into a place of deep hurt for Rick.

"I do understand, believe me," is all he says.

"You're not exploiting my daughter," I say after a moment.

He nods solemnly, then raises his hands as if extolling calm.

"Look, this is a tad awkward for everyone, but the power's out up and down the Keys. Please, come in, dry off, relax a bit. Marla, I'll get you a towel, and you can call for help." He sweeps his arm, inviting her in farther.

Marla peeks behind Rick as if someone might jump out at her.

I can't tell if Rick believes part of what she's saying, but her emotion feels completely authentic.

I think back to the bruise on her elbow.

"Or...you're welcome to stand on the front porch until the mysterious truck comes back for you, but I'm going inside."

"Here," I unlock my phone and hand it to Marla. "Call the police." We watch as she presses the numbers on the screen, 9-1-1, her eyes darting around. From the tiny speaker, I hear three tones and a recording.

She scowls, her teeth gritted. "It's just some error message! All circuits are busy, or something like that."

She hands me back my phone, and I check the time, seeing that it's nearly noon. I also notice that my battery power is down to eleven percent, which I know I should conserve.

"Then I guess you're riding with us," I say. "Unless you're staying here."

"Thank you, but *hell* no," she says, running a hand over her hair. A breeze blows in through the open window facing the water. When I glance over, I see an expanse of blue sky opening over the tops of the palm trees.

Every part of me wants to get Quinn in the Volvo and get back to the mainland, but what can I do? I think back to her car, parked at the odd angle in the street. I want so badly not to believe her, but his old F-150 is easy to identify. How can I say no to someone who's just been through what Marla has?

Even if that person is Marla.

I start calculating the time it will take to drive her to the Sheriff Substation.

"We're leaving. If you're not coming with us, my advice is to wait here for the police."

But Quinn is at my sleeve. "Mom, wait, we still need to get Dad's old typewriter and his other things. We can't leave it."

The thought of going back into that room makes me start to sweat. "That stuff is going to have to wait. I'm sorry."

"Mom, it'll take two seconds for us to run in and grab it."

The thought sends a chill up my spine. "They're just things, Quinn."

"Jesus Christ, Mom. I'll go with you if you're so scared."

I turn on my heel. "Hey!"

Quinn clenches her jaw. I can tell she knows she's gone too far.

I have to remember I'm talking to a teenager, a human with no developmental concept of risk. She'll find the slimmest of margins to get to what she wants; I admire the determination while it scares me to death. She's been talking about retrieving Cam's typewriter since the week he passed. I force myself to breathe. What are the odds that whoever attacked Marla is still hiding in the estate now? Slim, but there's no way I want her setting foot inside. I say something I regret, even as it leaves my lips: "No," I say. "I'll go in."

But she leans closer to me. Close enough that only I can hear her whisper, "Mom, *no*. I want to go with you. I found something. Something I want you to see *now*. Someone hurt Dad." She lays her hand on my shoulder and continues. "Granddad wasn't with me the whole night. Or early this morning."

When my gaze flicks back up to Rick, his expression has changed. Maybe his intuition tells him he's being talked about.

It's the first time I've ever seen his façade fail him.

Marla sees it, too.

"Quinn..." he says.

"Don't leave me alone," Quinn asks me, her earlier confidence now shaken. "He's hiding something."

Chapter
EIGHT

SUMMER 1998

"You're dead wrong."

Jess shook her head with absolute certainty. "It came out on *Some Great Reward*."

"Sorry, it's on *Catching Up*. I *have Catching Up...*"

The day after being offered the new part, I was again sitting on the room floor where the extras for *Breathless* waited, listening to Cassie and Jess argue about which Depeche Mode album featured the song "Somebody."

A thunderstorm had blown in, and the sound of rain pounding against the windows combined with the occasional gust of wind against the old walls made the Pinecrest seem even more ghostly than it already did. Parts of the house may have been reconstructed, but the room we sat in had floorboards so splintery that pinpricks of light peeked up from below. I hugged my knees against my chest when a crack of thunder made us all jump.

Ann had offered me a lanyard that gave me more access to the set, but I decided not to ditch my friends. But Cassie and Jess had been arguing for long enough that I'd caught a few of the other extras shooting looks in their directions. "Guys, please," I finally interrupted.

Cassie stretched and sighed to disguise her annoyance. Jess folded her arms, her expression pouty, "Just let me finish. If you'd be quiet for one second, I can explain. It's on *Catching Up with Depeche Mode* because *Catching Up* is a compilation with a bunch of their singles. But the *album* it came out on was *Some Great Reward*."

"It's...whatever," Cassie said as if the whole debate was stupid now that there was evidence to refute her point. She turned to me. "You missed the big excitement while you were doing your thing."

"What big excitement?"

"Yesterday? A nail flew right through that wall."

I looked at Cassie blankly, then she pointed, and my gaze followed her fingertip to a small metal point sticking out of the plaster. "What the hell?"

"Exactly. One of the guys working the set came in and gave everyone the fifth degree about whether any of the extras had messed with their stuff. Of course, we're all just sitting in here, bored, talking about movies."

"But someone had?"

She shrugged. "Maybe? Apparently, there's a safety thing on nail guns that has to be depressed for them to fire, and you have to press the tip against something hard, like wood, to shoot a nail out."

"So?"

"So, the safety was pulled back with some kind of band on the one he was holding. He didn't think it could fire, but it did, so..." She pointed again. "Wham, right through that wall. Freaked him out more than us, I guess."

I pictured the repairs to one of the docks the summer before last, the velocity and sickening thumping sound those guns made each time they fired.

"That's kind of scary," I said, my mind pushing away thoughts of someone in its path.

"It's just an accident, nothing you have to worry about now that you're...a star. Are you supposed to be in here among us regular people still?"

"Stop, I'm supposed to get some kind of briefing or something, but honestly, I'm feeling a little guilty about not helping Don."

Cassie blew out in a puff of disbelief. "Well, *that* makes sense. Go ahead and take off now, but tell them I volunteered to take the part? I feel like starring in a movie."

Jess knocked her leg lightly against mine. "She's right, you know. The marina's going to be there when you're done. You *have* to do this."

I liked few things less than being told I had to do something, but I could see Jess's point, and I felt grateful, but the waiting made me anxious. I knew the set would be like this, but I also knew how impossibly hard Don must have been working since he was covering for me.

I looked again at my watch, which had hardly moved. "I just wish this guy Cam would hurry up."

Cassie sat up straight. "Cam? The one who came to the drama department? You mean to tell me the director's *son* is the one giving you acting lessons? I'm dead."

"They're not acting lessons. Mr. Plummer told me it wasn't even really going to be acting. I'm supposed to just do what I feel in the moment, but in kind of a choreographed way, if that makes sense."

I could see in their expressions that it didn't, which was fine because I didn't fully understand, either.

There was a quick knock on the door, and as if on cue, a younger, slightly taller version of Rick stepped through the door. He wore torn jeans and a black T-shirt, had sandy, chin-length hair, and scanned the room right to left before asking, "Um, Lexi?"

I raised my hand, and he nodded, smiling, before walking over and reaching his hand down to help me up. I could feel Jess's and Cassie's eyes on me and wanted to tell them to stop, whatever they were thinking, to *just stop*, because I was nervous enough without the pressure of their gazes.

"I'm supposed to show you around the set and tell you a few things about the shoot today. Ready?" He sounded genuine, which was a departure from the kind of sincerity-with-a-motive feeling I got from his father the day before.

I waved bye to Cassie and Jess and followed him into the hall, rolling my eyes as Cassie flashed me a big thumbs-up while Jess tried to cover her hand. Two assistants hurriedly approached just as we entered the hall, Cam and I leaning back to let them pass. One carried a severed arm, and the other held a metal bucket in each hand. "Coming through!" the first called out.

"The props can seem a little weird if you're not used to this kind of stuff," Cam said as we started again. I didn't mention that I'd seen more blood splashed over docks than I had so far on the set. He pointed at two black boxes fastened to the top of the banister, each with a few small separate bulbs visible inside. "Those strobes will flicker to make it look like a lightning flash. They add the thunder later."

I thought of the real thunder that had made me jump a few minutes before.

"Most of the scenes are supposed to be at night, so sometimes the lighting accentuates shadows on faces and the sides of walls, or looks like the moon if they have to reshoot during the day." He pointed overhead as blue-toned lights popped on. With the windows blacked out, it might have seemed like faint moonlight if the chatter of extras wasn't filtering in from the lobby. "Oh hey, Dave," Cam said, exchanging a wave with a man carrying a butcher knife as he led me out to the pool deck.

"They're set up to shoot upstairs and working in the kitchen area, so it's a little quieter if we walk around the outside of the estate to where you need to go. Take a walk?"

"Sounds good."

"Before I launch into the blocking for your scene, is there anything you're just curious about?"

I didn't want to sound unsophisticated, but I also knew this was my chance. "I mean, I'm learning a little as we go, but I don't completely understand some of the job titles. Do you have one?" The question came out more flirtatious than I'd intended.

Cam shrugged and smiled. "Dad doesn't have an enormous budget, so everyone's doing a few jobs at once. Technically, I'm the second assistant director, but that doesn't mean much in this film. I'm here because I can do a lot of behind-the-scenes stuff without being trained. I was supposed to intern at a newspaper this summer, but Dad needed the help, so here I am." Another smile. I liked that he seemed to take things in stride, unlike the goofy, beer-drinking boys I knew on the island, and I understood helping out his family even though he had other plans. Cam had a winsome confidence about him that made it seem like everything would be easy. I wondered if that came from growing up well-off.

We passed through a gate and set out onto the grounds. Typical for Florida, the downpour had already stopped, but heavy raindrops still fell from tree branches above, dotting my shirt.

"What's a 'grip'?" I asked.

"It's a funny name, I know. You know the cameras? Grips are in charge of everything they sit on, which keeps them in place. Usually, there are a few different angles in one shot. Dad doesn't use any stunt doubles or green screens. You've...probably heard a little about how he directs?" He raised an eyebrow, asking.

"Some. The stunts and bloody stuff don't bother me. I've stepped on nails, gotten plenty of rope burns at the marina where I work." I turned my palms up to show him my calluses, and his eyebrows scrunched down.

"Ouch," he said, his voice lowering a little.

From somewhere in the distance came a blood-curdling scream.

We both stopped walking for a second. "That...happens, some-times," he said apologetically. "Some of the effects get added later, but it's pretty minimal. The fire is a real fire. The actors' falls hurt. It can be pretty hard on the cast, but luckily no one's been injured so far." He paused as if recalling a memory. "I mean, *seriously* injured."

"If you don't mind me asking, what happened to the actress play-ing the part I took? The original Casey? Your dad didn't say exactly."

Cam hesitated. "Sure you want to know?"

"Yes. Obviously."

"I don't mean to be mysterious." He rubbed the back of his neck. "You've probably heard some about this place, that it's cursed."

"Since I was a kid, but just the kind of stories kids tell each other at sleepovers. Everyone's told me to avoid this place, but I've never heard good reasons why."

"What I'm about to tell you might change that," he said. We walked stride for stride while I waited for him to elaborate, remem-bering what Cassie had just told me about the nail gun. "I've seen a few things, and so did Dawn, before she left. I didn't know her very well, but she seemed pretty chill to me, at least not someone who would make things up. Being in this movie was a big break for her. But her personal items kept going missing, for one thing...things there'd be no reason to steal—a favorite hairbrush, her shoes—mostly it turned up after a few hours, but it seemed like someone was messing with her. Then there was... Are you sure you want to hear this stuff?" He smiled like we were about to conspire.

"Are you kidding?! Yes. What were you about to say?"

"One morning, she found an electrical cord tied into a noose in her dressing room. No one should have access to that room but her. It could have been one of the techs practicing for a prop, but there's no noose in this film. It sure seemed like someone laid it out for her, which if you think about it is very, very..."

"Creepy," I finished. I folded my arms as we walked along the back of the estate, passing a crew spread out on drop cloths, filling balloons with red dye.

"Exactly. Then, two days ago? She said she went to shoot, *locking her door* before she left, then came back to find all the glass in her room smashed—TV, mirror, everything. She freaked out, understandably, rambling about the curse. Whether the rumors got to her, or she was just stressed out, I don't know. But she left in a hurry."

"Wow," I said, taking everything in.

"I don't mean to dump that on you, but you asked, and truthfully you deserve to know," he said.

"I guess your dad probably hired more security or figured out a way to keep the set more secure?"

Cam laughed a little and shook his head. "Security? You think that because you don't know my dad. There's a rumor that he's the one who's doing it all."

I hesitated. "Do you think there's any chance...?"

Cam shrugged playfully. "I...I don't know. But I think the truth is almost worse. He *enjoys* it, as sick as that sounds. He likes the cast and crew being on edge because he thinks tension makes for better art, whatever that means. He's already telling reporters about what happened to Dawn. And you know what? They're eating it up."

I didn't know what to say, so we walked in silence for a while. When we got to the door that would lead up to wardrobe, we paused. Cam opened his mouth to say something more when a deep thunder rumbled inside the house. Artificial, as far as I could tell. Cam nodded in the direction. "The sound techs are geniuses at getting things to sound extremely nasty with just household stuff. Like a bone breaking is usually a set of crab legs. Last year, they made a monster-eating-a-person-sound by twisting a head of romaine lettuce."

"Sorry," I said. I couldn't help but laugh. Maybe I needed to release some tension after hearing about Dawn.

But Cam laughed, too. "No, I get it. It sounded funny to me the first time I heard that, too. It's a lot of fun to watch. You should come out to..."

He stopped himself.

Was he about to invite me to Los Angeles?

I'd go, I realized. Somehow, I knew I would. I'd known him for less than ten minutes and realized I'd go to California with him, no questions, without thinking twice about it.

What was happening?

I swallowed as I paused at the door, wanting to extend the moment. "So, what about you?" I asked. "You wanted a regular internship? You don't want to go into the family business?"

"You don't beat around the bush, do you? I guess I don't, no. It's interesting, but not exactly for me. I'm more of a writer."

I'd never heard anyone say that they wanted to write for a living, but I didn't want to admit how blue-collar I felt, so I smiled and nodded as if he'd just said the most natural thing in the world.

Cam nodded at the door. His voice softened. "So, let me tell you a little about how it will go upstairs. You'll go into wardrobe and then to makeup, probably for about fifteen minutes each. Then someone, probably Ann or my Dad, will place you on the set. You'll stay kind of frozen while the crew tests the lighting and sound. I mean, you don't have to stay *mime*-still, but try to stay put. Then, Dad will say, "Action," and everything will start. You'll walk from the bathroom to the bedroom and start getting ready for bed. Your character's a little on edge because of the hotel's unexpected guest, but you'll be trying to keep yourself calm because you just want a good night's sleep." He paused, then added bashfully, "Then, at some point, you'll tangle with a serial killer."

"At some point?"

"You may run through the scene a few times or go a long stretch where nothing happens. Most of the actors just try to stay in character. Dad likes the jump-scares to be real. I think it's too nerve-racking, but it's his method. Truly, you can back out if you feel uncomfortable."

"I'll be alright," I said. I thought back to the actor's exasperation the day before. He'd described the process as "cruel."

Cam shook his head a little as a smile crept across his face. "It's anxiety-provoking, I get it. But, you know, this *is* a horror movie. Some things are inevitable."

I turned the doorknob and looked up the dark stairwell. "Meaning?"

His smile widened. "Meaning, not many characters survive Dad's movies. At any moment, someone might jump out and kill you."

Chapter
NINE

OCTOBER 31ST

A serpentine vein is now prominent on Rick's temple. "Now wait a second, even if something did happen to Marla last night, which frankly I have no reason to believe, I had nothing to do with it." His eyes shift around to Quinn and me. "Nor did I have anything to do with Cam's disappearing last year. And honestly, how dare you? How *dare* you even insinuate otherwise? What gives any of you the nerve to assert I would..."

"Because you created the mystique, right?" I interrupt, sharply but calmly. "You played up every unexplained and tragic event happening here to promote your work. Are you surprised you're suspicious? Drop the righteous indignation and just tell us where you went this morning."

"I need to do no such thing," he replies, his tone returning to its usual cool timbre as he glares at Quinn. "I shouldn't have to remind you I was with you, in the main building. After the worst of the wind passed, while you were asleep, I went outside once or twice, *briefly*, to have a look at the damage to the estate. The sun wasn't fully up, so I went back out for a long walk this morning. You might have noticed there's a lot to check in the ten acres, including my cottage?"

The cottage itself is a nondescript beige, in-mode for Florida builders around the mid-eighties. What's striking is how usual it is; hardly where one might expect a famous horror director to reside. The last time I was inside, it didn't appear updated but wasn't run down, either, existing in that strange time warp of appearing neither new nor old. I remember what Cam told me last year about his father keeping to himself. "You've been staying at the cottage for a while now," I say.

Rick blinks quickly like the question has caught him off guard. "I have been, but so what?"

It feels like he's leaving out some information. "Why? You always adored the main house. You built the cottage a decade ago for guests. Why move in there yourself?"

"I can sleep wherever I like," he says. "But since you asked, I was keeping the main house clean and ready for read-throughs and then filming. No one's been up in the guest rooms since last year."

"I was," Quinn interjects, then looks down as everyone turns their eyes toward her. "I went upstairs yesterday afternoon while we were closing up the house." She glances up at me. "He hasn't been letting anyone up there during filming. The cast and crew weren't staying in the guest rooms."

Rick's face flashes genuine surprise.

Rick, what are you hiding?

"I say we try the police again," Marla says insistently.

"My cell is dead," Quinn announces.

Rick taps his pocket. "Mine too."

Marla's expression says she doesn't believe him, and I'm not sure I do either, even though his phone being nonfunctional is plausible.

I check mine, even though Marla had already tried to call for help. It looks like there's a signal, but no bars lit up. "I have a little charge left and want to save what I have for the drive home, but I'll try again if you'd like."

She nods.

If you saw what I did during the drive down, I think, *you'd know we shouldn't bother.* I think back to what the soldier said when I entered the Keys: *We're on our own.*

While Quinn tugs at my sleeve, I redial 9-1-1 and get the same error message as Marla. "You need to see what I found."

"The call won't connect," I say, pocketing my phone and letting Quinn lead me toward the front entrance to the Pinecrest.

Marla calls out that she doesn't want to be alone with Rick, but now I'm too curious about what's driving Quinn to fully care. Rick may be dangerous, but he's not crazy enough to hurt her when we're so nearby.

Besides, I've heard Marla scream before—if something happens, we'll know.

I hear Marla continuing to berate Rick, then take a deep breath before Quinn and I step over downed branches along the shaded path between sea grape trees. I look back toward the road as the wind brushes in. There's no one else in sight because none of the other residents were unlucky enough to have taken an impromptu boat trip the day before. Or no one else was that dumb. They all saw the weather forecasts, took calls and texts from relatives, or checked their email. Then, they got the hell out of the Keys when evacuating was still possible. I remember the expression on the National Guard soldier's face, and a chill runs up my spine.

Here's what Cam would say: *First, the warning from the guard. Now we're here, in this remote, desolate location.*

What comes next?

I duck beneath a circuitous branch then push inside the front door. Daylight fights its way inside at the far end of the lobby. I flick the light switch, but of course, nothing happens. I see Quinn and Rick's efforts to board up before the storm—slats of plywood nailed up at odd angles and a few bits of whatever cardboard they could find. Puddles splay out in places where rainwater blew in. Something about the darkness of the interior during the day makes the lobby seem larger than it is. "People are afraid of the dark," Rick told me once, years ago. "They project all their fears onto it. Shapes get transformed and distorted. We struggle to make sense of what we can't see, filling in the pieces with our fears."

As we make our way toward the staircase, I hold Quinn's hand, our footsteps squeaking through the water on the floorboards. We pass what used to be the front desk from when the Pinecrest was a functioning hotel. Rick kept it in place because he liked it.

"Come on, Mom," she says, tugging. She can feel my reluctance.

"I'm coming," I say.

Places hold a presence. *Amityville, Texas Chainsaw,* a hundred examples when going into buildings like this are bad ideas. Part of me wants to call Cam's name as I look around the expansive lobby.

I swallow.

This is ridiculous, I think. *Get up the stairs and see what Quinn's talking about.*

Do I really think the place is haunted? That I'm about to see a ghost?

I think to Cam: *Remember that chapter in your manual titled, "Not Listening to Your Intuition," about how characters put themselves in terrible positions when they should know better? You mentioned* The Silence of the Lambs.

I picture Clarice Starling entering the house of Buffalo Bill near the end of the film. She's there to ask him a few questions but notices some clues about his identity—spools of thread, and then finally, a moth. By the time he asks about suspects, she readies her pistol. Only the audience can see Bill's revolver laying on a stove in the next room, just out of her sight.

She should have had her gun drawn from the time she knocked on Bill's door.

Part of her already knew he was the killer.

Ready yourself, if you're so nervous, Cam says in my mind.

I look around, scanning the room. I hate guns, so it's not like I can just retrieve one from my car. A lamp? Not useful. A side table I could detach a leg from? Possibly. A piece of the broken glass scattered across the floor? I'd more than likely cut my hand.

Then, my eyes settle on it.

The knife that stabbed me in *Breathless* hangs in a black shadow box above the mostly ornamental fireplace in the foyer. It's the one Marla couldn't find during her scene because it was already in her killer's hand. I'm no weapons expert, but I happen to know it's a dive knife—a serrated edge for cutting fishing line—meant for emergencies, maybe to tap on an air tank to get someone's attention.

It wasn't designed as a weapon, but it'll do.

"Mom? What are you doing?"

"Hang on." Regardless of the arguing outside, someone cut Marla's tires. And if that person is still here, I don't plan on encountering them unarmed.

I stand on my toes to pull it off the wall. The box is heavier than I'd thought—the wood is thick, and I see the top is covered with a coat of dust. I flip it face down on the floor, pop open the back, then pull apart the plastic straps that hold the knife in place. I know it has value to someone, a collector, maybe, but that's unimportant now. "Sorry, Rick," I mumble. The long blade gleams in the faint light as I test the weight in my hand and switch the knife to my other hand so I can grasp the banister, then step over the rope Rick had strung up across the stairwell.

"I'll go first," I say.

Cam had looked down the stairs—these stairs—during our last call when he'd stayed here and he noticed a light had been left on.

What had he seen?

"We're going to the room at the end of the hall," Quinn says. "The one he used as an office."

When we reach the landing, I see a branch poking through a window down the hall, warm air wafting through the rupture. I hear the early afternoon call of crickets and wipe the sweat from my brow. Without air conditioning, the temperature is only slightly cooler inside than out, and I notice it heat up even more as I move onto the second floor, kicking aside shards of broken glass as I go. Beside each door is a small gold oval preserved from when the Pinecrest was a hotel. Instead of a number, each bears the name of a native bird, written in cursive: *Osprey, Pelican, Heron*.

Cam's room during the summer we met, his first in the Keys, was *Ibis*. I haven't been upstairs since he and I were teenagers. It's the room where we first kissed, where I first let him undress me. I assume it's empty, but I push the door open. I have to look.

The shades are drawn, but everything appears intact, and I realize that since the storm came in from the west, it most likely spared this side of the estate the heaviest damage. Like most remembered places, it's smaller than I remember, but the smell—a blend of furniture polish and salt air—is exactly the same. My eyes settle on the bed, my mind drifting just long enough to feel myself blush.

A sound coming from the end of the hall snaps me back.

My head jerks around, the knife's rubber handle feels warm in my palm.

"Hello?"

There's just the sound of the breeze whistling through the broken glass.

"It's nothing, Mom, come on."

My eyes adjust, and I let go of the breath I'm holding. I half expect to see twin girls in matching blue dresses when I look down the hall.

We make my way toward the final room, where Cam finished his book last year, the suite with the best view of the water. Despite all my reservations about this estate, I have to admit the view is spectacular. He could watch the waves from the second floor, the tide roll in and out.

The suite's door is open, and the room is filled with light. Shattered glass covers Cam's desk, and loose sheets of paper blow around everywhere. Below, the bay looks tranquil, like a child on best behavior after a terrible tantrum.

Bits of glass and fronds from the trees crunch under my shoes. "What are we looking for here?" A paperweight with Hemingway's face rests at an angle. A lamp is on its side, the bulb broken, the filament so vulnerable-seeming, emerging like a bud. I recognize some of his things. Others he bought down here. Their unfamiliarity reminds me of how long we were apart while he worked on the book. He came here to isolate himself. No distractions. My eyes sweep over the bed, the fold under the pillow tucked in a way that tells me Cam made it. It looks the way his side of our bed looked for two decades. There's a knocked-over lamp on the bedside table, and I stand it up and straighten the shade.

"There," she points to the typewriter. I step to it as she lingers in the doorway, tucking the knife into my jeans before I try to make sense of the chaos of paper on the desktop. Some are upside down and wet. Others are torn or are blotchy from where the typewriter ink has run. None of them are numbered. He'd been so romantic about this book, insisting on using the old-fashioned Smith Corona. It had taken him the better part of a year. Now, the finished product was out in the world, immortal. Looking at the pages, I shiver, transported back to when I first saw the manuscript. I put my hand on the edge of the desk as the feelings rush back.

My hands shake as heat rises through the floor. I read bits of sentences here and there, fragments I recognize from when I proof-read his first draft.

"Not those," Quinn says. "The one he was working on."

I don't know how my eyes didn't settle on this immediately. A single sheet of paper is inside the typewriter. The desk chair's rollers squeak as I push it aside. I lift the mechanism that holds the paper in place, find a roller on the side of the machine, then turn it, so the page advances out.

There is writing about two-thirds of the way down.

I cover my mouth with one hand as I read.

been spending too much time alone. I may be losing my mind. Either that, or the rumors—ones I've never wanted to believe—are true. My fingers ache from stabbing at the keys of this sixty-five-year-old typewriter. I thought solitude would help me work, this place without the flood of information from modern life.

It helped, at least in the beginning.

Now, it's with a sense of dread that I remind myself: I wanted this.

Some places are empty for a reason. I hadn't thought of that.

I keep losing things—my keys, my wallet—despite going very few places and spending most days by myself. Now, I can't find my journal. Maybe I'm consumed by what I'm working on, but I don't think so. It feels like it's more than that. I feel a familiar presence that I can't explain even though I'm alone here.

Sometimes, at night there are sounds downstairs or in the hall. I've gotten up to check before but found no one in either place, nothing disturbed. I've wondered: am I imagining them? Hours blur from so much time in the quiet. Maybe my senses have blurred too. I sometimes forget the day of the week and the date.

Now my shadow seems distorted. How strangely it twists on the pine floor and on the colorful paint in the halls.

Can life become a horror film?

Can you get lost in what you create?

Through the second story window, I've watched the water in the bay become more uneasy each day. I sense unrest all around me.

I think a storm is coming.

The floor creaks as I step backward, my heel crushing a piece of glass as my calf knocks into the wooden bed frame. This was not a page I edited. It wasn't written for publication. Cam wrote it because he wanted to document what was happening. It feels foreign in my hand, and I set it back on the desk because I want to be away from it. The tone is nothing like the campy, satirical tone of all the rest of the book. These words sounded sincere.

Suspicious.

And afraid.

And too much like the summer when we were first here.

When the terrible things started to happen.

"Well?" Quinn asks.

My stomach hollows as I try to answer, the words from his page still replaying in my head.

I may be losing my mind.

My eyes stay fixed on the tucked bedspread. He was the last one to sleep here. *I might be losing my mind because now fear runs hot in my veins.*

"Someone was messing with him. You can see that, *right*? This proves Dad didn't just *disappear.*"

I don't know what it proves, but I know we need to leave.

"We have to get out of here," I say.

The Pinecrest and the Keys.

The desktop presses into my thighs as I reach around the base of the typewriter to pull out the page. But a twinge of pain makes me snap my hand back. My hair falls around my face as I search the desktop for what just bit me, a tiny drop of blood rising on the pad of my index finger.

My eyes refocus on a single gold earring lying behind the typewriter.

I pick it up and examine it in the stream of light through the broken window. It's a unique design, like a long teardrop. Nothing like one Quinn would wear, with her black nail polish and extra-long shorts. I test the edge against my skin—it's not especially sharp—I must have rolled onto it at just the wrong angle—but pointed enough to break my skin.

It's been more than a year since Cam was here.

Right?

Rick hasn't come upstairs. A woman's earrings don't show up by chance in a man's bedroom. Had someone spent the night with Cam last year?

I look at Quinn, knowing full well I would never voice this thought to her even as my skin flushes with anger.

I never imagined Cam would cheat on me, and I never sensed he was.

But was he having an affair while he was here last summer?

Or running from something else when he vanished?

↝

Sunlight is hot on my face as I burst out the front door onto the porch, dragging Quinn by the hand. I stop just long enough to turn the lock on the doorknob to lock it before drawing in a deep breath to fill my lungs with fresh air.

"Wait, Mom, shouldn't we take that to the police? That's new evidence, right? Why aren't you saying anything?" she asks.

I'm too confused and furious to string words together but manage the self-restraint to not vent about my suspicions to Quinn. From the porch, I can see Rick and Marla. We've only been away for a few minutes, but part of me is relieved they're in the same position as when we left—him trying to explain something while Marla shakes her head.

"You're sure what you heard was a *gunshot*?" I hear Rick interject, smirking.

"I lived in New York City for fifteen years. I know what a gun sounds like, just like I know your truck," she says.

Quinn is beside me. "That was a journal entry, not part of the book, Mom. We can't just run away from this!" Quinn grips my shoulder, spinning me to face her, the urgency in her eyes confirming why she's here: she accepted Rick's invitation as an opportunity to look for clues about Cam's disappearance. My heart aches for her.

I drop my voice, trying to keep myself steady. "Call it running if you want, but yes, we're leaving this place, and we're leaving now. Do you need me to remind you that you shouldn't have been down here to begin with?"

She yanks her wrist away from my hand with angry force. "But we're *here*, *now*. We're not leaving without showing what we found to the police or without Dad's things."

"Let's go."

I step off the porch, but she doesn't budge.

"You're that ready to move on? You've got a new boyfriend now and can just walk away from what happened?"

"That's unfair. You know it's not like that. Now, come on."

"Why? So you can just bury your head in the sand like you're so good at doing?"

This comment stops me dead in my tracks. She'd meant to hurt me and did, her accusation cutting to the bone, even if she didn't know it would go so deep. Years ago, I did the same thing. I know that. I denied what I saw, and then I got out. I'm not sure I ever forgave myself. Now, it's happening again. "Quinn!"

She looks up and away but doesn't answer.

I step back onto the porch, breathing slowly to try to keep calm. I rest my hands on her arms. "Listen, you're not wrong, but it's not the time to sort through everything. We need to get Marla to the police, get to a safe space, and report this ourselves. I need you to help me now, okay?" She doesn't answer. "Quinn, *okay?*"

Don't you know how scared I am? Of what we both just read? Of so much changing? Things you don't even know yet...

This morning I was afraid I would lose you, too. Now all I want to do is leave.

"Fine," she says.

~

Quinn and I settle in that uncomfortable parent-child operating mode we use when we're mad at each other, but there's no time to talk. For now, we play it cool as we make our way back toward Marla and Rick.

"Well?" Marla's pulled her hair back, but her eyes are still as wild as they were earlier. "Did you two find whatever it was you were looking for?"

"Not exactly," I say, purposefully avoiding eye contact with Rick. "But it's time to get on the road. The Sheriff Substation is about a mile north. I don't know what to expect there, but I'm sure they'll keep you safe." I picture the sand-colored building with the green roof and shutters. Unlike a few of my friends, snagged by petty crimes as teens, I'd had no reason to go in and had always driven past without looking twice.

"I don't even know how I *can* leave *now*," Marla says.

Rick looks at her confoundedly.

"The *tires?* On my rental? It's not moving anywhere."

He shrugs and pats his jeans pocket before extracting a key and tossing it to her. "Here. The crew brought down another rental from Miami. I was going to move it closer to the house anyway. Just drop it off at the airport."

She grips it in her fist and glances at the white compact sedan. "Fine."

Quinn runs into the cottage to retrieve her things, then emerges a minute later. She tosses her bag in the trunk, glances at Rick, then climbs into the backseat. Marla drops into the passenger seat, and I hear the zip of her seatbelt. I nod at Rick because I have nothing to say.

Maybe we'll talk again. Maybe we won't.

"Really?" Rick asks, his tone like a teenager who's angry because he's gotten in trouble.

I get in the car and drive off, catching a quick glimpse of him in the rearview mirror as he turns and heads toward the dark cottage.

"Just a few minutes to the station," I voice to Marla, just to have something to say. I feel like I do when I'm at work at the high school, when a student needs my help—they've forgotten money for lunch and need to borrow five dollars, or they're having a tough time at home and need a few minutes in a quiet space. Except now, the stakes are vastly different. She stares straight ahead, her silhouette calm and unreadable. Dramatic people can drain you, but I remind myself that this is a woman who survived an attack. She needs to get to the police and be taken safely to her car.

Giving her a ride is the least I can do.

Did she really hear a gunshot? A flicker of doubt flashes through my mind. My foot leans on the gas. The road hypnotizes me for an instant with the heat waves coming off, and I wipe the back of my wrist across my forehead. I feel the press of fatigue from not having slept and wonder if I should let Quinn drive part of the way home. We pass another building that looks as if a bomb went off inside. Glass and bits of colored plastic are scattered around what remains of the front lawn. The other side of the building looks untouched—a picture from another day in paradise.

Marla clears her throat tentatively. "I know you're in a hurry, trying to get home. So, thanks, really."

"This won't take any time," I say, trying not to tap my fingers impatiently. Occasionally, I glance in her direction, the sunbaked road and the downed trees flying by in the window beside her.

"Marla, how long had you been down here in the Keys?"

"Three weeks. I came down a few days early because I wanted to see Key West."

It seems a little random, but so does Marla's life, and I'm reminded that she didn't grow up here.

"Just visited some places," she clarifies, "Ate at Louie's. I hadn't been there in years."

"Nice," I say. I picture her wandering around in a guayabera and Kinos, her money stolen from a scam tour she booked at a kiosk. The tourist line is "Locals celebrate sunset every night!" but really the locals set up new and unique ways to separate you from your money as *you* celebrate. The buskers are cute, though. There's a dog who wears pants, innumerable Tarot readers, musicians of all sorts. If she'd emailed me in some alternate world before she went down, I would have told her to tour the Hemingway House and the Audubon House and eat at Captain Tony's and the Green Parrot and try to avoid the day's cruise ships docked there.

"You must miss it here," she says quietly. She's so much calmer now than she was at Rick's. I wonder if her anger has burned off or if she realizes I must not be her enemy.

I swallow. "I did work a lot as a kid. Too much, really. I took off from here as soon as I got the chance."

"I'm sure you were sick of all the people like me who come down and don't know what they're doing."

I shrug, thinking of the guys from New Jersey, Philadelphia, or

Indianapolis who thought they were masters of the sea because they understood finance or law or watched *The Greatest Catch.* "Most of the time, it was pretty amusing. Other times, it could be slightly dangerous."

"Yeah?"

I look at her. She's fragile and tense enough, so I don't want to go into it under the circumstances. Boats sink every day at marinas; it's more dangerous than most people realize.

Maybe she does realize it after the explosion that took Doug's life.

Maybe Marla realizes the dangers all too well.

Quiet strikes me as we drive. No buzz of boat engines or rumbling on trucks. Just the dead calm of a deserted space. As we make our way up US 1, the tires catch on sand that's spilled onto the road. I slow as we come over the next bridge, passing a dive shop where a dozen bright yellow air tanks rest in the parking lot as if they'd been tossed out the front door. Beyond, a patch of Australian Pines stands along the coast. As a teenager, I walked there with boys vacationing from faraway states—New York, Connecticut, Michigan—places that sounded exotic, then. I wondered what brought them to our island when they could have gone anywhere. They might share a kiss and feel their warm hands on the sunburn beneath my T-shirt, watching the steady lights of ocean vessels on the ghostly horizon.

I tell her, "I camped on that beach with Girl Scouts when I was a kid. I searched those dunes with flashlights, looking for crabs after sunset."

I hear her cough, and when I look over, I realize she's sobbing.

"Marla, are you okay with making this report? It's just a little farther."

"No. I mean, I don't know. Coming here early was a mistake. I didn't expect to wake up alone in my car or get caught in the storm or any of this. I'm not tough, like you." She fidgets with the string on her dress. "You were always so strong, even back then. When you stepped on that set twenty-five years ago, you were fearless."

I nearly laugh, caught off guard. I search the mirror for Quinn's eyes, but she's looking out the window. "I'm glad I carried it off. But you were pretty tough on that set if you remember. I started as an extra. You were the star."

A shadow falls at an angle against Marla's cheek as she looks passively at the wreckage around us. "I should have known better than to come back to the Pinecrest after what happened to Doug... Rick wanted everyone who threatened him out of his way..." she mumbles like she recalls the fragments of some rueful dream. She looks down at her hands, and the hair on the back of my neck stands up.

I swallow, not wanting Quinn to hear this but feeling like she should. Maybe hearing someone else's impression of Rick will finally show her how dangerous he is. I think of the skepticism Marla faced over the years, how terrible it must have felt to be doubted. I feel my heart speed up and force my attention back on the road. "You think *Rick* had something to do with the accident back then?"

Her eyes flash in surprise, just a flicker before she waves my question away. "No, no. Actually, Rick's the only filmmaker I've *ever* trusted on set if I'm being honest. Back then, I broke down to him about what was happening all around, the accidents, the broken and missing things. And I wasn't the only one. You know that's why Dawn left."

The original Casey. I lose my breath for a second. "I...knew a little." What Marla's saying makes my stomach tighten as history shifts in my head.

"She got spooked. Left before filming her scene. That's why Rick needed someone else for her part." She looks at me. "You. You hear those stories, those old rumors about how some film sets are cursed. I always wondered if *Breathless* was."

"Like *The Exorcist*," I say, automatically, practically quoting Cam. I stop myself from saying more.

"Exactly like *The Exorcist*," she says. "Darkness was all around that film. You know two of the actors who get killed in the script died in real life before post-production? *Seven* people associated with that film died. Ellen Burstyn had a permanent spine injury when her harness broke. Linda Blair had a mental breakdown."

"Come on." The words slip out of my mouth.

"I'm serious. Objects levitated in the room when William Blatty wrote the novel—not to mention the unexplained fire. Everything except Regen's room burned," Marla says, a little trancelike now. "It delayed shooting for six weeks. Some sets were known as cursed. When Landis was filming *The Twilight Zone* movie, a helicopter crash killed several people. Or, you know, *The Wizard of Oz*, of course."

"That was just a rumor." I want her to please stop talking, but I know she's not wrong. I can't count the number of blog posts and YouTube videos that have been made about the filming of *Breathless* and about how Doug died. The folklore is fuel for curiosity. Marla's word doubted at every turn, while Rick, all the while, poured that fuel on the fire.

I swerve to avoid what looks like a washing machine flipped upside down. Sand has accumulated in tiny dunes around two palm trees that have blown over, emerald-green fronds sticking up at odd angles.

Marla's voice continues to rise. "I'm not crazy, Lexi. It *happens*. Films get cursed. Especially horror films. And it just makes them more popular, doesn't it? The curses just publicize them. It all becomes part of the *legend*."

The topic feels like quicksand. The harder I try to get out, the faster I'm getting pulled in. It's like I'm watching a scary movie through my fingers, exploring and avoiding simultaneously. I try to interject, but Marla talks over me.

"Maybe this whole place is cursed too? I only came to restart my career, and now I'm barely making it out alive. The fucking Pinecrest. I know what happened last night and what I saw on that set. *I saw a ghost.*"

"Stop!" I cry, the sound coming out more forceful than intended.

Now Quinn sits up straight behind us. Her eyes dart back and forth between Marla and me.

"The Pinecrest isn't *cursed*. What happened was just a bunch of weird coincidences that Rick played up, and what happened at the end of *Breathless* was an *accident*. Whatever happened to you last night was something else entirely. Maybe Rick was involved, maybe not. That's going to be up to the police to figure out."

Her eyes say she doesn't believe me.

Do I believe myself?

I point up ahead to the substation we're approaching on our left. The parking lot is empty, aside from two service vehicles parked near the entrance. The bushes along the driveway are uprooted, the floodwater ripples in the ditches on either side—but the building itself seems intact.

"There. Hopefully, someone's inside."

"I..." Marla pauses, stumbling over her resistance to what she wants to say. "I need to ask you something. And I need you to be honest." Her voice is shaking.

My nerves are on edge from raising my voice, but I answer calmly. "What is it?"

Another pause, then, "Do you remember seeing a little boy on the set of *Breathless*?"

"I..."

Before I can respond, a patrol car pulls behind us, its breaks squeaking as it slows to a stop. The sun reflects off the windshield at an angle that makes it impossible to tell who's driving.

When its blue lights flash, I jump.

⌇

Marla looks over her shoulder, a vein throbbing in her neck. "He's coming up here," she says, a slight tremor in her voice as if we're kids about to get in trouble. We haven't seen another moving vehicle since we left Rick's cottage, but this cop is acting like he's pulled me over. It's the third or fourth time I've spoken to an on-duty cop, but I know Marla's led a different life.

She wrings her hands in her lap as the thump of the cruiser door closing hits us. She's muttering as if rehearsing what she means to say to the cop, "I was leaving last night, didn't want to stay the night here...slashed tires."

I reach for Marla's hand, but she moves it away, and I wonder why she's working so hard to keep her story straight.

"We have to tell him what we found upstairs," Quinn says behind me.

Marla looks at her, but Quinn's words don't seem to register.

"Soon," I answer.

The cruiser's blue lights flash, reflecting off the broken windows of a one-story home across the street. When I catch a glimpse of the officer's face in the rearview mirror, I realize it's familiar. My gut remembers him before my mind does, a wave of disappointment rising from where I stored high school acquaintances.

I sigh.

Marla's head turns, her eyes a little frantic. "What is it?"

"I know him," I whisper, rolling my eyes in a way that would put Quinn to shame. "*Knew him*, I mean, a long time ago."

I roll down the window, and he leans forward, peering into the car. The sweetness of whatever body spray, or whatever he's recently used, hits me as my mind search through memory fragments for his name. Maybe he played baseball? Or had a class with me?

"Morning, ladies. Well, almost good afternoon."

His blond hair has thinned but spiked in the same teenage way, and the beginning of a belly budges over his belt. His forehead has puukened from years of sun exposure, and his cheeks show the stubble of someone who normally shaves but skipped today.

For obvious reasons.

He looks older than the National Guard soldiers, with touches of gray around his temples and eyes betraying fatigue that rivals my own.

"Hi, we were hoping to fill out a report," I say.

His gaze sweeps around the car at Marla and Quinn before he shakes his head once, quickly. We drift through the awkward moment of pre-acknowledgment until his expression transforms. "Wait, I know you two. You're Marla Moretti, right?"

Her expression brightens as she answers in a voice completely different from the one she used a moment earlier, "Hi, Officer. Good to see you this morning."

Always acting.

The officer takes off his sunglasses, and his face brightens. Anyone who thinks celebrity means nothing has never witnessed someone realize they'll have a story to tell later.

"And *Lexi*?" he says. "I didn't recognize you at first! I don't know if you remember me? Dustin Reynolds? You were a grade ahead of me, but I think we had History together? You're in town? *Now*?"

Dustin. Where to begin? "I'm here to get my daughter home. But the three of us are here, right now, because of what happened to Marla."

He squeezes his eyes shut for a second as if overwhelmed by so much information. "Sorry, I've been running around like *crazy* this morning. Fortunately, most people weren't stubborn about evacuating when the call came before landfall. They say when Jim Cantore shows up, it's time to leave."

There's something vaguely accusatory about the way he says this, but I manage a smile at the thought of Jim Cantore holding onto his hat. "Just to back up, we're actually here right now to file a police report. Marla was attacked last night during the storm."

"Attacked?" His expression makes him look thirteen. He takes a step back.

Now, I remember. Good guy. Silly in class, but nice to everyone.

Bumbling, Cam says in my mind.

"Let me go turn off these lights. Hang on. You guys don't have to stay in the car." I notice a dark patch of sweat in the center of his back as he trots back to the cruiser.

Marla pulls down the visor and straightens her hair.

Cam's manual whispers in my head: *It's one of the biggest clichés that cops are useless in times like this. They say things like, "Slow down" and "Take a deep breath." Then, characters like yours say, "You have to help us," and "You don't understand." Usually, by the time cops appear, the main characters are completely hysterical.*

I glance at Marla, her hand visibly shaking.

Maybe worst of all, cops are usually in danger themselves but don't realize it. When they die, the main character usually seems to feel a mix of terror and frustration—a sense like, "I told him so."

I tell myself to stop. A breeze tilts the branches of a Poinciana tree that survived the wind, a scattering of red blooms on the ground below. The blue sky is so midmorning perfect, it seems computer generated as if all of this is part of some production or surreal dream: Dustin as an adult cop, the hurricane, the earring, Marla's attack.

Dustin returns, flips open a notepad, and clicks a blue ballpoint pen. I hear a muted snap as Marla flips her visor up, then the jostle of her car door opening, then closing. She explains everything to give him a full picture of what's happened: her coming to the Keys to read for the *Breathless* sequel, how I'm here to find Quinn, and how we met her and Rick at the Pinecrest earlier. Then, Marla folds her arms over her chest, going through the conflict with Rick and how she found her tires slashed. Her voice breaks as she recalls being chased this morning. When she describes the gun going off, I grip the side of the car seat.

But Dustin laughs. "Wait, you were at the *Pinecrest* this morning." Dustin turns to ask me, "You know what that means?"

I want to ask, "Meaning what?" But his expression tells me he's heard every rumor.

I brace for what's about to happen, I can feel it coming, and I hate it for Marla: more disbelief. Dustin clicks the pen closed, tucks it into the front shirt pocket, then squints as if preparing to deliver bad news. "You both were in that movie, right? *Breathless*? And you said you were in the Keys because you're working on a sequel? Any chance what happened was set up to be filmed?"

"No," Marla says, her voice flat now. "It was nothing like that."

"And you're absolutely sure it was Rick's truck that you think tried to hit you?"

"Yes?" Now it's Marla's turn to be incredulous.

Dustin raises his hands. "Listen, all I'm saying is I've been called to the Pinecrest before, usually by a tourist who doesn't know its history and sees Rick Plummer messing around with some special effect. And a lot of people were in a hurry yesterday. You said you heard a gun go off, but could it have been anything else? Lightning? A tree branch snapping can be loud. So can a gutter coming undone."

Only then do I hear the deep tiredness in his voice. I want to believe his dismissals, but I can't. *Maybe he's exhausted,* I think. Maybe he's trying to delude himself. I have a paranoid thought that he knows more than he's letting on, but I quickly push it away.

"You guys did the right thing by reporting this, and I'm sorry it happened. There's no telling who you ran into last night. There aren't many vehicles out today, and you're clearly not here to clear debris. Unfortunately, some people come onto an island after a hurricane, which is why I pulled you over. I hate to say it, but there's nothing much I can do until things get back in order and there's power on the island."

"*Nothing much?* It's attempted murder!" Marla's telling the truth, or a better actress than the world gives her credit for.

"*Everything's* an emergency right now, frankly. Dispatch has us running all over. The storm blew in quicker than anyone guessed. Right before I saw you, I was getting an elderly couple to the hospital." He nods westward. "When I leave, I'm going to help pull a yacht out of someone's living room. At least one fatality at the scene."

"I understand," Marla acknowledges quietly.

Dustin scratches tiredly at his eyebrow, his expression changing like a shadow passing over the bay. He looks for a second as if he might say something but doesn't, and remember that I've had this feeling with police before—a sense that there's a joke I'm not in on. "I'll take down this information and share it with the dispatchers. They'll let everyone know to keep an eye out, but I'll be honest, I don't know how much help you're going to get on this. At least not right now. Our department, the Coast Guard, and the National Guard are all pretty much all putting out fires. Literally, in some cases. I don't mean to discourage you, but it's true. But I promise I'll drive by the estate and have a look around."

And have a look around, I think.

He at least manages not to scold us for being on the island at all.

"The best advice I have for you both right now is to get to your vehicles and drive north. Come back down when things are at least slightly more normal in about a week. Your car is at the café?" he asks Marla.

She nods. "About a block from there, yeah. But since the tires... I'm going to take a different rental that's still at the Pinecrest."

"I'll drive you. Maybe you'll remember more details on the way."

My stomach tightens. This doesn't feel right. I remember how rattled she sounded on the way here, so I speak up, "I'll drive her, I have to stop to get my daughter, it's..." but Dustin shakes his head quickly.

"This way will be better," he says, stopping me.

Don't split up, Cam says in my mind. I look at Marla, and she looks away.

Maybe Officer Dustin is starstruck and wants the chance to talk with Marla without an audience, I think. And maybe Marla would feel safer riding with a police officer. I can't tell. I try to catch her eye again but can't.

"You said you have cell service?"

I nod. "It seems spotty, but yeah."

Dustin finds his pen, clicks it open again, then pulls a card from his front shirt pocket and scribbles on it before handing it to me.

"Officer Reynolds," I read aloud.

"That's my direct line. Call or text me if there's anything else. I'll be pretty much on duty for the next twenty-four hours." He slips his sunglasses back on.

"I guess I'll follow you back." I tuck the pink streak in my hair behind my ear and slip the card into my jeans.

I can't tell if he can hear me as he walks back to the cruiser, opens the passenger side door, then circles around the back of the car and gets in himself.

"You're okay to go with him?" I ask Marla.

She glances over at the patrol car, then turns back to me. "I'm getting the hell off this island as fast as I can."

That's not an answer, I think.

People in horror movies make such terrible decisions.

"You know what's a little crazy?" she says as she walks away. "How much all of this is just like a movie."

"Mom," Quinn says, "Mom, we have to tell him."

"Later," I say. I call Marla's name again, but she looks back blankly like she's lost in a dream or in her memories of the haunting she'd described earlier. She languidly waves before Dustin cuts the wheel, and they turn toward the main road.

The quiet gives her question from before room to resurface in my mind: *"Do you remember seeing a little boy on the set of* Breathless?*"*

Maybe I've never wanted to admit it because before Dustin pulled up, I froze.

I didn't get to tell Marla that I saw the little boy, too.

Most people don't understand they're in danger until it's too late. They don't get how fragile their lives are, how they can change instantly. I watched the storm veer east days ago, the sour-sweet smell of spilled beer rising around

me from the concrete floor. Key West was oblivious, but it was like I could feel Hurricane Stephen would turn before it did. Calculations began right then. How long, how far, how much.

The bartender, an anchor tattooed on his neck, asked me when did I get so interested in the weather? At the other side of the bar, the jukebox played the Allman Brothers song, "Ramblin' Man." It was the song playing in the bar scene in The Exorcist.

You'd know that I'm sure.

I looked out the salty window at the pink edges of sunset, listening to the bass thump from the stereo of a passing car. Overhead, a chevron of seagulls passed. I walked out the back door to the steaming street, opened a new burner phone, and forgot the name I'd been using.

You're unlucky, Marla Moretti.

Or do you make your own bad luck?

You want to shut down the movie, but that simply can't happen.

Now, you need a minute to get yourself together. You and your vices. Your pills and your vodka sodas, and back then, your cigarettes.

Maybe you were always a little lost.

You're the final girl? Right?

You bury your face in your hands. Your shoulders heave. You're alone in a rental car, white paint dulled by the sun, the glass flecked with wet leaves from the storm. The island is so still a day later, but debris is everywhere, and I'm careful as I approach, stepping on fronds and shingles not to leave tracks in the sand.

I grab the passenger door handle just as you start the engine. I drop beside you before you can touch the gas. Your eyes go wide.

Are you relieved? To know you're not crazy?

At least you have that now.

But when you see the gun, you open your mouth to scream.

I press it to your neck and tell you, "Quiet."

I point southward.

If we were in one of your movies, this would all be happening at night, tense music playing in the background to let everyone know bad things were about to happen. But now there's just the sound of broken tree limbs crunching under the tires, the air conditioning rushing through the vents, the harsh glare of daylight.

You're crying, shaking, your hands around your face like you're trying to push away reality. "No, no, no..." you say, again and again.

You really shouldn't try to run.

~

"You keep ignoring me!"

Quinn flops back into the car seat before kicking off her sandals and tucking one of her feet under her.

A wave of fatigue stops me as I start to explain. I take a breath and try again. "Honey, it wasn't the time. You heard what he said, *'Come back in a week when things have calmed down.'*"

"So what, we just say nothing now? About what we found?" She's exasperated, and I don't blame her.

I touch her shoulder. "We'll report it, I promise. I don't know if it's evidence, but I'll make sure the police have another look at it and around that room. After we get home and the power is back on here, we'll call and schedule a time to file a real report."

Her chest rises and falls as she makes a hopeful face.

I want to come to terms with what might have happened, even if it's awful. Or dangerous. I'm pulling out of the parking lot when her arm shoots forward, pointing, "Mom, look *out!*"

We skid a few feet until the brakes catch. We nearly avoid a mailbox sticking up diagonally, half-buried in the sand. I'd missed it while

I was rubbing my eyes. "Sorry," I say, my heart pounding. "I'm more tired than I realized."

I remember Marla telling me about spending the night inside the coffee shop and seeing the silhouette inside this morning as we passed by. I cut the wheel and start back in the direction of the Pinecrest, and Quinn makes a quizzical expression. "I need some coffee or something to eat before I drive. And weirdly enough, there's a place open up here."

"Sure," she says.

We pass a shop for rods and tackle, and then another that sells souvenirs. The yellow paint on the side of the buildings looks fresh, almost as if the storm buffed it. Across the street, three beach cruiser bicycles tilt languidly beneath the unforgiving sun. The familiarity strikes me, even in its ruin. I hardly returned here once I got out. "Let's take a half-mile detour," I say. Two blocks later, I head down another street, then take a left, where a stop sign now bends at the corner. I take my foot off the gas, and we slow to a halt.

The house where I grew up looks like the others on the island—two stories with a carport on stilts. Two of the second-floor windows have been cracked, presumably from flying debris, and one on the first floor is spiderwebbed like it had been hit squarely by a base-ball. Duct tape reflects the sunlight, and for just a second, the surface seems to shine—three glowing strips holding the glass in place.

"Your old house," Quinn says, sitting up. "We've been by, but I didn't realize how close it is to the Pinecrest."

"Close enough that your dad and I could walk and meet halfway."

The upstairs windows haven't been tended to, I notice. Most likely, whoever lives here now didn't have a chance to secure them, a fact that makes my stomach sink at the probable mess inside.

Quinn asks, "Do you think there's a connection between what happened to Marla and what happened to Dad?"

The question startles me, even though I've been wondering the same thing since we found the page on his typewriter. "I hope not."

I look for the last time at my old house and turn the engine back on. The willow I climbed as a girl languidly hangs like it's been made drowsy by the sun, its fronds scattered about on the ground.

This is just a place I happened to grow up, I remind myself, *a bedroom where my mother once tucked me in at night, a kitchen where I ate my meals, and a living room where I laid on the floor and talked to Cam on the phone.*

My eyes sweep over the driveway that I pulled out of when I left.

Then, I drive away, the crunch of gravel noisy beneath my tires. I take us back to the main road, and a little farther down, I see the sign for the Sea Shell Café. I start to park in front, but the lot is coated with sprays of sand, downed branches, and shingles from roofs. I see a dark shape move inside and circle to park in the back, where the structure must have partially blocked the wind because the pavement is clear.

"Come in with me?" I ask Quinn, slumped in her seat.

"Do you mind if I stay in the car? I'm not hungry."

The front door, which stands open, is fewer than thirty feet away, but I still feel uneasy. "You don't have to eat. I don't want to be apart." She groans and follows me in.

Beside the door is a chalkboard decorated with pastel letters reading, "We Survived! Come in for a cup." A surprisingly ornate illustration of the sun completes the picture. Something about it reminds me of the mandalas painstakingly created by Tibetan monks that are trampled seconds after completion. *Survived,* I think, *what a choice word.*

My phone dings, and I see that Luke has texted to ask how we are. I'm about to respond when I look up at Quinn, frowning at me.

Her sixth sense about Luke and my interactions with him has evidently been activated. "Come on," I say, pocketing my phone, relieved that my cell service seems to be working again.

A bell clinks as we nudge the door, my eyes adjusting as I step into the shop. Inside smells like suntan lotion and sea salt and like fresh ground coffee. A server in her early twenties stands behind the counter—her strawberry blond hair pulled into a high ponytail. She holds a dishtowel and glances at Quinn as she slides into a booth beside the door. Everything seems eerily quiet until I remember there's none of the usual background noise: murmurs of conversation, silverware on dishes.

"You came back," the server says, showing a slightly chipped front tooth as she smiles. "I watched your car pass by earlier." Her being so observant strikes me as odd before I realize she's probably as weary and on edge as everyone else. The smile I return must convey my curiosity about how she's made coffee without power because she adds, "We have a propane camping stove that came in handy."

"One large cup of coffee then, please." It's just the three of us. I take a seat at the counter and glance at her name tag: *Audrey*. Then I remember Marla's story. The rum drink, the blackout, waking up in her car. "I'm lucky you're open," I say. "Actually, we may have an acquaintance in common. Were you the one who helped out Marla Moretti during the storm?"

Audrey pours the cup, then sets it on the counter in front of me. "Guilty as charged. She'd pulled over about a block away when the storm started getting bad. I think she was waiting for the rain to slow down, but it was only going to get worse. So I brought her into the central office here. It's not much, but safer than being in her car. She was pretty rattled, so I had a drink with her. When she nodded off later, I went to my apartment during a break in the rain. I assume she let herself out and left this morning. You...know her?"

"Old acquaintances," I answer. I don't say anything about Marla's story, but Audrey smiles like she's letting me in on a secret. "I served coffee to the cast and crew over the last few weeks, who all seemed to forget I can hear because they talked about all *kinds* of things while they waited. Marla definitely took a *lot* of calls. She didn't want that movie ever to get made."

Something about how she says the last sentence makes me check to ensure Quinn is safe. I glance and see the top edge of her flip flop bobbing beside the booth, then sip my coffee—lukewarm but hitting the spot, the caffeine doing its work in my brain. "I take it you heard something?"

Audrey's face falters as she seems to gauge my curiosity.

I hold up my palms. "I don't mean to be nosey, sorry."

She grabs a cloth and began wiping the countertop absently. "I guess there's no real secret here. I'm just trying not to gossip. Marla probably told *everyone on the island* she would stop the production. I probably overheard her say it three times, myself. She kept saying something about not wanting the role she was cast in?"

My heart breaks for Marla all of a sudden, willing to be *that* unpopular.

"But honestly? She wasn't the one who hated the film production the most. Not at all."

This makes my ears perk up. I try not to sound too inquisitive. "Who do you mean?"

"The local cop, Officer...something or other. The blond guy. He *hates* Rick."

She obviously means Dustin. I blink in surprise and start to imagine why, when I think: *Who hasn't hated Rick at certain times?*

I'm recalling how angry I was at him earlier when Audrey goes on, "Listen, Marla Moretti told everyone who'd listen she was going to get a lawyer to shut everything down. But I could never tell how serious she was, and at least one person legit rolled their eyes in her face. But when the cop—sorry, I forget his name—when *he* talked about hating Rick, it made the hair on the back of my neck stand. He wasn't specific about what happened between them in the past, but whatever it was drove him crazy. One time, he went down to the estate at the end of the day and wrote everyone in sight a ticket for having an open container. That's ridiculous in the Keys. He was just trying to mess with them however he could."

If there hadn't been real fear in Marla's voice and eyes earlier, I'd have chuckled at Dustin strutting around, absurdly ticketing crew members for hoisting celebratory beers. After all, there's not much to do in Islamorada once the sun goes down. Drinking is a local pastime. A few beers on the dirt road beside the property is hardly enough to draw the attention of the police.

I can't resist trying for a little more information. "Rick's...a regular here, too?"

"Interns got the coffee when they started making the movie, but before that, Rick came in every day, always leaving enormous tips." Audrey twirls her hair.

The consummate charmer, I think.

I notice the cuts on her hands, the taut tensions inside her elbow. She may look young, but working down here has toughened her. Audrey acts like she wants to tell more but is nervous about doing it. Her voice brightens when she says, "Actually, this *shop* is amazingly lucky. Hardly any damage last night. I didn't know what to expect when I came back this morning."

"First hurricane?" I ask.

She nods. "Somehow hadn't factored those in when I decided to move down from Cincinnati."

My exhaustion may be making the coffee seem more delicious than it is, but I don't care. I'm content to chat just to savor it a bit longer. "Why here?"

She smiles mysteriously and shrugs. "The romance of living in the islands, I guess. I went all the way to Key West, but the bar scene was too much. I got caught up with a rough crowd and woke up a few too many times on the floor. Not the best season of my life, and not how I'd pictured myself living when I moved. I wanted my life to be less bleak, not more. I guess a lot of people hurry to get away from where they're from."

Don't I know it.

"So, you left Key West?"

She smiles. "I met a guy working as an EMT down there. He shoved someone off me one night who wouldn't take no for an answer, maybe a little too roughly, but it was nice to have someone looking out for me. He said he'd lived in this part of the Keys for a while, and I remembered liking this area when I stopped here, so when he asked me to come back with him, I said I would. That's my boyfriend now." She points at the chalk drawing.

"I'm impressed."

"I don't mean to talk your ear off," she says, resting a hand on her chest. "I'm Audrey."

"Not at all," I say, now feeling a little guilty for prying earlier. "I'm Lexi. I'm glad you made your way back. It's a lot quieter than Key West. Will you guys stay long?"

"I don't really know. He wants to get out as soon as we can afford it. He wants to study graphic design and has incredible talent, even though he never went to school for it. Too expensive, he always says.

Maybe someday." She points to a board behind her, a chalk drawing beside the list of yesterday's specials. "I wish I had his energy."

Maybe she reminds me of a younger version of myself: scrappy, hardworking, dreaming about getting away from this resort town. She's met a guy and wants to create a life with him. I reach for my credit card but realize that there will be no way to run it without power. Instead, I dig a twenty-dollar bill from my wallet and set it on the counter. "I wish you and your boyfriend the best of luck wherever life takes you."

"Oh, my gosh, thank you!" she says. She refills my cup before we say goodbye, then I turn and start back toward the parking lot. I hesitate, realizing I'm headed back to reality, away from small talk and well-wishes about young couples starting out, and I push my way back into the blinding sun. My eyes settle on the distant shingles of the Pinecrest's roof, poking out above the pines. It's like it's slightly inescapable and watching me, and not the other way around.

The door slaps closed behind me. "Looks like you hit the jackpot," Quinn says, stretching as she follows me out. I'm so distracted by what Audrey said that there's a half-second delay before I realize Quinn's taking the coffee I'm holding. I have no idea what to think about Audrey's take on Dustin, nor can I imagine what he could have against Rick, aside from the inconvenience of the cast and crew drinking near the estate. But how much trouble could they have been, especially in a tourist-driven economy? Still, her emphasis on the word *hate* lingered.

We climb into the car, but I turn to Quinn before I start the engine. "I have to ask you something. When I pulled up this morning, you were holding that box cutter. I didn't mention it in front of anyone because of how it looked." My suspicions are reignited by Audrey's assumption that Marla had already left.

She bites her lip sullenly, her eyes staring forward.

"Where did you find it?" I prod.

"Can we just go?"

"It's what could've cut Marla's tires. You know that. Tell me."

Quinn wrings her hands and looks out the window. "I know how it'll sound."

I take her by the shoulder, her eyes teary and fearful. "Tell. Me."

"*It was in Grandad's truck! Okay?*"

My stomach tumbles into freefall, maybe because this makes so much sense. I struggle to find the right words when a loud sound shatters the silence. Quinn grips my arm.

It's a gunshot.

~

"Stay in the car!" I yell at Quinn before running back to the café entrance, my footsteps crunching over the palm fronds I'd parked around back to avoid. "Hello?" I call into the dark space, but there's no answer, no sign of Audrey. Did she hear the shot and run? How did she leave so quickly? I look around for the source of the noise, but everything around is chaos—buildings half torn down, tree limbs scattered everywhere.

I'm circling back toward the Volvo when I see it—two blocks away but recognizable—the faded white paint of the rental car Rick had tossed Marla the key to earlier, parked at an odd, diagonal angle at the edge of the street. My heart beats so hard, my pulse throbs in my ears.

From the direction of the Volvo, Quinn calls, "Mom?"

"Stay here," I say, the air still, seeming to swallow my voice. It tears at me to leave her even for a minute, but I don't want to push her toward danger, and I have to see what's happened. The white car seems less than a hundred yards away, but it's hard to tell because of the mess strewn everywhere. I rush toward it, my unease mounting until my hand clasps over my mouth.

The passenger side door hangs open.

The windshield is cracked and flecked with bright red.

Marla Moretti is slumped over the steering wheel.

Chapter
TEN

SUMMER 1998

"Things keep breaking, Rick!" a voice said.

I was waiting in the Pinecrest's kitchen while Rick and Ann consulted on how to replace yet another crew member who had abandoned the production when a door opened, then slammed closed. "And I don't care if anyone hears me," the voice continued.

Three of the crew had departed, and two cast members also left because of the "bad energy," which had started being discussed openly in this, our third and penultimate week of shooting.

The curse of the Pinecrest was on everyone's lips.

Even the extras were getting fidgety. Cassie had scoffed and said she didn't believe in curses, but Jess had misgivings about staying on any longer. Both had jumped when a camera rig collapsed during a shoot the previous night. Later, another cord was found frayed, the wire inside shooting sparks beside a timeworn curtain. Doug had rushed in with a fire extinguisher and covered the area. Afterward, Cam told me confidentially that he wasn't sure what was happening but that he'd never seen anything like it. "At this point, I think Dad wants to finish this thing now before anyone else leaves."

"He's not scared?" I'd asked.

Cam shook his head. "I think in some twisted way, he likes watching the cast freaking out. He doesn't get scared, but that's just him."

I folded my arms and held my tongue, trying not to dislike the father of the man I was falling for. I was still working at the marina in the mornings, but the filming for my big scene had been delayed to nearly the end of the shoot, giving me hours and hours to spend on set with Cam.

I could see an actress with red curly hair placing her hands on her hips from where I sat in the kitchen. "The mirror in my dressing room is smashed, and there're shards of glass everywhere!"

"You found it like that just now?" Rick's shadow moved across the wall as he leaned to touch her shoulder.

"They're *all* like that *now*. I can't take any more of this."

"It's an old house. It's just settling, probably. Things get hot because of the lights and then are cooled by the fog machine."

"This is *not from the house settling*," the woman yelled. "There's something wrong here. *Really* wrong."

"We're at the end, dear," Rick told her. "The last full week of shooting."

"Good thing, because I'm on the next bus, or boat, or *hydrofoil* off of this island," she muttered before storming off.

Rick bounced a little on his heels, his giddiness showing before he followed the actress to see what was going on. "This is getting better each day. She's practically hysterical."

Ann shook her head at him, then came over and sat beside me, sighing as she hugged her clipboard to her chest.

The air was thick despite a fan oscillating in the corner. The card table's surface was sticky with some kind of special effect goo, which

I wiped off the back of my arm. "Do you mind me asking what you think is going on?"

Her weary eyes alone were an answer. She didn't know, either. "*Breathless* is the third film I've worked on with Rick. The budget we're working with is less like *Pet Sematary*, more like *Plan 9 from Outer Space*. You just kind of have to go with things, you know? It'll all be over soon."

She was too smart to be so tuned out. Ann was either kidding herself or too afraid to recognize the circumstances around her.

"Sure," I said.

She stood and started toward the door. "It's almost time for your scene. Go ahead and get dressed. You can hang your clothes in the closet there," she said, pointing.

More like undressed, I thought, eyeing the nightgown we'd chosen for wardrobe to lay out for me.

"I'll be back in a minute," Ann said before striding off, studying a list in her hand.

This was the scene I'd been building toward all summer since first putting on Casey's costume.

I started to answer her when another knock at the door on the far side of the room interrupted me. "Oh, it's Doug," someone hollered. "Doug!" a few people called—the way Norm was welcomed on *Cheers*. I'd seen him around for weeks now—a tall man with a slightly British accent and a warm smile. "...Marla's boyfriend," I heard someone whisper. "Good afternoon, everybody," he said. He stepped into the now-crowded room, wearing a denim button-down and cowboy boots that clapped softly on the hardwood. He waved politely to everyone before extending his hand to me.

"Casey?" he asked, smiling. Bits of brush were glued in various places to his chest. I could see what I assumed was a painted-on scar jagged across his cheek.

"That's me," I said.

"Very nice to meet you," Doug said, pumping my hand once. "I'll be playing your assailant today. Bit of a psychopathic killer."

Someone chuckled.

"I've done this a hundred times, but just let me know if anything feels off? Rick likes surprises, but between you and me, I'll likely be in that closet, there." He pointed. "Or coming from that hallway. I'll *probably* be going your way about ten seconds after we start rolling, I believe. I think the basic plan is for you to grab the phone and for me to knock it from your hand. You'll hit me, and then I'll make like I'm strangling you. Oh, and are you right-handed?"

"I am," I said. I was starting to feel slightly dizzy from so much information at once. Cam and I had walked through the blocking on more than one occasion, but now that it was actually happening, my mind was reeling.

Rick approached us in the hallway, his deep voice unmistakable as he came in the door. "Great, great, you two look ready. Five minutes, everyone?"

Someone handed Doug a dive knife that he toyed with before half closing the closet door, then leaning in, listening to the hinges.

Rick showed me where he wanted me to sit, then all the assistants retreated. Voices lowered, and I could hear the crew's footsteps around heading in a dozen different directions. Everyone headed to their places before the camera started rolling. The lights on the vanity in front of me dimmed, making me think of what Cam showed my first week on the set. I was looking at my reflection as they adjusted, and the effect in the mirror was like watching myself fade. First, the edges of my cheeks began to recede, my brown hair, then my face became invisible. Only my eyes stared back at me, still visible in the indoor twilight.

It's only a movie, I told myself. *Breathe.* There's nothing to be afraid of.

I won't really vanish. I'm not really about to die.

I'm eighteen and have my whole life in front of me.

Then, I heard Marla's voice. "Break a leg. And you," she said to Doug, "Try to look scary."

Someone laughed.

I saw her kiss Doug's cheek in the corner of the mirror, then squeeze Rick's arm before turning on her heel and storming off. "Eyes closed, Lexi," Marla called.

"We're good?" Doug called before slipping away.

"All set," Rick called back, then quieted the set.

Through my eyelids, I could sense the overhead lights dim fully away, and for a few seconds, everything was black.

In the next ten minutes, I was murdered three times.

I'd never felt more alive.

Chapter
ELEVEN

OCTOBER 31ST

"Eyes closed, Lexi," I hear as an echo. It was what Marla told me before I was murdered in my famous scene.

Now her eyes are wide open, except they're dull, lifeless as she stares forward.

The gunshot also echoes in my mind.

It rang out less than two minutes ago. Whoever fired it is still close by. I feel a prickle on the back of my neck as the rest of my body goes numb. Am I imagining it? Or am I being watched right now?

I turn and run back to where I've left Quinn, my mind spinning from the horrible sureality of what I've just seen.

I run back to the car, climb inside, slam the door and lock it.

"Mom? Is everything okay?" Quinn can already tell it isn't.

My eyes dart around as I start the car. I'm prepared to stomp on the gas if I see someone, but I need to call Dustin first. My hand shakes so violently that when I finally pull his card from my pocket, I can hardly dial his number into my phone.

He answers on the first ring. "Reynolds."

"Dustin, it's Lexi. We—we were just with you." I'm talking faster than I can think, the pace of my speech blurred by fear and denial of what I've just seen.

"Back up," he says. "You're where, now?"

"We're at the coffee shop in the *middle of the island*," I say, my exasperation edging toward hysteria. "Marla's car is a block from here. You must have just left her. Dustin, she's dead."

Beside me, Quinn gasps.

In the distance, a police siren begins to wail.

⌇

Quinn spirals in front of me. "What?" she says, her voice breaking wildly. "She can't be dead. That's *wrong*. It has to be. She was just with us."

Dustin arrives in less than two minutes, his patrol car lights flashing. He's making a call as he pulls up, then puts away his radio and closes the door, sending an echo across the sunbaked parking lot. I walk with him to the car and watch as he looks inside, then follow him back to his cruiser, where he makes another call.

Disbelief blurs his expression, my sense of time, everything. Did Dustin understand what Marla had seen? Had she shown him her tires? He looks angered by what he's about to ask, the excitement he'd flashed earlier from talking with a celebrity having drained away. He pops his thumb like he's clicking a pen and takes a statement from Quinn and me. Her hands clench and unclench as she talks about going inside the coffee shop, then coming out to the car.

Dustin goes inside the shop and calls out several times, then comes back outside, shaking his head after a few seconds. "No one's here."

"She said she was just about to close. Maybe she left, ran when she heard the shot."

Maybe, I think.

"Do you happen to know where Rick was when this happened?"

"I don't know," I answer, even though all I can think of is Quinn finding the box cutter in his truck.

"I called this in. What little help there is should be on the way."

He steps away, and moments later, I hear brakes squeak, then more doors close. When Dustin reappears, his expression is stiff and formal. "Another officer came up to secure the crime scene, but there's no medical examiner anywhere on the islands. I need you two to follow me back to the Pinecrest. We need to talk to Rick and find out what he heard. Let's go."

I start the car and follow Dustin's cruiser onto the road, passing Marla's white rental car and an unmarked vehicle now beside it. I put my hand on Quinn's knee, and she puts her hand on top of mine, her expression terrified. As of right now, she's the only one I can be sure had nothing to do with what happened to Marla.

"Do you think he took Marla straight to her car after we watched them pull out?" she asks.

"I think so," I say.

As far as I know, Dustin was the last one to see her alive.

⌒

I lower the air conditioning temperature until chilled air pumps through the vents as the tires thump rhythmically over the old girders. The sun has crossed the meridian as we ascend the bridge, radiating heat. The Pinecrest sits on the west side of the Key, but on the other, a roof lays in pieces, a dock juts jaggedly into the ocean, snapped like kindling. Marla may not have known the difference between acting and living, but I do. But what happens when your life begins to resemble a script? The evacuated Keys, the bumbling cop. It feels so unreal.

We enter the Pinecrest's gates, park, and walk past the old house toward the cottage. I wonder briefly if his neighbors know who Rick is and the kinds of films he's made before remembering he's one of the most gregarious, charismatic people I've ever known. I realize he's probably had anyone who will listen over for dinner parties and cocktails.

Rick descends the front stairs, a white towel wrapped around his hand. I look past him out to the bay, where the water is still in the afternoon sun. The sky is clear blue with only traces of wispy clouds along the horizon. He looks confused. "What are you two doing back here? Dustin?" There's something in his voice, but I can't interpret it. I watch as he rewraps his hand in the towel, pink and red streaks around the edges.

Dustin steps forward, his chest puffed out. "Marla Moretti was killed, Rick, less than a mile from here."

"What? Lexi, what's going on?"

"It's true," I say. "I found her."

"Oh my God," Rick's eyes turn vacant for a moment, his shock genuine. I see it mirrored in Quinn. Know it can be found on me as well.

"I took a report from her in which she said you meant to harm her."

"I can't believe this."

"I need to ask—"

"Shut up for a second and drop the cop act, Dustin," Rick barks, suddenly, his facial expression cycling through the first edges of pain. He looks unsteady like his legs might buckle beneath him. "You were taking her to file a report," he says to me. "Then Dustin, you brought Marla back here to get the other rental car? I...think I heard the engine start," Rick says.

"You *think*?" Dustin asks sharply, his aggression surprising. "How long ago?"

Rick's gaze begins to cloud. He taps his fist against his lips. "I..."

"Come on, Rick. A woman is dead. Try harder. Have you been here in this cottage? No one else has come or gone?"

"Just me. No, no one has come by," he answers mildly.

"He's taking this in, give him a second," I say to Dustin.

"I'm not so sure," Dustin says. He tightens his jaw as if grinding his teeth. "He's usually got everything all figured out."

"Let's go inside," Rick suggests, leading us.

I notice Dustin's hand rests on the holster of his pistol.

We enter a foyer that smells strongly of coconut sunscreen and vaguely of alcohol. Beyond it, odd shadows spill across terra-cotta tile. The furniture is modern without being uncomfortable or the tacky pastel I associate with the Keys. The walls are decorated with contemporary paintings that probably cost the equivalent of my librarian's salary. Stainless steel appliances make the kitchen look like a showroom catalog. I can hear birds calling outside, the distant tear of an emergency vehicle rushing somewhere. Maybe to the scene of where Marla was found, I realize.

When Rick closes the door behind us, I jump. He suggests we go into the living room, and we do, spreading out on his L-shaped white leather couch while Quinn disappears into a bedroom. I hear the shuffle of his footsteps down the short hall, then his bathroom door closes.

Dustin stands at the foot of the couch, clearly not intending to sit down. "So tell me what happened, starting yesterday. Ms. Moretti had been staying at the estate?"

Rick goes over the timeline, starting with Marla working with the cast and crew earlier in the week, then showing back up with Quinn and me that morning. I feel waves of sadness and shock from knowing Marla's gone—*gone*—that make me want to throw up.

The afternoon light reflects dully off Dustin's handcuffs. A cold shadow passes over his expression as he listens. At the substation, he said he'd been awake for twenty-four hours already. Maybe what I'm noticing is his exhaustion. Or is it something more?

"And there's absolutely no way what happened with her tires, or the gunshot she heard, was part of your little production? A piece of the film being shot at the estate? Maybe to take advantage of the wreckage after the hurricane?"

"Absolutely not."

Quinn returns and perches herself on the far end of the sofa with an eye on the doors as if she's waiting for better news to arrive.

"Did you tell him about what I found?" Quinn asks.

Dustin looks at Quinn and then back at me.

Why am I reluctant to share it? Because the situation is so nightmarish already. And because I'm more frightened than I want to admit.

Dustin speaks directly to Quinn, looking over my shoulder. "And what's that?"

"Evidence that my dad was murdered last summer," Quinn answers in a matter-of-fact way only a teenager can.

Rick's expression darkens as the words reach his ears. He doesn't want to believe Cam was murdered, and neither do I. It's a prospect that's too starkly threatening, too terrible, and yet how can we not consider it?

Especially now.

Maybe this is the right time.

"What's the evidence?" Dustin asks her. He's taken the tone cops use when talking to teenagers as if trying to lull her into some kind of confession.

"A letter left on his typewriter upstairs. It looked like part of the book he was writing at first, but it *isn't*. It sounded more like a diary or something he wrote saying strange things were happening. It's from right before he died."

His expression softens, slightly but perceptibly, and I remember his skepticism when Marla and I met with him earlier. I can almost read his thoughts: *A teenager found a letter.* "This was found in a room in the Pinecrest?" he asks, simply.

"Yes," Quinn answers, either unable to read his disbelief or not acknowledging it.

Rick nods, adding softly. "I'd blocked those rooms off. No one's been in his writing room since last summer as far as I know, so apparently, it's been there since then."

Dustin rubs his hands over his face. "The detectives went through that space last year?"

"I believe so," Rick says.

"You believe. You think. This is great." Dustin coughs. "No one goes in or out of that room for now, okay? It's unclear whether that's relevant to the current investigation or a separate matter, but it should be left undisturbed. Someone will likely take a look in the next few days."

Rick nods.

Quinn shakes her head. "That's it?"

"Maybe you don't understand how the Keys are operating right now, but—"

"Never mind," Quinn interrupts. She stands and walks out onto the deck, pulling the sliding glass door closed behind her.

Dustin clears his throat. "Ms. Moretti told me a few other things before I left her at her car that will be part of my report. She told me she planned to stop the production of your next movie, Rick, and that you tried to stop her. She said you've sunk a lot of your own money into the film and would stand to lose it all if she went through with it. Something about breaking your contract with her? Ring a bell?"

"It's...a little distasteful to speak about it right now, isn't it?" Rick asks. "But I can assure you Marla doesn't—*didn't*—have a case."

"Sure," Dustin says dismissively. "Just something she mentioned. What happened to your hand, Rick?" Dustin nods at the towel.

It's funny to hear the question from his mouth, his suspicions so clear. I'd been wondering the same thing.

"I'm starting to find this insulting, Dustin. The cut is from brush I was clearing," Rick says, beginning to loosen the towel. "Would you like to see?"

"That won't be necessary." Dustin holds up his hands. "A lot of brush to clear."

I notice the smoldering in Rick's eyes, like he wants to strangle Dustin right now. His sedate demeanor has disappeared.

"I have to ask, Rick, if you've had any threats against you in the last few weeks. Anything unusual at all. Anyone from your past, maybe, made contact?"

No, I think, filling in the blank for him.

Of course not.

Except, instead of answering, he looks at me, his eyes communicating...something.

The hair on the back of my neck stands up like there's an electric current nearby, a presence.

Dustin lowers his voice. "Rick, I'll ask again. Has there been any unusual contact over the past few weeks?"

Over his shoulder, I see Quinn standing with her back to us, her white shirt billowing like a ghost in the soft breeze.

"Last summer," Rick begins. "There was something, but I didn't know what to make of it."

I could hardly believe him. I feel my cheeks flush hot with anger. "*What?*"

So many secrets.

Did he know Marla was in danger? Or that Quinn was when he brought her down? I grip the side of the couch to keep my thoughts from spinning.

Rick's eyes narrow as he nods. "I *still* don't know what to make of it. I'm not sure if I trust my memory of it. And I don't know what it would have to do with Marla."

"Go on..."

What Cam told me last year floats to where my memory puts information it means to forget. *My dad doesn't want to stay here. He tried to get me to stay at the cottage with him.* Cam had sounded confused about it but jovial, secretly pleased to enjoy the freedom of having the place to himself.

"I was at the Pinecrest, alone..." Rick begins. "Even last summer, I mostly stayed here at the cottage. Occasionally, I'd lease out the estate for private events, but I kept it open for the second half of the summer so Cam could finish his book uninterrupted. But the house takes a lot of upkeep, so I decided to stay in one of the bedrooms the week before he came down to get it ready." He rubs the back of his neck. "It started out fine. I didn't leave once, not even for groceries. I felt relaxed and actually began wondering whether I should move back in. I own the place after all, and it started to seem like I'd been wasting it. In the middle of the fourth night, something woke me. I thought I'd been dreaming at first. It was dark, and I wasn't wearing my glasses but started to sense someone was in the room with me. When my eyes adjusted, I made out a shape. I thought it was Cam for a second. Even though that didn't make sense, he wasn't there yet. But I...saw *someone*. Who? I wasn't sure. He was in my bedroom, standing over my bed. I called out, and the shape froze. I started to stand, but I knocked over a glass, and he ran away, left my door open on the way out."

"Did you report anything at the time?"

"A cop came out, had a look around with me, but nothing was missing, and I wasn't sure who or what I saw. Nothing was disrupted downstairs, no broken pane of glass or pried open door. No sign of a break-in." Rick shrugs. "And I knew what it sounded like. A crazy old man, the horror director, seeing things. I wondered if someone was trying to give me a taste of my own medicine, hoping to scare me. I don't know if the cop who came even documented anything. There was no evidence of forced entry or anything stolen, and I was unhurt. The cop was a nice kid and had heard the place's legend. I felt terrible dragging him out in the middle of the night. He asked for an autograph before he left, and I tried to laugh it off with him as a bad dream."

I hear the tremor in his voice.

Is this why you didn't want Quinn to come here?

Cam, what did you see last year?

I suddenly thought back to Marla's question. *Do you remember seeing a little boy on the set of* Breathless? My mind spun. What happened all those years before, just last summer, now? What was it about this place that somehow made horror real?

Dustin takes down the details as Rick stumbles through, answering his questions. *What date? Which night of the week?*

Dustin asks, "Who else has access to keys to the estate beside you?"

"Just Lexi," he says, nodding at me.

"And Lexi, you were up in Fort Myers during that time. No trips down here?"

"No." I shake my head.

"I want you to stay on Islamorada," Dustin says. "All three of you."

"You don't think she or my granddaughter have *anything* to do with this," Rick says, leaning protectively in front of me. "They both have to be free to go."

Dustin puts his face in his hands for half a second. Then, he looks at me. "Yes, technically, they are. And honestly, no, I don't think she or Quinn have anything to do with it. But what counts as probable cause can get pretty loose in an emergency, and I'm sure we could find a DA who would ask a judge to issue a warrant, but I don't want to do any of that. I just want you to agree to..."

"You want us to stay the night?" I glance again at Quinn.

"Unfortunately," Dustin says, "The other factor is that you're probably safest here, if you want to know the truth."

"*Here?*"

He nods solemnly. "I hate to say so, but it's true. The Keys in both directions are the Wild West right now. If you start driving north, I have no way to know where you are and no way to protect you from whoever's out there." He nods toward the door. "Probably tomorrow morning will be a different story. Crews are working on the towers, and last I heard, power may come back by morning." He looks me directly in the eyes. "Even if I didn't need your help, I would strongly recommend spending the night. You have the safety of locked doors and of being together. I'll be on patrol for the next twelve hours and won't leave this Key. Any sign of trouble, and I'll be back here in minutes."

I want to object, but the feeling is like pulling over to make room for an ambulance when you're running late. Dustin isn't asking us to stay because he wants more to do. Marla has been murdered. Her killer is somewhere outside.

I think.

Until a few minutes ago, all I wanted was to get Quinn out of the islands, but he's right. Everything is different now.

"Okay," I say, the word coming out bitterly.

Rick grips his hands together.

"I don't like this situation any more than you do, trust me." Dustin again rests his hand on his gun. I feel my muscles tense as his eyes shift back and forth between Rick and me.

I lean forward. "Before you said there were *things, plural,* Marla told you when you dropped her off," I say.

"Oh, yeah, thanks for reminding me. One would be of interest to you. She told me that twenty-five years ago when her boyfriend was killed in that boat explosion. Here, in fact. The one at the wrap of *Breathless*? She said the last person she saw on the boat before it went up in flames was you."

I feel dizzy for a second. My chest tightens.

Dustin cocks his head. "Sound familiar?"

Chapter
TWELVE

SUMMER 1998

About an hour after my scene, I changed back into my regular clothes and set out to find Cassie and Jess, my skin as flushed as if a heater had been left on. Tourists who described the Keys as having a sea breeze obviously never spent much time on second stories. A week earlier, I'd watched Rick Plummer wipe sweat from his forehead and quote *Body Heat*: "'When the temperature rises, the suspense begins.'" Heat raised tensions every summer, not just in the movies. I saw how snappy people got when the summer got to them. Irritable. Edgy. I felt a measure of relief as I pushed open the back door, as if I was escaping something, when I literally ran into Ann. "Your friends said to tell you they were headed home for the day. They didn't know how long you were going to be."

Great, I thought. I felt like I'd abandoned them without meaning to. I didn't mind walking the two miles home, but I'd been eager to tell them all about the scene. I found the pool area empty except for one of the other actresses, the redhead with beautiful freckles who had confronted Rick weeks before. She sat on the pool's edge in a black bikini and wove her legs dreamily through the water, her eyes closed behind her tortoiseshell sunglasses. Beside her on the pool deck were the burned remains of a joint. So much for her taking the first lift out of the Keys. I noticed the black cord of her headphones as I got closer. She seemed to have a boyfriend when the shoot began, but I hadn't seen him in several weeks. She straightened when she sensed my shadow, scowling before shifting her expression into a polite smile. She pulled out an earbud, letting it drop to her side.

"Yes?"

My feet shuffled backward, the grit of sand between the bleached tile and my sandals. I realized I didn't know her name. "Sorry, do you know where Cam is?"

Asking made me realize it was him I'd begun looking for.

She shook her head as she picked a leaf from the pool's surface, then wordlessly replaced her earbud and resumed her trance. I passed empty lounge chairs, where traces of coconut lotion still lingered in the air, pushing open a wooden gate, then snapping my hand away. The pain made my eyes water, and a single drop of blood rose at the base of my palm where a splinter had lodged. I remembered hearing a warning from childhood about how splinters travel through a person's bloodstream to their heart but told myself that was nonsense. There was no way to remove it with my mouth, so I jammed my hand into my pocket and continued to a side door that led to the kitchen area.

Which was locked.

I listened for signs of activity but heard nothing. I shaded my forehead with my hand to peer through the glass but saw no movement in the downstairs hall, just a bright oil painting of egrets and the pale green rug lit ruby red by the glow of an ancient Exit sign. A sense of isolation washed over me as if everyone had departed abruptly.

I paced to the service entrance, pushed the door open, and found myself in a short hallway. "Hello?" I called. The throaty chug of an ice maker was the only sound.

That was when I heard my name. I turned to see Cam leaning against the trunk of a banyan tree, a paperback resting on the leg of his jeans. "I watched your big scene. You did great for it being your first time," he said.

He stood, and I could see once again how much he resembled Rick: same straw-colored hair, same jaw. Later, I'd learn that his parents had been divorced for less than a year, and while he still spoke to her often, you'd see no trace of his mother in his face. He moved the bookmark to mark his page and slipped the book into his back pocket. "You're leaving?"

As soon as he asked, I realized I didn't want to. I didn't want to find something to eat in my refrigerator or start laundry for Don. I wanted to stay in this crazy, dysfunctional, bloody, wonderful world for its final two weeks. When I explained how my friends left, Cam smiled. "Well, then why not stick around?" he asked.

And that was how we started *really* talking.

We talked and talked about everything. About how he was reading *On the Road* and what he wanted to write one day. About how I helped run the marina and couldn't wait to leave the Keys. We walked the estate, the shoreline, the house, and the words flowed effortlessly between us. When we covered the last square inch of the Pinecrest, landing right where we began, Cam turned to me, his voice sure, hopeful.

"Want me to drive you home?"

And I nodded.

Before we left the set, we ran into Rick, out of breath but with his signature trained smile.

Cam leaned in. "Dad? Everything okay? You seem a little preoccupied."

Rick flashed a smile. "Do I? Not to worry, it's absolutely nothing to do with you." He ruffled Cam's hair like he was a little boy and not a young man, already in college. Rick seemed to read the inquisitiveness in Cam's eyes, then cleared his throat. His smile looked sad before he said, "I got some news earlier today. I'm still trying to make sense of it, that's all. Probably nothing. People come out of the woodwork sometimes, don't they?"

Then, Rick was off, his voice echoing off the hallway as he called out directions.

Cam and I exchanged a glance as we intertwined fingers. There was no time to worry about what Rick meant. We drove to the end of a street where there was a particularly nice view of the water, abandoning all thought of turning toward home, and started a conversation that lasted twenty-four more years.

～

Two weeks later, on the day filming wrapped, I looked for Cam around sunset, planning to head to the wrap party together. Since playing my part, I had an unofficial pass to wander where I wanted. Either that or with the production finally over and the props and scaffolding down, no one minded. Suddenly, as I was walking, the reality that Cam would be leaving soon rushed toward me with startling speed. I had no sense of the world's scale or what it meant to fall in love. The boat channels were crystal clear in my mind, but I could count the times I'd been north of Miami on one hand. And felt like this about someone? Well, that was completely new.

Before me, the Pinecrest's front door was open, which was

unusual, so I tromped upstairs to look for him in "Ibis." His room—empty antique bed, hardwood floor splotched with polish—was dark and so quiet I could hear the ceiling fan's motor hum as its lazy blades rolled the curtains. The energized voices of adults engaged in animated conversations came through the air vent. I could make out only fragments, laughter, playful taunting.

I started into the hallway as a woman's scream broke the quiet, instantly cutting away every other sound. I rested my hand on my chest as the hair on my forearms prickled.

A second later, my mind caught up: Filming was over. That was Marla Moretti I'd heard, probably showing off her trademarked scream one more time. I let out a breath because my reflexes still didn't know the difference between her showing off and the real thing.

Or was Marla just that great of an actress?

Maybe I should have gotten used to screams or been less unsettled by the sight of blood, but did a person ever really get used to those things? What does it mean if they stop bothering you?

Was Cam used to them?

Was Rick?

I descended the stairs and walked out the back. That's when I spotted them, down by the water—all thirty-five people remaining in the cast and crew. On the bay, a large white boat was tethered to the dock. The water behind was glassy, ending in a shimmering line touching the sky. The last of the day's sun warmed my face.

Even at a distance, I could see that everyone was recklessly drunk. Alcohol was part of living in the Keys, and I knew the vibe of cast parties, but the scene in front of me was something else. Someone had run an extension cord out to two large speakers that were thumping music so loud I could feel it in my chest. Near the water, two people I recognized from the crew chased each other with sparklers until one stopped and aimed a bottle rocket at the other, then lit it. When it barely missed, they both doubled over, laughing. On the dock, one of the actors teetered, catching himself on a piling at the last second, a woman I didn't recognize screaming at him. I was taking in the frenetic charge, the chaos before me, as someone passed with a tray of lime jello shots.

But even with the reckless joy of finally wrapping, something seemed wrong. Something I couldn't identify. There was a buzz in the air. A man with a gold Sharpie, asking people to sign a clapboard as a souvenir—the old kind, with the scene number written in chalk—walked past as Marla brushed her hair from her forehead. She was stretched out on a lounge chair someone had pulled over from the pool area. When she turned, I saw that her other cheek showed a bloody gash of stage makeup, which had begun to peel at the edges, her scream from a moment ago forgotten. It was sometimes strange to see an actor out of character, their shifted identities unsettling in a way I couldn't name. It was starting to feel like a very bad dream.

I steadied myself, scanning the scene intently, looking for Cam.

A moment later, I spotted him, standing beside his father.

Rick's eyes were invisible through his sunglasses, and the sunset reflected in the lenses. He usually dressed with a quirky formality but now wore a black polo shirt. The heat had worn him down. Days of shooting outside had turned his forehead pink. His beard had grown thick, as though he was too busy for any grooming whatsoever, and was the same obsidian color as his shirt, I noticed. He swished a tumbler of amber liquid in his hand, which, I'd learned, meant he had finished work for the day, as the people around him began to laugh at something he said. Rick was the sort of man whose jokes people laughed at whether they were funny or not.

It was the casting director, Ann, who saw me approach. She waved me forward as she touched Rick's forearm to let him know I was coming. Her touch, I noticed, was very familiar.

Cam saw me then and closed the distance between him and me in the yard. He took my hand.

"Well, hi there, you two," Ann said as we approached, more as an announcement to the others than a greeting. Were Cam and I being recognized as a couple? It felt that way.

Marla pinched the stem of a full wineglass wobbling dangerously.

Rick took off his sunglasses and hung them in his shirt collar as he stepped away from the conversation. "You're just in time. It's been a long few weeks, and everyone's a little strung out, so I was thinking of taking the boat out. Interested?"

Cam and I looked at each other.

"Sure," I said.

"Maybe," Cam answered at the same time, then looked at me. "Dad rented it through the end of the week."

Rick motioned out toward the bay—the sun's reflection in the water was knife-shaped and blindingly bright. Ann told Rick, "Lexi's the expert on boats here. Maybe we'd better let her drive it, at least off of the dock."

Rick swished the liquor in his glass and smiled as if puzzled, then finished his drink and shrugged. His eyes looked glassy. I knew what a drunk tourist looked like.

Cam whispered in my ear, "I don't think he knows how to start the boat, let alone get it away from the dock."

"I can hear you," Rick said, his head turning sharply.

"Well, it's no matter," Ann began, stepping forward with a nervous laugh. "Why not let the expert handle it? Lexi, do you mind making sure the boat's ready to go and maybe getting us going?"

"Not at all," I said, "I'm happy to drive out and back." Tourists usually thought they wanted to drive a boat until they started doing it. They usually realized pretty quickly how much there was to know. The smart ones did, at least.

I made my way over and pulled myself onto the boat, which rocked slightly against the dock from being tied up too loosely. I glanced at the rope and saw maybe four feet, including the slack, then shook my head. The console was clean enough, but I noticed dark footprints all over the deck, headed in every direction. That was when the smell of gasoline hit me. I went to the back and saw the rust-colored liquid across the back deck, sloshing forward each time the boat rocked. My heart sped, the checklist forming in my mind. *Flush the bilge, find the leak, patch it, clean the deck...* I was muttering to myself as I climbed down, my pulse racing as if I'd just stumbled upon a loaded gun, a real one, lying on the dock.

I went to Cam first. "No one can get on that boat. There's gas everywhere."

"What?" he asked, his expression turning serious. "How?"

He looked over my shoulder as Doug climbed aboard and began fiddling with the controls, apparently eager to put to use some of the nautical lessons he'd learned researching his role.

"No," I yelled, my heart picking up. "Doug, get off!"

I noticed Marla watching him, walking in his direction with her hand on her hip, her hair tied up with a pale-pink ribbon, the gash on her face vibrant. Rick followed my gaze to watch for himself. Grabbing my arm and patting it in a placating gesture. "I don't think there's much damage Doug can do up there, right?"

He kept talking, but his words strung into a light buzz, the ear-ringing hum you might hear after a concert. I jerked my arm out of his, startling him.

"No, Rick, he has to get off, now!"

It felt like my voice was drowning in the conversation around me, in the twisted dissolution of a nightmare.

"...ended up being the perfect place for a sense of isolation."

"...dangerous laughter."

The mind blurs memories just *before* a traumatic event. The trauma itself forms in surreal clarity. Or did I just sense what was about to happen? The hair on the back of my neck began to stand up. I attempted to rush forward.

Sound emptied from the air before a whoosh of flames rolled with the force of a wave over the boat, rocking it. Rick started toward it as a row of bright yellow flames rose from the stern, Doug swatting at them helplessly. They shot up both sides toward the bow, engulfing the console along the way.

Cam was grabbing my hand, pulling. "Lexi, stay back."

A loud, shrill scream cut through the party. I'd heard it earlier, knew it was Marla. Except that this time it was not for show. She was running now, her arms outstretched. Around me, every conversation stopped. Every head turned toward the water, feet ran, and bodies moved toward the dock.

When the boat exploded, the force was so great it knocked them all down, the heat so intense I could feel it in my cheeks. Around the dock was a rolling plume of autumn orange, outlined by a ring of black smoke that would soon turn the air all around us hazy gray. Around us was the chaos of screams, some of them coming from the boat as the sharp smell of burning gasoline filled the air.

This is really happening.

I saw Doug's body tumble into the water. A man costumed as clergy ran past me yelling about calling the fire department. When I turned, I saw a small shadow dart through the treeline at the edge of the property. Not a crooked branch, or the shadow of a black-winged bird, I saw a shape, small, fleeing.

I sensed, right then, that I would see that shape again. I would understand it someday.

I just didn't know when.

Chapter
THIRTEEN

OCTOBER 31ST

A few more minutes to verify my contact information, and Dustin leaves. The blue lights flash in the wet palm fronds as Dustin pulls out of the driveway. I check the porch for Quinn, who continues staring out at the waves, evidently needing a break.

I suddenly realize I haven't eaten all day, and Quinn will need food soon. I find a flashlight and start looking through the pantry shelves. I see enough pasta and canned goods to feed us for a week right away. I turn the cans around, read the labels—peas, beans, tuna, none expired. I feel my shoulders relax. It's like some postapocalyptic scene that Rick knew to prepare us for. One less problem, at least.

"We'll be safe here," Rick says, and I jump. When I turn, he's standing behind me, rubbing his beard.

"Jesus, Rick," I say. "Are you ever going to get enough of frightening people? And I'm not sure why you think we're safe here at all." I push past him to get out of the pantry, making my way to the other side of the kitchen, so the island is between us. "And what does Dustin Reynolds have against you?"

"Dustin and I do go back, but it's nothing terrible. He thinks he's a scriptwriter like so many other people and wanted me to look at some of his stuff a few years ago. He caught me at the wrong time once, and he left in a huff."

I know firsthand how writers can react to being rejected. "You don't have a habit of encouraging other people's work," I say.

"Fair," he agrees quietly. "But the thing about his script couldn't have been a big deal. Where'd you hear that, anyway?"

"Small island," I say. There's an edge to my voice from processing too many thoughts at once. "What were you saying about someone breaking in this summer? You didn't want to mention that before now?"

"I know I should have. It's hard to explain."

"Well, what stopped you? Why didn't you tell *me* a man broke into the Pinecrest?"

He looks at the floor. The air is still.

"Truthfully? Because I wasn't sure it was a man."

I just stare at him. Part of me thinks, *Oh, please,* but not all of me. I've seen too much now.

So had Marla.

"I didn't want to bother you with something like that when I didn't know what to believe, myself. You already..."

"I already what?"

"You already had enough on your plate, picking up the pieces. And it's not like we've remained close."

A stab of sorrow hits my chest, sharp and fast. "Rick, what is going *on?*" A sob escapes from my throat. "Marla made a point to tell Dustin I was the last one on the boat before the explosion at the wrap party for *Breathless.*"

He waves off the concern. "That's only because you were the only one who knew anything about boats. It was a miracle you..." He looks at me, then pauses for just a beat. "Got off in time," he finishes vaguely.

"Meaning what?"

"We'll get answers soon," he says. "The police, Dustin, will be patrolling tonight. We'll be fine here. I just wish..." He sounds wistful suddenly. "I mean, it's *terrible* to say. But I wish she'd finished shooting all her scenes. Even though, with what we have, I'm sure there'll be a way to work her into the final cut."

I feel my hands tighten into fists. My chest feels hot. "I know you're not being serious right now. You're not actually thinking about how Marla dying will impact your movie."

"She would have wanted..."

"*She's dead, Rick!* There's no way to know what she would've wanted except to stop the production altogether. She was murdered in the last hour, and all you can think about is your damn movie!"

"I...misspoke."

"No, you didn't." This is Rick's maniacal pursuit of filmmaking, case in point. He has zero perspective about anything else that isn't his movies. I almost say this alienated his son, but I bite my tongue.

"I *know* I sound awful. I don't expect you to understand. Movies are how I control the uncontrollable. They're how I process fear, how I make sense of grief. I *have to* make them about what terrifies, or else I'd lose my mind." Rick wrings his hands.

"You're sick," I say, headed toward the sliding glass door, the waves behind the dock glaring in the sun.

I can't stand him, but even as I walk away, I wonder if I'm making a mistake. *Don't split up,* I think.

But what I say is, "Stay away from Quinn."

⌒

I close the sliding glass door behind me while Quinn faces the water. I put my hand on the rail beside hers. The breeze feels warm against my skin, and I smell the salt in the air. There's a kind of pressure from her refusal to look at me.

Quinn's voice cracks as she stares straight ahead. "Mom, what happened to her?"

She's so poised, so grown up at times, but right now, she sounds like the child I still remember. I feel for her—she's been jerked around all day, unmoored and witness to something terrible. One minute I'm in a hurry to leave as fast as we can. The next, we're not going anywhere. And all the while, she's trying to wrap her mind around a murder.

"They don't know yet. She reported being attacked last night, and now this."

"You don't think Grandad...?"

"Quinn, tell me about the box cutter."

"I had just found it when you pulled up. Then I heard Marla was yelling at him the day before, and anyone could assume... I don't know. *I don't know* why it was there in his truck. This was before what *happened to her*." Quinn sounds the way she does when I ask who was at a party or who she was texting so late at night, but there's also sincerity in her voice. I want to believe she doesn't know how it got into Rick's truck.

"I believe you," I say. I reach for her hand and squeeze it.

"But you're going to tell the police about it when it comes up, aren't you?"

"Yes, probably." I realize as I say this that if telling the police about the box cutter means implicating Quinn in any way, then I won't say a word. "What we need to focus on right now is getting through tonight."

I chose to avoid saying the word *survive*.

"Mom, I'm scared."

"I am, too. But it looks like we're staying the night here. There's running water, and I checked the pantry for food, but I need to make sure we have other supplies in case the power doesn't come back on all night, like candles."

"And weapons?"

"Those too," I say.

"Mom, what did the police officer mean when he said you were the last one on the boat before it exploded? Is that true?"

I shiver. "It's true, but it's a misunderstanding. Marla was upset."

"She thought you caused the explosion?"

It's something I'd always minimized. Her asking the question so directly shocks me. I can't answer. Even saying, "I don't know," sounds wrong.

That's when my phone rings.

When I look down, I realize the text is from Luke. He's also called once, which I must've missed. His text says: Things going okay? You're on the way back? Just checking in.

I start to text back when I feel Quinn glancing over my shoulder, a hint of incredulity in her eye. "Your *boyfriend's* texting you?"

"Luke," I say. "He's just checking to see if we're on the way home. I'm about to break the bad news."

"I wish my phone worked," she mutters. I catch another look from her, somewhere between frustration and indifference. How to even begin to explain to Luke what's happened? I type, It looks like we're staying the night. I pause, then add I miss you before closing my phone, thinking for just a second about how sincere and right it felt to type those words.

I do miss him, truthfully.

Especially now.

~~~

A memory flashes in my head from two months ago. Luke's voice in my ear asking, "Can I ask what we are?"

"You can, but I don't know," I said, trying not to be obvious about checking the green numbers on the clock beside his bed. Quinn had gone to her high school's football game. I wanted to get back to our apartment before she did.

Cam and I had chattered even through the duller seasons of our marriage. We liked words. But Luke could be contemplative, quiet. I didn't know what to do in those spaces. I fidgeted.

"I mean, are you seeing anyone else?" he asked.

The only light was a flaxen glow from the hallway. I searched for my shirt, then stopped. "No."

I didn't have to ask if he was. I could tell he was only seeing me. That was what scared me. I wasn't ready to be anything to anyone.

His head shifted across his pillow. He may have been smiling—I couldn't tell in the dark.

Cam had been gone for a year, and I'd been meeting Luke like this for five months. I didn't want Quinn to know I was seeing him but didn't understand *why* I didn't, except for some vague notion that it was too soon. My subtlety had become a secret. I wouldn't admit the reality of the relationship, even to myself.

He was too much like where I was from. The marina, the men there. His lack of ambition and imagination, maybe.

How could I ever say that to him? I suspected he knew and was hurt by it but chose me anyway. I hid behind not being ready.

He wore a Saint Christopher medal on a thin silver chain that dangled as he sat up. He said, "I want us to be more than this. I haven't read as much as you, and I don't come from a famous family, but I do care about you. A lot."

I sat on the edge of the bed and pulled my jeans on, then walked briskly to my apartment, leaving his words unacknowledged. The crowd noise from the football game carried on the wind, play still evidently going on.

I never anticipated living as a widow. Sometimes you get lost in your own life, and Luke deserved better than to be kept at arm's length. I found a bottle of wine in the refrigerator, set my shoes by the door. I picked my phone off the counter in the lonely fluorescent kitchen light: I don't think we should see each other for a while.

I watched the message until it was clear he had read it, then I typed another:

I'm not ready for a commitment.

Then, another:

I'm so sorry.

It would be two weeks before we spoke again when he would call me on my frantic drive to the Keys after the hurricane.

I checked the phone on and off until later when Quinn burst in the door. She tossed her bag down, eager to convey the details of the game and some exchange between her friends. She stopped in her tracks when she saw me.

She asked, "Mom, are you crying?" Her voice, so frighteningly nurturing.

My phone rings as I'm putting it away.

Luke.

Quinn glances down. "Need to take that?" she asks.

The truth is that I do. Luke's persistent and still prefers old-fashioned phone calls over incessant texting. He'll just keep calling until I pick up, and talking with him, right now, is nothing I want to do in front of Quinn. I tell Quinn, "I'll be right back," step off the porch, and walk around the front of the cottage. My battery is at seven percent, so I better make this fast. I dial his number. My shoulders tighten when he answers.

"Just calling you back," I say.

"I wasn't sure the call went through but had to try. I guess this is what spotty cell service means: signals might come for a time, then drop. What's going on down there?"

"Quinn and Rick are safe, but it's not good, Luke." I brace the phone between my cheek and shoulder as I tell him about Marla being attacked, us filing the police report, then learning that she was dead.

"Where are *you* now?"

"Outside Rick's cottage at the Pinecrest. Rick's inside, Quinn's on the back porch."

I hear the faint clicking of keys in the background of the call. "I've been looking online into the Pinecrest Estate, actually," Luke says.

I ask, "Yeah?" Part of me is touched that he sounds worried. What could he possibly have read online about the Pinecrest that I haven't already heard?

"I'm not superstitious, but it's pretty interesting. How much do you know about it?"

"I heard rumors as a kid, like everyone, but Luke, probably half of them were made up, just kids talking. I guess their imaginations were vivid enough that Don used to avoid driving past when he could."

"You said your ex...I mean, your former father-in-law owns the place? Rick Plummer?"

"The one and only," I say. "He bought it in the early nineties when I was in high school."

"Hmm," Luke curiously says like he's fitting pieces of information together in his mind. "I'm reading its history, and this is some pretty crazy stuff..."

I nudge some debris with the toe of my shoe. "Are you trying to build the suspense here?"

"Did you know the original owners belonged to a *cult*? That's according to two articles I dug up and the property records."

"Where *are* you?" I ask, confused.

"In my apartment. I did Realtor training last year and learned a few ways to pull records online."

I'd forgotten this.

"Don't sound so surprised. I *do* know how to operate a computer, despite being a charter guide." I picture the edge of his smile, a silver moon in a summer sky.

"Sorry, I'm just rattled," I say. "Did you say a *cult*?"

John Cassavetes's eyes in *Rosemary's Baby* flash in my mind.

"*Cult* was the word the article used, but these guys sound pretty laid back. Kooky, maybe, but pretty harmless. They built what became the Pinecrest as a hotel and gave their guests what was referred to as 'the salt cure' to heal ailments of all kinds." The way he says "salt cure" makes me imagine air quotes around the words. "It mostly involved swimming. It was used to treat arthritis but also sometimes serious ailments like cancer, and you'll like this, lunacy."

"Sounds legitimate," I say sarcastically. "But actually swimming in saltwater doesn't sound so bad."

"For all we know, it worked. The hotel had been around since the twenties, but the new owners took over in 1961. They gave their guests the treatments for the next two years. Harmless, right? Except some of the locals didn't think so. In June of '62, someone took a torch to the place. Half of it burned before the fire department could get here."

I knew that. I picture the wooden staircase, something about special pine being used in the floors. "It's a wonder it didn't all burn," I say.

"Most people got out, but not everybody. Two people died in the fire that night, trapped inside."

I feel my heart start to pound in my chest, the seatbelt resting against my throat. "That's awful."

I remember Marla's question again, the one I never answered: *Do you remember seeing a little boy on the set?*

And Rick, just a few minutes earlier: *I wasn't sure it was a man.*

My stomach begins to feel nauseous.

"Awful and true," Luke says. "The group or cult or whatever you want to call them left afterward, and the place was abandoned. The locals didn't trust what they were doing. They meant for the place to burn. The land sold at auction, and a couple bought what remained. They rebuilt the parts that were lost in the fire and renamed the place 'The Pinecrest.' Based on what I saw in the records, they added the pool and the dock. I'm guessing the land was valuable enough they thought they could make it work and that tourists wouldn't know about what happened or would forget. It was at least somewhat successful because they operated for nearly thirty years before they sold it in 1997."

I'm processing what he's saying.

I'm also thinking about what I'm not telling him.

It must be that I'm quiet for a beat too long because Luke asks, "Lex? Still there?"

"Yes, sorry," I answer, trying to keep from getting lost in my thoughts. "Luke, can we have a conversation later?" I ask suddenly. I regret the question the instant it leaves my mouth.

There's a pause. I picture him leaning forward, his brow furrowed. "Of course. Everything okay? I mean, aside from the obvious?"

I'm doing exactly the opposite of what I intend. I'm creating anticipation.

I lie. "Yeah, absolutely. Just stuff that's better to talk about when I'm not running on no sleep, you know?"

I hear the dishonesty in my voice. I wonder if he does, too.

"No," he answers slowly. "I...don't completely know. You're sure you're okay? What can I do to help? I'm a little powerless here."

I straighten in my seat and tap my fingers against the wheel. I need to finish this call.

"Wait, Lexi, there's something else. I hate to tell you, your cat seems to be trapped on your patio."

I hear her meow in the background.

Shit.

Phoebe. My first thought is, *How could I have?* But I know exactly how. I haven't been able to think clearly since the weather alert flashed on my phone screen yesterday afternoon. I remember petting her earlier this morning, giving her food and water before leaving. She must have slipped past me before I closed and locked the porch door somehow.

"Do...you want me to let her in? I don't mean to get in your business, just thought I'd offer. Is there a key anywhere?"

Cats are independent, but not giving her food or water for hours is simply irresponsible.

He's being kind. You have to trust a little. Besides, what choice do you have?

I wince and run a hand through my hair. "*Yes*, thank you, Luke. The spare key is buried in the river rocks beneath the downspout."

"I'm on it," he says like we're just the regular sort of neighbors who might do a favor for one another occasionally. As if nothing's happened between us.

"Thanks," I say.

I let out a breath, forcing myself to relax and watch shadows begin to form over the façade of Rick's cottage. I was inside less than an hour earlier, but it feels like so much has happened.

I think of Dustin Reynolds claiming he'd been called to the Pinecrest Estate by tourists because of Rick playing with special effects. And of Luke saying, "*Two people died there.*" I remember Rick, years ago, boasting that he couldn't believe how little the owners had asked for the Pinecrest. He planned to retire here eventually, which I suppose, is exactly what he did.

"*Like an ancient burial ground,*" Cam said about settings in some movies. "*Like a place can hold on to evil.*"

Can a place can hold a memory?

I realize I've always believed it could.

Just like the memory I have of what I saw at the Pinecrest, of the explosion that killed Doug when I was Quinn's age.

Luke only knows part of the story.

More than two people have died here.

~⌐

After I end the call, I step out of the car, and I see the boat Rick bought years ago—twenty-two feet, twin 250 outboards, fastback, gray stripe, incredibly fast—tied up at on the dock, and maybe from muscle memory decide to walk down to make sure it's secure. You can take the girl out of the Keys, but you cannot take the Keys out of the girl.

My feet sink into the grass, so I maneuver onto a rock path leading to the water. From the way my shoes slosh through the yard, I can tell the storm surge was about ten feet beyond the seawall. I test the first plank of the dock with the edge of my shoe. When it holds, I step on.

I pull myself nearer the *Pursuit*'s hull, bend to examine the spot where it would have collided with the pylons. An extra line is tied over the console, and two more are tight across the cleats on the stern. I grasp one of the ropes, tug on it.

I'm shocked to find everything looks to be in perfect condition.

When would Rick have had time to tie everything off?

Chapter
FOURTEEN

1999

Rick paced a worn-out strip of his Miami condo's hardwood floor in front of an enormous window facing Biscayne Bay, a cordless phone pressed against his cheek. *Breathless* was released two weeks earlier and was currently the number one movie in the world. Rick was making money hand over fist and was, at least until we showed up, completely alone. Back and forth he went, gnawing the cuticle of his free hand. He didn't bother to greet us when we came in. Until Cam caught his eye, I was unsure if he even knew we were there. The temperature outside was still in the low nineties, but the living room felt frigid as Cam and I took a seat.

"I'm sorry about this," Cam said. "If he's not done in a few minutes, we can just go ahead and leave. We're not going to miss your birthday dinner." I touched Cam's arm, not sure how to respond. Rick was my former employer, technically, but I wanted to stay out of the conflict between him and his son.

"It's okay," I said, squeezing his hand.

"No, it isn't. He's being rude. He's lucky he's invited at all. He's not going to ruin it."

Aside from the sofa and a coffee table, the place was nearly empty of furniture. Takeout containers were stacked on the kitchen counter, beside them an overflowing ashtray. Rick was barking at whoever he was talking to. "Fine, but for twice that, strike while the iron is hot. If they're selling out at one-fifty, why not try selling them for three hundred? Change the font on the lanyards and call them special editions."

Cam plucked a *Rolling Stone* magazine with Marla's face on the cover off the coffee table, then dropped it on the floor. "This is disgusting," he said.

I didn't say a word. Rick and Marla's lives weren't the only ones that had changed—mine was different too, not only because I'd started college and deepened my relationship with Cam since the movie wrapped, but because I'd experienced a measure of fame myself. I had just enough recognition to know it was something I didn't want. Since *Breathless* came out, I occasionally heard whispers when I was in a grocery store or shopping center, only to look up in time to see someone avert their gaze. People made stabbing motions at me a few times, which made me smile once but became less and less amusing each time afterward. "I'm looking forward to this being over," I told Cam after my most recent encounter.

But Cam had said Rick wanted the exact opposite, that he wouldn't be happy till fan reaction reached a fever pitch, something more than *Scream* and *Hellraiser* combined.

That desire was on full display in front of us.

The phone beeped as Rick hung up. He walked over to us with a searching look in his eyes, as if trying to remember exactly why we'd come.

"We're running late," Cam said. "What were you so busy talking about?"

"There's a VIP promotion the studio wants to do for the midnight shows. The tickets will come with souvenirs. Little pieces recovered from the *actual* dock."

I felt my stomach turn and turned my eyes to the expanse of water beyond the window, trying not to think. His new place occupied the twentieth floor of the high rise and had a view like I'd never seen before.

"You're not serious," Cam said. "That's actually insane. You're talking about the dock where a man died, where *Doug* died…"

"Exactly."

Cam shook his head.

"They're just little pieces of wood in envelopes. I'm promoting my film. This is part of it."

"I have no respect for using other people's pain to make your little movie successful."

"It's not a little movie anymore, is it?" Rick asked.

I felt so uneasy I leaned forward, wondering if I was about to get sick.

"I heard this morning it's going to stay at number one next week, too."

Cam stood. "That's what you really care about? And then what? It won't *ever* be enough, will it?"

Rick's phone rang again.

"We have to go, Dad. We're already going to miss the reservation. It's Lexi's birthday."

"Happy birthday," Rick said, then answered the call, saying, "Call back in five minutes," before hanging up again. "It's not a great time for me to go out. Sorry."

"You should have said so before we came to get you." Cam made room for me to pass, and we started toward the door. "Should you be talking about some of this stuff with a lawyer at least?"

"That's a hard *no*. I trust lawyers less than anybody. You know that."

"Dad, look at you. You're alone! And acting crazy."

Rick turned and looked out at the water. His body language was dismissive, but his voice sounded raw. He seemed completely strung out. "Filmmaking is my passion, and I'm not apologizing for it."

"It's your *obsession*. There's a difference."

"Know what? Drive is something you never understood. I didn't set out to make a *successful* film, I wanted to make the biggest fucking horror blockbuster of this decade, and it won't grow if I'm shy about it or too scared someone's precious feelings might get hurt. The deal I made with the actors was that if they gave their all, so would I. And they gave their blood, sweat, and tears to that movie—literally."

"The ones who survived."

"At least I'm not afraid to be ambitious," Rick said under his breath.

"What did you say?" Cam stopped in his tracks.

Rick arched his eyebrow as his phone began ringing again. "You heard me. I'll be working. Go enjoy dinner."

I watched Cam's jaw clench before he turned and asked, "Would you wait outside for me for one minute, please?"

"Sure," I said, then waited beside the elevator. Through the door, I could hear them shouting at each other. When Cam emerged, his eyes were black with rage. He apologized several times and shook it off so we could have a nice dinner, but he never would tell me what was said.

Chapter FIFTEEN

OCTOBER 31ST

Rick tends to the cut on his hand, which, I notice, does indeed look like scratches from thorns. He looks up when I approach. "Quinn's gone inside, but the only breeze is out here. You look troubled," he says.

I'm still a little out of breath from trudging slightly uphill. Some part of me feels guilty for assuming he'd cut Marla's tires or had something to do with her death. "You managed to secure the boat beautifully. It didn't move an inch. The knots are a mess, but they held by some miracle."

"I guess one of the crew tied it up?" He looks puzzled.

"Lucky you," I say. I think back to how quickly he could alienate his own son and wonder who might have gone out of their way to do a favor for Rick. When we left his condo on my nineteenth birthday, it took two years before they spoke again. Cam didn't reach out again until we learned we would have Quinn. It surprised us both, and I knew Cam would need support.

"He deserves to know," I'd said.

"She deserves to be protected," he'd answered. I hadn't been sure encouraging him to reach back out was the right thing to do, even as he picked up the phone. Now, I think back to everything Luke mentioned on the phone—how a cult operated the Pinecrest for a time, how a fire burned half of it to the ground. "Can I ask you a question? Why did you buy the Pinecrest?"

Rick wipes the sweat from his forehead, smiles mischievously. "Seems like an odd choice, doesn't it? It's a pretty long story."

"Go ahead," I say. "It looks like none of us are leaving for a little while."

Rick smirks. "Fair enough. I'd vacationed down here a few times, up near Largo. I met a woman who lived there named June. She had a connection to the place and brought me down here to show it to me. We weren't much of a couple, but I'd never seen any place like it. Right away, I pictured shooting here."

"June?" I ask.

He nods dismissively. "Cam's mom and I were on and off at the time. Sounds very 'Hollywood,' right?"

I don't know what it sounds like, but I don't say anything.

"This was years before the *Breathless* script landed on my desk. When it did, when I read the part about the evacuated island after a hurricane, I knew the Pinecrest was the place. You could say I was a little reckless with money in the nineties and was flush with cash. I made a call." He points back to the boat we'd just secured as if to support his point. "Truth be told, the property wasn't expensive. The previous owners couldn't keep it up and were pretty desperate to sell. It was run-down at that time if you remember. Their revenue per room went down year after year. By then, Cam's mom had fully moved on. I saw myself making a life here after the movie wrapped."

"And the woman you were seeing? June?"

"We had a falling out."

His smile fades in a way that makes it clear he wants to drop the subject, but I can't help but press, just a little. "Does she still live down here?"

"I wouldn't know. It's a bad story, Lexi. She turned out to be not a very good person. She lied, a *lot*, about things that were obvious, silly things. One morning, I caught her stealing from my hotel room. I asked her to leave, and she didn't take it well. She visited unexpectedly during the shoot. It was a strange time, and we were in the middle of filming. I never believed half of what she said. I never knew what to make of her, honestly."

A memory flashes through my mind of the time Cam and I ran into Rick on the set when he said he'd gotten some unexpected news. I wonder if that's what he's talking about.

I wobble a bit, and Rick catches my arm. "Sorry. I didn't sleep last night."

"Lie down for a while? I'll let you know if we hear anything from Dustin."

"Maybe," I say. I don't trust Rick one bit, but I can't see a reason he'd harm Quinn—he would have had plenty of chances to do so before now if that had been his intention.

I check in with Quinn, telling her I'll be ten feet away, and to stay inside, and to yell for me at the first sign anything is amiss, then I take a look at the guest bed. It's housekeeper-tidy, cloud-white.

I slide the window soundlessly open on its track, then tug the curtains closed. The room darkens almost hypnotically.

There's no way I'll make it through another night without sleep, I think. I have to rest, and maybe I should before sunset. I practically tip over onto the pillow, the fabric brushing my cheek.

A few seconds later, I hear a seagull's sharp call somewhere in the distance.

I close my eyes.

When I open them, I pull back the curtain and see the milky white sky. A scrim of clouds has blown in. Panic stabs at me, then recedes just as quickly when I remember where I am and why my stomach feels sick.

Marla. I flirt with the idea her death had been a bad dream. That surely Dustin will return, shrugging, embarrassed as he shares the news that he'd been mistaken. I reach the nightstand for my phone, wondering if he's been in touch, and tap the screen—no new calls or texts. Still, five percent battery left. Surely Rick would have woken me up if there was news.

When I look at the corner of the screen, I realize it's nearly 6 p.m. So much was happening it felt irresponsible and even dangerous to sleep, even though I needed it. I make my way to the living room, where Quinn leafs through a magazine.

"You're up," she says through a tired smile. She's more resilient, stronger than me, I think, digging a granule of sleep from the corner of my eye. Across the kitchen, Rick stands on a chair, pulling a lamp from the cabinet above the refrigerator. He sets it on the counter beside an identical one, then climbs down as I approach. "Help me with this? I don't know how soon we'll have power, and I don't want to figure these out after nightfall."

"Anything from Dustin?" I ask.

He shakes his head and retrieves a clear plastic container beneath the sink. The sticker on the side says *Lamp Oil.*

Thunder calls in the distance, the air still and warm as I pad in his direction. Through the kitchen window, lightning reaches across the wild-looking clouds above the horizon, the sky faintly purple. I tilt the first lamp sideways while he unscrews the cap and pours in the oil, which is flaxen-colored and the consistency of a thin syrup. The sharp smell hits me, and we do the same with the second lamp, then Rick stores the container beneath the sink again. He washes and dries his hands, then strikes a match, making a sizzling sound. He touches the match to the wick of each lamp, then lowers a glass cover onto both before carrying the lamps to the dining room table, turning the room a rusty orange color, despite the early evening light.

"Quinn mentioned these last night. I haven't seen old-fashioned oil lamps since I was a kid. My family used to lose power all the time. It wasn't until living in a college dorm that I learned lights usually stay on. My roommate freshman year kept wondering why I wanted a flashlight by my bed. She laughed when I told her."

"I remember you going off to school that year. It gets so dark down here. We're far enough from Miami that there's a sense of the ocean." His voice is gentle, and it occurs to me that, of course, he remembers that time. I was already with Cam.

The shadow of my hair waves against the wall.

"I was never afraid of the dark. I guess I didn't know any different."

Rick and I both pull out our chairs and sink into them. I glance over at Quinn, facing the other direction, still reading. Rick notices the shift in my posture.

"What is it?" he asks.

"I'm still thinking about something Marla said this morning. She— she asked me something strange. She asked if I thought what was happening here, the circumstances, seemed like the plot of *Breathless*."

Rick knowingly smiles, like he's withholding sarcasm. "You'd have to tell me more."

I walk through Marla's observations, linking them together, repeating a theory I don't believe. "Maybe it does sound a little crazy. A hurricane that knocks out power, then there's an unexpected visitor. After that, a skeptical cop takes a report. Then, a death. Odd, right?" Saying it to anyone else would feel insane, but Rick's contemplative disposition sets me at ease in explaining the theory.

"So if that's the script, what happens next?" I ask hypothetically.

He sits still for a moment. "She wasn't wrong. The sequence is heavy into the horror tropes of most movies, but I don't know... I'll answer that question with another. Do you believe in synchronicity? Events so similar they can't be coincidental?"

My mind whirls back two decades to a psychology class, listening to a lecture about Carl Jung, and I ask: "As in, when situations co-occur, symmetrically, meaning something? I guess I do. But would that apply to horror movies?"

"Why not to horror movies? And especially on Halloween. And if we were characters here, we'd need no further proof that we were in the middle of a horror film." I love and hate this about Rick: he's so imaginative, he won't give a straight answer. Don, my stepfather, would have simply said no.

I fold my hands and let them rest on a soft cloth napkin. "I'm sorry about before. I didn't mean to raise my voice at you."

"Completely understandable under the circumstances. You can see why I was reluctant to tell you about the break-in. Dustin and that other cop didn't know what to make of it either."

"Especially in light of the stories about the cult?" I ask, watching his reaction.

Rick doesn't blink. "The stories about the cult, if you want to call it that, are true. And about the fire and the people who died."

Luke's description plays in my mind, *"The locals didn't trust what they were doing. They meant for the place to burn."*

Rick's chin lowers like he's shy, and all other sounds fall away. "I'd heard about the place being haunted, the same as everyone else. Of course, part of me wanted to believe them. I played it up! I can't explain why but I've always been fascinated with ghosts, haunted places. I've wanted to encounter the numinous all my life. I work in horror, after all. I thought the rumors might create an atmosphere during filming." He stops, touches his beard, then finally looks up at me. "I never took any of it seriously until last year."

"Until the break-in, or whatever it was?"

"It wasn't just me. Lexi, Cam told me he saw the ghost while he was working on his book." Rick lets go of the chair back and runs his hands over his beard like he's releasing the memory and returning to the present moment. "This was the week before the boat disappeared. I told the police about it during the investigation, but nothing came of it. Too many ghost stories around here for it to raise much suspicion, maybe."

"You didn't think to tell me?" I think back to the night Cam and I were on the phone, the night before he vanished. Something had been off. I could feel it.

This is being with Rick: waves of frustration, followed by charm.

"Maybe you both scared off burglars?"

The reflection of the flame wobbles on the face of Rick's dive watch. "I don't think so. When I woke up that night, something about the experience *felt* different. I've had my share of bad dreams, and it wasn't that. I don't know how to explain it. The shape I saw stood still. It watched me. It *felt* familiar if that makes any sense. Nothing was missing, but what would they be stealing even if it was a break-in? There's hardly anything modern in the place, which is part of the charm. No electronics or anything like that worth pawning."

"Jewelry?"

He gives me a wry look. He doesn't wear any, and he's been divorced for more than twenty years.

"There's a safe in the office where I keep legal documents, but that's all. And it's tiny, more of a fireproof box. Even our housekeepers through the years knew that all that was inside were my papers. Whatever it was scared me enough that I packed my things and moved back into the cottage the next morning. When Quinn insisted on coming I tried to say no, but she laughed it off. When I could see she was set on coming, I installed the cameras with her."

"Cameras?"

"They mostly catch owls and raccoons, an occasional key deer. Or they're *supposed* to, even if the power goes out. It sends a live feed to an app I can watch on my phone, like a nanny-cam that never turns off. It's a little eerie watching it, actually, like some of those video footage films from the early 2000s, *Paranormal Activity*, *The Blair Witch Project*, movies like that, not that there was much to see. But for now...it's cocktail hour," he announces suddenly, evidently eager to change the subject. "And there's no guarantee of power any time soon. So, glass of wine?"

"I better not. One of us needs to stay alert."

He's already selected a bottle from an overhead rack and is twisting a corkscrew into the top. "One glass?" he asks, a tad mischievously. "My doctor said it's healthy." Rick always kept better vintages than most restaurants. He walked Cam and me through a vertical flight one Christmas Eve that left me hungover for the better part of the holiday.

"Really, I'm okay."

He calls to Quinn as he lets the wine breathe. "Hungry over there?"

"I'm starving." She drops the magazine emphatically and joins us to help see what we can find to eat. My mouth waters as Rick swishes Syrah around in a bulbous glass, and soon the three of us sit at the lamplit kitchen table, a board of cut fruit, cheese, and crackers between us. Our shadows play, exaggerated on the wall as Rick tells stories and asks Quinn about her senior year. Beneath the cloud of Marla's death, it's a small joy to watch how hungrily Quinn still eats. For a moment, the scene approaches normalcy, as if we'd chosen our circumstances, like we're just a regular family, picnicking at sunset on the island.

I'm laughing at one of Quinn's stories when the noise starts. It begins as a low rumble, a slight vibration, before deepening, like plate tectonics shifting. The three of us share glances as the lights flicker, then pop on all at once, as if they'd waited for the chance. The refrigerator emits several loud, electronic beeps, followed by a high-pitched hum, and a breath of warm air from the overhead vent hits my shoulders.

"Power," Rick says.

I look up. In a few minutes, that air will turn cool.

I wonder if I should be more relieved than I am. Relieved that the police can investigate what happened more accurately. And that we won't spend the night fending off the dark.

I should be thankful for the sense of order returning and reassured, but I'm not.

Quinn rushes to her phone as summoned and seconds later calls, "Mom, do you know where the charger is?" *Of course*, I think, *her first concern is her phone.*

Rick drains his glass and moves to refill it. "Maybe if they're able to communicate with you, the Sheriff's office will be fine with you two going home," he says.

"Found it," Quinn calls. I picture the white cord dangling from her hand, the satisfying thump of her securing the plug into an active outlet, a lightning bolt icon appearing at the top of her screen.

A thought occurs to me. "You know those cameras you were talking about earlier? Think there's footage from them?"

Quinn shrugs. "I'll check."

Rick slides open the door, and the legion of other air conditioners turning on all at once sounds like a swarm of insects. The air temperature begins dropping noticeably, the sheen of sweat on my skin threatening to chill.

"Mom, I..." Quinn's voice erupts, quivering with fear.

No, with something else.

Excitement.

She makes her way between him and me and props herself onto an arm of the sofa. Rick leans in from one side. I lean in from the other. She raises her phone, and the screen reflects the overhead light like a mirror. "Before my phone died, I downloaded the app that gave me access to the stream. I just used your login. Sorry, not sorry. So now it's working, I think, and a bunch of notifications popped up. The camera stayed on all night during the storm even though the power was out." A horizontal line rises and lowers over the icon on her screen as the app loads. Then, the screen changes to a menu, and one of the notifications pops up.

"What do those mean?" I point.

"The notifications? There's an alert any time something moves. The cameras start recording any time a motion-sensors registers movement nearby. In the last twenty-four hours, they kept kicking on."

No kidding, I think, before something else occurs to me. What if there's evidence about Marla's death? Her words about hearing the gunshot run through my mind. "Wait."

Rick's body stiffens as well. He understands. "Should we call Dustin? Is there any chance we're about to see the person Marla encountered?"

Quinn shifts the phone gently between her hands then lays it on the coffee table like it's suddenly too hot to hold.

"I don't know why we didn't think of this before." Rick says, "The cameras record audio, too, when the sensor turns them on. If it's close enough to where she said she was, it may have caught what happened." Rick motions toward the phone. "Does the app keep the clips after they play? Or do they disappear?"

"It should store everything, but let me check." Quinn keeps the app open her phone while she digs mine out of my purse, and with the last of the battery life, searches the app maker's website for instructions, the light of my phone's screen reflected in her eyes as she reads. "No, it's fine," she pipes up. "The clips are permanently stored until you decide to delete them." She touches the screen, scrolls down. The beaded friendship bracelets she and her camp friends exchanged last summer dangle from her wrist. "Seventy-eight clips total," she says. "All thirty seconds each."

Rick whistles.

"They won't delete, Mom," Quinn implores.

She and Rick sound confident enough that I lean back. "Fine," I say, feeling myself exhale.

Quinn leans forward and pushes play before I can reconsider.

⁓

The first clip is from the camera facing the office door. The image is blurred slightly by water droplets on the lens. It's bright. Morning, obviously, and the post-storm wreckage looks exactly as when I arrived. Green palm fronds and limbs from a gumbo-limbo lie scattered across the wet ground. One twists on the steps like a snake trying to crawl.

"How are these ordered?" I ask.

Quinn squints at the screen. She moves her fingertip to the arrow that shifts the cue to advance the video. "Reverse chronological, it looks like, starting with a little while ago."

The next clip is from the camera positioned above the office door. I see wreckage there, too, extending from the back step to the hedges that line the pool deck—hedges Rick's landscaper had been neglecting to trim. I watch for a few more seconds before seeing the motion that activated the camera. I have to lean forward to see it, but it's plain as day. A curious seagull pokes curiously between the downed branches, seeming oblivious that there even was a storm. I feel the muscles in my shoulders relax a little as Quinn scrolls to the following clip.

The next three videos are dark. A howl escapes from the tiny speakers that make the hair on the back of my neck stand. I lived through three hurricanes, and there's no mistaking the noise they make; it's like a train made out of the rain, running on the wind, plowing over everything. I squint at the screen, and the images show devastation in realtime. We watch a telephone pole snap in half like a twig. Another angle shows a house I passed earlier, near where I'd first seen Quinn. Patches of the roof blow apart, the remains falling into the wooded lot beside it.

I check the timestamps on the clips captured throughout the night: 5:12 a.m., 4:44 a.m., 3:58 a.m., and imagine Rick and Quinn inside the center room during that time, while Marla was drunk, tucked in the café.

I jump when my phone rings.

Quinn glances at me before turning back to the security footage, but Rick starts to stand before I wave away his concern. I rest my hand on my chest and can feel my heart pounding. "Sorry," I say. I grab the phone from where Quinn set it a second ago and check.

Luke.

Battery life: three percent.

Calling back this soon, intuition tells me why.

Quinn and Rick stay glued to Quinn's phone as I step onto the porch and close the door behind me. It's gotten later than I'd realized. My eyes had adjusted to the electric light inside the cottage, but the sky now is darkening to a dusty pink as the crooked shapes of gulls pass silently overhead. I draw a breath and swipe my finger across the screen, hug myself with my free arm. "Hi. Everything okay?"

"Lexi, I need to ask you about something. Are you alone?"

The wind whips my hair around my face. I look over my shoulder, then back out at the ocean. Down the coast, lights blink like Christmas decorations in the distant dark. "Yes."

"I know the timing of this call is bad, but this really can't wait."

I feel the skin on the sides of my arms start to go numb the way it always does during the "big" moments in life, when I sense, like right now, the strangeness of the fact that what's happening is *actually happening.* Because I've known since yesterday morning that sooner or later we'd have this conversation. We needed to talk sometime, and right now is going to be that time.

"You know I wouldn't invade your privacy. I didn't *mean* to, and I'm only in your apartment because you asked," he says.

"Luke," I start, but he doesn't seem to hear me.

"I wasn't snooping. I want you to know that. I washed my hands in the bathroom before I left just now when I looked down into the wastebasket. I saw a..."

"Luke."

"A box that caught my eye. I couldn't help it. And I wondered why you would buy a test..."

"Luke, I'm pregnant."

There's a pause during which I try to imagine his expression, what his eyes might say about what he's feeling. I'm thinking of what to say next when Quinn screams from the far side of the cottage.

The timing is so absolutely terrible. It's nearly comical. "I'll call you back. Something is happening. Call you in one minute, promise."

I hang up before he can object, then glance at the phone screen before it fades out. Three percent battery still left.

Quinn flings open the sliding glass door before I can grab the handle. A puff of the cool indoor air washes over me. "You need to see this," she says. "Right now." The phone shakes in her hand. Her expression is one I've never seen before. Her eyes have widened to a point beyond sanity. Behind her, Rick stands, his face pale.

"Is it Marla?" I ask.

Quinn huffs in tiny, shallow breaths, just short of hyperventilating, unable to answer.

I look up at Rick. Time slows down, the seconds expand. We all three sit where we had a few minutes earlier, and Quinn sets her phone on the coffee table. Her eyes fill with tears as she nods at it. Her voice shakes. "It's Dad. He's on the video."

Half a second of disbelief passes before my jaw falls open. I have to swallow to shut it.

I look at the phone, my voice cracking as I say, "That's impossible."

Rick runs his hands over his hair. "Play it, Quinn. She has to see."

"Impossible," I repeat. I think of the numb semi-awareness of the funeral and the gaping emptiness that followed.

The room feels airless like we're floating in space or another dimension.

I'm not about to see Cam.

We said goodbye a year ago.

"Play it," Rick tells Quinn again, this time with a slight edge to his voice.

She can't. She looks at the phone like it's a snake biting her. She pulls her knees to her chest and rocks. I pick the phone up and press the play arrow on the screen. The time stamp on the video says 8:31, just after the storm peaked, about two hours after Quinn and Rick came in off the water, secured what they could, and hunkered down in the interior of the estate. Marla would arrive at the café within an hour. There is just enough light to recognize the back entrance, dozens of fronds spilled over the tile, the rush of water in unrelenting sheets, the hurt animal howl of the wind.

"I don't see..."

A figure moves into the frame. My back arches as I sit up on the sofa. It's a man walking quickly, wearing a baseball cap. The collar of a raincoat is pulled up around his neck. His head swivels in a way that betrays his unawareness of the camera. He sets his hand on the doorknob, then quickly looks over his shoulder. In the dim light, the side of his face is clear.

I'm looking at Cam.

I can't be. The intellectual side of my brain knows this. I drop the phone as I scream.

Quinn's voice is in my ear, her hand gripping my shoulder. "Mom, you see him, right?"

My head nods up and down involuntarily.

I do.

I see him, too.

Chapter
SIXTEEN

OCTOBER 31ST

I'd half expected her to have caught someone breaking into the hotel, looting it. Now, the implications of what we've just watched filter down to a single word: *How?*

How am I seeing Cam?

I press the back arrow and start the clip again. My pulse throbs, but there's a comfort to being able to see the same sequence repeated; it confirms I haven't just hallucinated.

I watch again: he approaches the door, rests his hand on the doorknob, turns his head. I haven't lost my mind. Or at least, I haven't lost it alone. We're all three looking at the same thing. I'm gripping the phone so hard it begins to bend, so I lay it flat on the coffee table and wipe my palms over my jeans. I look at the expressions of Quinn, Rick.

They're as blindsided as I am.

As haunted as me.

It's *him*. It has to be. I would recognize his shape anywhere—the way he carries himself as he walks, the curve of his jawline into the slight jut of his chin—it's Cam. I am not dreaming. I'm reminded of how he was never found and how Quinn begged me to look for him.

My eyes sweep over to the couch as I retell myself the story of what had happened so far that morning: I sped across the Everglades, found Quinn and Rick, went with Marla to the police, then met Dustin when he arrived with news. Those things happened before now.

My eyes drop to the bottom of the video screen, where I find a set of double arrows on either side of the play triangle. I touch my fingertip to the first set and restart the clip, then watch intently, again.

"How many more of these are there?"

"Nineteen," Quinn answers.

Rick draws a breath as I skip to the next clip.

The scene is even darker. This time Cam opens the door and slips inside.

Just that.

I watch it several times before skipping ahead to the next.

Cam leaves in the third clip just as he did in the first one, except this time, he seems to take extra care by locking the door behind him. He then pulls something from his pocket—a rag of some kind—and wipes down the door handle before leaving.

Thoughts fly too quickly to explore. What we're seeing is not possible. But even supposing for a second that it is, I wonder what he's looking for at the estate. Where is he living? Where has he gotten those clothes? Or a car to get around?

Why did he disappear? I shiver so violently my teeth clatter. What if we're watching his ghost?

I feel the pressure of tears behind my eyes, but a thought stops me: There clips, somehow both awful but precious, don't auto-delete, but could they disappear if the phone loses power? *What if I could never retrieve these again?*

I check the battery icon on her screen, and it's red, the battery life showing three percent from the charge, same as mine.

"Get your charger," I tell Quinn. She nods, rushes into the bedroom, and returns, waving the cord. She plugs it into the wall, then into her phone. I briefly picture us, raving, trying to explain to...who? I've given no one in my life a reason not to trust my judgment, but who could believe us? My hand shakes as I take a screenshot of the paused image.

"*Now* should we call the police?" she asks.

"I don't know," I say. Maybe I need to see more to be sure. Maybe I want more time with these clips before I share them. I watch them each again. How many times, I don't know. I want to pore over every pixel, analyze each frame—our own private Zapruder film.

"We're one hundred percent sure this is from the camera you installed a few days ago? There's no way this is from before? Last year?"

"Completely sure," Rick says.

Quinn rubs her eyes. She looks at me in a way that lets me know what's coming next. "I want to go over there."

"Hold on, hold on." I stand up, pace the room, my feet squeaking slightly on the hardwood, still wet from when I'd been standing on the porch. Two realities swirl at once. "I have to do something."

"Mom, *what?*"

I find my phone, touch the screen. The battery is now down to two percent after the conversation with Luke.

I scroll through my contacts to be certain I'm not misremembering Cam's number. I couldn't bear deleting it from my phone, even after everything settled down, just like I couldn't manage to delete two old voicemails from him. I need that connection, his presence, digitally, if he can't be here in person. When Cam's number comes up, I touch the screen and hold my breath as the phone begins to ring.

"You're calling him?" Quinn asks.

I nod and raise my index finger. Maybe he'll answer—just pick up and explain away the last year. Maybe.

Three rings pass, and a recording begins, saying the call could not be completed as dialed. No, the call would go to some kind of voicemail if it was in use by him. I catch a glance at Rick's expression, and his eyes are cloudy with confusion as he rubs his palms together. I touch his shoulder, squeeze it.

I glance again at the image frozen on Quinn's screen. *Cam, what are you doing?* I try to slow my thoughts and rationally consider the best course as Quinn's frantic energy radiates off her, but I know I'm stalling, buying time to take in all of this.

"Mom!"

"Okay, okay." She wants to see her father. I get it. I want to feel that flood of relief, too. As surreal as it would be, I want nothing more right now than for Cam to walk in the front door of the cottage and for us to celebrate with a glass of wine or four. But I can't even begin to hope until I know: *How? Why? Why wouldn't you have contacted us?*

"I need a minute," I say. "I have to make a quick call. Then we can figure this out."

"Figure it out? What quick call?" Quinn's voice cracks, exasperation so pure it approaches pure anger. "Who could you *possibly* need to call right now besides the police?"

I'm already near the sliding glass door. "Quinn, give me two minutes." I glance at my phone, the battery holding steady at two percent.

"Mom, *what are you doing?*"

"I need to finish a call. Please. I need just a minute."

I look to Rick for backup, but his face is pale, still in shock.

"*What?* You're calling your boyfriend? *Now?*"

She doesn't understand. She can't. Now isn't the time to explain. I have to do the right thing, and that means calling Luke. It won't take long. Not doing that, leaving him hanging halfway through the last conversation would be cruel, no matter what. I have to be a good human being. I'm stepping back onto the balcony, into that previous reality. Through the glass, I see her exasperated expression, her eyes glassy with tears, her hands on her hips. I gesture with my hands about holding on, but I know it looks helpless to us both. Warm ocean air feels heavy as I take as deep a breath as possible. I'll push aside the last five minutes, compartmentalize the image of Cam. I'm good at that; compartmentalizing is how I deal.

She wheels around, and I return to the quiet sunset-over-destruction landscape I'd been looking out at a minute earlier. I release a breath, thinking, *I'll handle one surreal life event at a time.*

I sink onto the wooden porch floor, moisture from the pooled water rising through the fabric of my jeans. Not ideal, but Cam's image has dizzied me, made my legs feel hollow. I tell myself I'll make sense of it, somehow, soon.

There has to be an explanation for what we just saw.

I check the phone and press his number to dial, the battery holding steady. Luke's now had five minutes to think about the situation. He answers before it can even ring. "Lexi?"

"Luke, before we say anything, something's going on here I can't explain. I have to handle it. Not ideal, but it's where we are. And my phone is about to die. If it cuts off, it means the battery died. I have one minute to talk, probably."

"I'm worried," he says. His voice is steadying, calm. "You and Quinn and Rick shouldn't be down there. It isn't safe."

"I'm a tad stuck at the moment." I swallow, trying not to sound scared.

"I mean, I get it." The buzz of this moment seems to crackle in the background.

"When did you find out?" he asks.

This conversation should not be happening now, and we both know it. "I suspected last week, I was late, and my body felt like it did with Quinn. I bought a test and took it yesterday morning. I needed a minute to take everything in before I was going to call you. Then the hurricane hit."

A loud knock on the glass startles me, and I nearly drop my phone over the railing. When I turn, Quinn stands at the door, her eyes aflame.

I can immediately see in her expression that she's been listening. My heart constricts.

I signal "one second" as she shakes her head and storms away. Knowing she knows dizzies me. I knew I'd have to talk with her. I just didn't think it would happen now, of all times.

I'm pulled in two directions at once. I hear Luke exhale as I check the phone battery. One percent now. I know this is when he might ask if I knew the baby was his. I'm bracing for the question when he says, "I wish I were there."

Words come out of my mouth that I don't consciously mean to say, "I wish you were, too."

I think back to the night he and I were last in bed—Quinn had gone to the football game—he'd asked me if I was seeing anyone else, and I told him I wasn't. That sufficed.

He believed me.

I hear the shushing sound of waves somewhere in the distance. "There's a lot to talk about when Quinn and I get home, which could be tomorrow morning. Hopefully. Right now, I've got to go. We…saw something. Someone who—I don't know how to say this. It looked like Quinn's dad."

"*What?*"

"Or, I don't know." I hear my voice break from the rush of emotions, the disbelief. "He's on a security camera. It sure looks like him. I'm sorry, Luke, I really have to get off the phone now, I..."

"I'm coming down," Luke says.

"No!" I say, too loudly. "I know this timing is awful, but no."

"It's only a three-and-a-half-hour drive."

"*Tonight?* I appreciate the gesture, but no."

I hear him moving in the background of the call—keys scraping against a countertop.

"Listen, the National Guard has the Keys blocked off at Marathon. Technically, they're supposed to be evacuating. Power and cell service are spotty. Even if the power is on here, much of the Keys will be pitch black in less than an hour. I appreciate the chivalry, but we'll have to talk when I get home. Try not to worry about it, okay?"

"I'm sorry, did you just say, 'Try not to worry'?"

"There'll be plenty of time to think about what we do. It's Halloween and Saturday night. Surely there's a party to go to or something. Don't you have a costume?"

"A...*costume?*" he asks, just as the line goes dead.

Chapter
SEVENTEEN

OCTOBER 31ST

I check the screen, the background dim in the rapidly gathering dark. I still have one percent battery life left, but the signal has dropped.

Great.

My adrenaline makes the glass door feel light and creates a swoosh sound in its track as I slide it open. I hear running water coming from one of the bathrooms and see a ribbon of light beneath the door, but the living room and kitchen are empty. The dinner from twenty minutes earlier lies abandoned on the table, three plates half-filled with peppery crackers and bits of white cheese. Rick's glass is empty except for a splash of crimson at the base. Had he heard me on the phone with Luke, too?

Had he guessed why I'd declined the wine he offered?

Gauging by her surprise after overhearing the news, I know Quinn hadn't guessed why I was so careful about having only a sip of my usual morning coffee. I call her name as I move toward her bedroom. I can see from the doorway that the overhead light is on but that she's not inside. The fan spins madly—its two metal pulls knocking together. I hit the light switch, power it off, and go back to the living room as I hear the bathroom faucet turn off.

The door handle clicks open, then Rick steps into the hall, toweling his face. His eyes register mild surprise.

"Where's Quinn?" I ask.

"I heard the front door open, but I thought it was you, stepping out for some air."

I look at the couch and the side table—her phone is in neither place. I rush out the front door and step onto the landing. Below, I see the back of Quinn's white T-shirt as she sprints through the trees toward the winding driveway. "Oh my God, she's headed to the main house."

If she even makes it that far, I think. It's getting darker by the second, and God knows what covers the ground. I try not to think about what I saw in the road on the drive down, the obstacles she could run into. But that's not the most dangerous part, I know.

Whoever killed Marla is out there, too.

Rick appears the doorframe, light from the chandelier haloing his head. "Let's go," he says, keys to the estate dangling from his hand. "We can't let..."

I snatch the keys from him, the hard ridges pressing into my palm. Halfway down the front steps, I yell, "Stay here. One of us needs to be here in case she comes back."

"Wait! The orange key opens the front and side door. The blue one opens every other door in the place." In my hand, there's a key with an orange base and an entirely blue key.

"Orange, front. Blue, every other," I say. "Got it."

I take off across the lawn, feeling the slight give in the patchy, sandy grass. I see mostly dark spaces in front of me and the dusky outlines of branches. Rick's cottage has power, but most other residents have evacuated, and their homes and businesses are unlit.

If this was a movie scene, right now is when Cam would warn the main character. He'd say Quinn leaving is an "irresistible bait," a lure the main character cannot *not* follow, an action that increases the danger and raises the stakes.

It's what puts the other characters at risk.

And you'd be right, I think as my heart pounds. *About the danger and that I'd follow our girl anywhere.*

Especially now, into this dark.

I yell Quinn's name, but there's no answer.

The estate is nearly fifteen acres. She could be turned around anywhere.

I stop long enough to find my phone and touch the screen. I call Quinn's phone, but there's just her voicemail, asynchronously cheerful. Navigating through the dark, I avoid a tire, an anchor, then something that might be a swing set. I crane my neck, scanning the horizon for her but seeing only the terrible blackness.

It's like the night swallowed her. Before wandering into the estate, there is a gulf of considerations—mine and Luke's. I could get lost, I realize, or worse, I could trip over something, break an ankle. Just guessing my way forward is not accurate enough.

The worries have to wait.

I can't stay put.

I look toward the rooftop's outline for guidance. During power outages when I was a kid, the brilliance of the night sky reminded us we lived on an island between an ocean and a gulf. But tonight's new moon offers no visibility or reassurance. Now, it's a cloak over a haunted fucking island, I think. An island now inhabited by a murderer.

The person who killed Marla.

And who knows who else.

Is it Cam? I don't *feel* like he's here, but were there parts of him that I never knew? The thought makes my mouth dry as I nearly run into the back of the Volvo. My hand finds the metal side, still warm from the sun. I use the shape to guide myself forward, sliding my way from the trunk to the hood. How far behind her could I have been? Three minutes? Four?

Just enough time to lose her.

I scream her name into the dark.

Quinn, please hear me. Come back.

I rub at my eyes then hesitate, estimating a path along the side of the road, measuring the distance to the estate in my mind. Four steps, the turn, then two more, and... Behind my eyelids are faint traces of color that remind me of testing out my senses when I was a kid, wondering what made it possible to see at all. If I had some battery left in my phone, I could use its flashlight to signal her, but there's no other option but to leave the truck running. Using my phone's flashlight function would give me maybe a few seconds of light but use the last one percent of my battery. Not worth it. I pause as I steady myself, the way Cam and I would when we would "make a break for it," caught in the rain in a car before running to get inside.

Different kind of dash now.

The warm autumn night wraps around me as I wade forward, my hands extended to keep me from walking into something. My pulse pounds in my throat, but I force myself to stand straight, to act fearlessly. I have to find her. That's all there is to think about. I yell again, "Quinn!"

Still no answer.

I step over a branch, nearly setting my foot down on a board with nails sticking straight up. They miss the edge of my shoe by an inch. I stop. I have to be careful.

This is like *Bird Box.*

Sandra Bullock made it. So can I.

I'm tempted to yell Cam's name into the dark, too. Somehow, I know I would sense his presence. But I also know what I saw with my own eyes.

I hear movement above me, the beating wings of some bird I've startled, cooing as it flies into the night. I can picture where I am on the grounds. A few more steps, and I locate the edge of the walkway, then feel what I assume are some of the stone steps leading to the front porch. I know there are probably fifteen to twenty of them leading toward the front door. I strain to hear some movement, see some light, maybe from Quinn's phone screen.

She must be using something to see by.

A few more steps, and I see them: A police cruiser parked in the driveway, its lights off. Behind it, an ambulance. Rick hadn't called them, there wasn't time, so what are they doing here?

"Quinn!" I yell again.

Darkness seems infinite. My heart is a whooshing sound I feel in my temples as fear strains my voice. "Hello?"

There's no sound now. Not even insects. This is what space is like, silence flooding in, the new moon tide impossibly far away. But then I hear twigs snapping, footsteps approaching. The hair on my arms stands up. I listen hard. Someone is behind me.

"Who's there?"

Then, closer, a brushing sound. Fabric on fabric.

A voice asking, "Lexi?"

A cellphone's light comes on and points to the ground, illuminating the bottoms of black jeans, maybe black shoes. It's hard to tell. Steps crunch hurriedly through the brush.

"I thought that was you," the voice comes again, warm as honey.

I slow my breathing and try to swallow. Questions burn as they take a few more steps. "I'm looking for my daughter," I say helplessly into the dark.

The phone turns upward, and blue-white light shows the bottom of a jaw, the soft edges of bleached hair. It's the girl from the coffee shop. Same clothes as this morning, same chipped tooth at the edge of her smile. Except now, the smile looks like a practiced expression, more nervous than sweet.

A breath leaves my lungs. "Audrey? I didn't know who you were. What are you doing out here?"

Her face glows ghostly in the faint light as she hands me a paper coffee cup. Her eyes look darker than they did this morning, as if her irises dilated to the edges of her corneas. "Sorry if I scared you. I *thought* it might be you walking up. Dustin stopped by and told me what happened, and honestly, I was worried about you and just wanted to check in. I brought you one of what you ordered this morning. He's here, too. I'm just—I'm so shook up about what happened to Marla, I figured you would feel the same."

The cup is warm in my hand. Coffee is the last thing I care about right now, but I sip the drink without thinking. It's nothing like what I ordered, but who even cares? "Audrey, listen, have you seen my daughter? She was with me before at the coffee shop?"

"Yes! She looks just like you! I think I saw her go inside. Come on, this way," she says. "I'll take you to her." She points to the porch, near the camera that caught the clearest image of Cam, then shines the phone's light at the steps as she pushes past, grabbing my wrist and tugging me behind her. I let her lead, unable to see a better option. At least I can see some from the light on her phone. We stomp up the steps, and I call out, "Quinn? Quinn, where are you? Audrey, you're sure she went this way?"

There are no lights on inside. Audrey reaches for the door when we reach the top. I nearly trip as she tugs my arm forward. She looks at me as her thumb presses the handle.

I stop.

"How did you get that unlocked?" My head spins as I climb the stairs after her. "Do you have a key to the Pinecrest?"

"Of course not," she says brightly. "It's just open. Everybody's inside."

I remember locking it when Quinn and I left this morning. I reach for her shoulder again, but she feels my grasp coming this time and slips out of my reach.

"Everybody?" Dustin? *Cam?* But she's in the hall before I can ask her to slow down. My heart beats so hard it feels like it could explode. I'm missing something. Why wouldn't he have come to the cottage if Dustin was here? And why is there an ambulance? Where are the EMTs? I need to turn around and run back. I feel like I'm losing my mind and that if I only had a moment to think, I could figure out what's going on. I stumble forward in the dark, keeping my focus on the light of Audrey's phone as it bobs into the lobby area. I take hold of *my* phone again as my shoulder brushes against the damp walls. I'm careful where I step, picturing the debris scattered across the floor when I was here this morning.

"Quinn?" I call.

As I enter the lobby, the light from Audrey's phone goes out. Everything is black again. Beneath my foot, a floorboard creaks. The sole of my shoe slips in water pooled there. My skin prickles—rage and fear burning under the surface. I can see only the outlines of things in the faint light escaping in from outside: a wall, a desk. "Hey, turn that back on?"

You're being stupid—a stupid character in a movie.

I hear Cam's voice: *The victims in horror movies always go places the audience knows they shouldn't. That they know they shouldn't.*

My elbow knocks into something wooden. I rub it and drop the paper cup I'm carrying. My hands search the walls, the texture of the old wallpaper rough under my fingertips. "Quinn?"

"This way," I hear Audrey say.

"What way?" I ask, shrilly now. Or *start* to ask.

I open my phone, but it slips from my hand as if I'd dropped it on purpose. I find the edge of a doorframe with the side of my foot and reach my hands out. When I grasp my hand around the doorknob, it slips off, slapping down against my thigh. The sensation is so strange. It takes me a second to feel afraid. I take another step, then stagger to catch myself.

I have to find my phone so that I can call for help.

"Audrey?"

Cam's voice is in my mind. *Lexi, you have to focus. Try to get back to the front door. Get outside. Maybe Dad or someone will hear you if you yell. That coffee she handed you had something in it. How many sips did you take?*

My thoughts lag sluggishly. They stutter.

Just one sip.

But I haven't found Quinn yet. I can't leave.

I nearly trip on my own foot.

"Cam?" I try to call. *If you're here,* I think, *show yourself.*

The world blurs. My head spins faster. When I turn, the floor rushes up, smashing against my knee. Pain shoots up my leg. I grit my teeth hard, my jaw flexing.

I want to stand. My heart races, but my eyelids turn heavy.

Audrey has vanished.

I press myself into a push-up position and try getting my left foot under me, but I topple onto my side. This time, I hit my head hard. Everything turns sideways. Each time I blink, it looks like my eyes are taking a photo at a crooked angle. I can feel a knot where my skull struck the floor. I try to yell, but my mouth feels lifeless. My breathing slows into short, shallow bursts, and I feel like a caught fish baking on a dock, wide awake and paralyzed.

I try raising my head, but it's impossibly heavy, a weight my neck could never support. My head crashes back against the hardwood onto the same spot I knocked into earlier and pain flashes over my field of vision.

The light from Audrey's phone pops back on in the corner of my eye. I can feel the thump of her footsteps on the floor as it weaves toward me. She comes near, crouches down, inspects me curiously. The look on her face is blank, her eyes fully black, like whatever soul or essence that had animated her before is missing. Her smile has disappeared. She wants to verify that whatever she gave me earlier is working, I realize.

The side of my cheek feels wet. I wonder if it's rainwater or blood as Audrey steps away again, the faint bluish light like a halo around her as she types something into her phone. She keeps her eyes turned away as if she prefers not to look at me now. As her phone drops to her side, I see the outline of a black boot at an odd angle on the floor.

I recognize it from earlier.

It belongs to Dustin.

Chapter
EIGHTEEN

OCTOBER 31ST

My brain restarts.

I open my eyes, but everything is black.

I'm sitting upright, my head hanging down. Something rests against my face—fabric, warm from the heat of my skin. Air flows in and out of my nose as if my body is just remembering what to do.

My arms are behind me, and my wrists burn. When I strain forward, they sting even more. I reach my fingertip around to explore the binding: thick rope, slightly wet, the kind used to secure sailboats to cleats on a dock.

My throat and the inside of my mouth taste metallic, and my head is cloudy, a haze of whatever drug I was given.

But I'm still at the Pinecrest. I can tell that from the smell of salt and wood polish. My guess is that I'm still downstairs, but not in the lobby—which means I'm in the room Rick converted to an office, the same place where he offered me the role of Casey. Down the hall was where I first heard him confronted by his terrified actors. Now, *Breathless* haunts us all.

I'm tempted to try to whistle or call out to gain a sense of where

I am through some sort of echolocation. My awareness shifts to my knee—the pain reminds me I hit the floor.

Now, everything has come full circle. Quinn and I can't die here on this set, which has somehow become real life.

A film I couldn't escape, like a dream within a dream. *Cam, I know I should have listened. Were you trying to warn us to stay away from this place?*

Like the psychologist in *The Sixth Sense*?

Was that your ghost?

Do you know that you're dead? I saw a boot in the corner just before I passed out. It belongs to someone who tried to help—Dustin, who meant well. That means he came here too, searching. Looking for evidence. Something must have brought him back, but I don't know what.

My thoughts blur. My heart drops from the aching rush of so much loss at once.

On my left, the hinges of a door creak. Heavy footsteps come toward me.

"Well, good morning. I didn't know if we were going to make it for a minute. You swallowed a good bit of ketamine."

My stomach clinches.

In my "coffee," an animal tranquilizer.

Don't think about that now.

What time could it be?

I ask where Quinn is, and a voice says, "We'll get to that, Lexi, now that you're finally awake. I need something from you. Quid pro quo, right?"

It's a man. He knows my name. His voice sounds half-familiar. Why do I know it?

The Hannibal Lecter reference throws me off. "Cam?"

"Sorry, no."

"Is Cam here? Is he *part* of this?"

Part of this. I don't even know what I'm asking. An hour earlier, a question about Cam being here would have sounded absurd, even cruel. But in the blindfold's darkness, visions of him walking in and out of this estate besiege me—of him entering rooms, laying atop the comforter in Ibis, donning his clothes for a stroll down the halls.

Do ghosts wear clothes?

Could he be back from the dead? *Stop.* Or maybe he never died at all. *Stop!*

That last thought is such a cruel taunt after all the grief Quinn and I, and Rick, went through. Except, I don't know how else to explain what I saw.

In fact, I don't know anything for sure, except that I need to find Quinn.

I need to get her out of here.

"What makes you think *he's* here?" The voice sounds slightly thrown off himself. Or maybe he thinks I'm even more disoriented than I am.

"What do you want?" I ask.

I hear the brush of his clothes as he stands. "Something easy," he says. "You and your daughter can walk out of here if you do it for me. You know how to open the estate's safe."

This is a *robbery*? All this trouble to rob the Pinecrest?

According to Rick, the safe keeps nearly nothing, but I need all the leverage I can get. If this guy thinks something valuable is there, maybe I can use that.

My fingertip moves back over the rope. I find one loop, then the edge of another.

The person who tied these knots didn't know what they were doing.

I ask, "You...killed that police officer?"

No answer. Then, "Just the safe, we're all done."

"More police will come, you know. They're probably already on their way."

He makes a tsk noise. "The power is still out over half the Keys. Half the roads are underwater."

"The owner of this place was right behind me. He'll call them. The ambulance—"

"The ambulance?" He laughs. "Nobody's coming."

His voice is steady. Something about it ignites the desire to taunt him like an angry sibling. I should keep my mouth shut but can't. "You don't know that."

"But I do. The brilliant Rick Plummer has probably already begun to drink himself to sleep by now."

I feel my breathing speed up and push more nausea away. Another piece falls into place. He knows Rick, it seems. He knows about us all. "He was right behind..."

"You texted Rick that you were leaving the Keys. He did his best to talk you out of it, but you insisted. Then, your phone died." He mumbles something else. "Lexi, your phone was on the floor beside you. Your thumbprint unlocked it."

I do throw up a little now. I feel the sting against the back of my throat. The terrible taste permeates my mouth. This son of a bitch went through my phone. He knows everything.

I give my head another clearing shake. I clear my throat. "There's nothing to talk about until I see Quinn. Maybe she's not here at all. Maybe she ran," I say. "She's smart and fast. Maybe I don't have to do anything for you."

In the distance, I hear her call out, "Mom!"

"Be careful," the voice says.

No. The adrenaline clears my head so fast. It's almost startling.

Sweat emerges on the center of my back and underarms, and my stomach feels tight like I'm in a car crash or being shoved to start a fight. The fabric slightly muffles my scream as I yell, "I'm right here!"

From a distance, her voice comes again, "Mom?"

Is she upstairs? Her second shout sounds like a question. I feel my jaw clamp down and shake my head again.

I start forming a plan.

I close my eyes and try to envision the knot behind my wrists. I trace the thick braid of the rope. The edge of my nail pulls one way, then another. The uppermost layer of rope loosens.

"Sounds like she didn't run," he says.

"Don't you dare hurt her," I command. "I'll get you whatever it is you're looking for here."

"Relax. She's safe and sound. Let's make this easy, okay?"

Safe is the furthest thing from what Quinn is.

That *voice*.

I picture Dustin's boot. A chill goes up my spine. He stumbled upon a robbery, maybe, but was Marla's death connected? Was Cam's? Why did they have to die?

I hear friction on my left, a match striking, and a small flame appears, dull and pixilated by the weave in the fabric. There's a crackling sound before the orange light grows. He's lit an oil lamp, like the ones in the cottage. Rick bought them for both places, I realize. The sharp smell of the oil is exactly the same.

I wonder why they're bothering with the lamplight at all. The estate has power.

Unless they *want* to keep everything dark. I realize they don't want their cellphones anywhere nearby, even if they're dead.

Of course.

They want no record of them being at the estate.

"You just want what's in the safe? I think I can get in," I lie. I *know* I can get in. The safe has a combination that Rick reminded Cam and me of every few years. It's Quinn's birthday.

"Oh, I'm completely confident you can. Old Rick sent you an email about it. Don't you remember?"

"You...read my email?"

Right, he had access to my phone. He's obviously done a lot with very little battery life. "I can try," I say. "I've never done it before."

It's the truth, but I need to keep this man talking, to know he's in front of me and can't see my hands. I'm disoriented, but I try to picture where we are in the house. If we're near the safe, which only makes sense considering what they want, we're on the first floor, most likely in the office. This also adds up because the sound of his voice, I realize, doesn't carry the way it would in a larger room.

My fingers loosen the knot's next layer. This one was even easier. It's tied like a large shoelace.

This is the person who tied up Rick's boat.

But why would he want *that* secure?

The door creaks again. Footsteps follow, gentler than his. I see a woman's shape through the fabric, a shadow that stops beside his.

It's Audrey, or whatever her real name is. "Or you could just tell me the combination," she says. Her tone is cruel now. I'm a mechanism to her, a thing standing in the way of what they want. Money, or whatever they think is in that safe. "No need for you to even get up."

I trusted her, and her betrayal burns in my stomach like something's boiling there. "I'm going to have to try a few sequences," I say. "But I think I can figure it out."

I pull at the last bit of rope as they whisper to each other. I can't make out exactly what they're saying.

"Easier if..."

"...step out."

"She's already seen *me*. And she needs to be able to see to do it..."

I pull the last knot, and the rope slackens in my hands. I hold it tight, so they won't notice how loose it is.

I have to be patient, even though my heart is pounding.

I don't want them to see I've broken free.

⌒

Footsteps shuffle away. The larger shape, his, is leaving the room. "*She's already seen me,*" Audrey said. That means they don't want me to see *him*, but why? Don't they just want to take what they want and be on their way?

The flame twists over the wick on my left. I roll forward and fill my lungs fully, my shoulders rounding forward. I push my sandals against the floor, tensing my quadriceps to test my bearing and to see if I can feel if the keys are still in my pocket. I shift my leg back and forth. *Please be there*, I think. I roll my thigh left and right until I feel the grooves of the keys press against my upper leg. Tears unexpectedly welled up behind my eyelids in relief. I needed this break. If either of them had taken the keys, I wouldn't know how to go about getting her out, short of smashing something.

I remember Rick's words: orange opens the front door, blue opens everything else. I hope I can figure out which is which in the dark.

Now Audrey's shape moves toward me. I imagine her blank expression. "Okay, let's get started, then. Just you and me, girlfriend," she says. Then, *woosh*, the cover whips off of my face, and she stands in front of me, her lip curled smugly. Behind her, the office is as I imagined it: disheveled from the storm and their apparent rooting around. The wall where Rick had once stapled Polaroids of actors is bare aside from the door to the safe. The modern painting that used to cover it lies on the desk. Surely, these two mean to steal that too.

Audrey puts her hands on her hips as she leans back to consider me for a second—her eyes twinkle victoriously. "Let's just get this done as quick as we can, okay? Then everyone can get on with their evening."

I need a few more seconds to get the circulation going again. I make my legs bounce like I'm nervous and ask, "You told me this morning your boyfriend is an EMT. I assume that's him in the next room?"

As soon as I ask, it clicks: he supplied whatever sedative she slipped me. Of course, he would have access to drugs in that role. Then, something else becomes clear: the oldest trick in any movie, horror or not. *Ocean's Eleven. Die Hard.* Dress like you're one of the good guys and slip away. Look official on the way out. Who has unquestioned access during an emergency? Emergency medical workers. *They might even take Dustin out on a stretcher.*

"The ambulance we passed, that's your cover for getting away."

Audrey shakes her head back and forth. "You're a smart one after all."

As she takes a step back, I realize something more: she's wearing a pair of hoop earrings, but above the left one is a small, empty hole. She's missing one. A gold teardrop, specifically.

She'd been looking through his things. *Of course,* I think, remembering the tone of Cam's letter on the typewriter and what Rick told me. Things had been going missing—his keys, his phone—just before he vanished. Did they have access then like they do now? These two have been searching the Pinecrest, hoping to find a way into the safe. Now that I'm here, they have one.

The thought of her in Cam's space makes my cheeks flush with anger.

"I love that you're so *inquisitive*," Audrey says. "But why don't you focus on what you need to do here, okay?"

My next move must be fast, and I need to time it perfectly. Energy surges through my whole body, but in a way, what Audrey's just said is spot on: I have to focus on what I need to do here.

She's leaning toward me when I clear my throat. "Audrey?"

She pauses. Maybe she thought I hadn't remembered her name?

"I have to tell you something."

A look of pure curiosity flashes in her eyes.

"I have your other earring."

I knock my forehead into the base of her chin as I spring forward. I hear a crack, then I fall to my knees, gathering balance as I prepare to run. I discover my left leg is half numb and still partly asleep despite my shaking it, but I stagger ahead as Audrey cups her jaw and stumbles backward, screaming. I push past, grabbing the lamp from the counter, knocking aside the matchbook there as I limp into the hall, the glass warm against my chest. I twist the lock on the inside, then slam the door closed behind me with a force that shakes the wall.

At least for the moment, she's stuck in there, in the dark—stunned. Good.

She'll get the door unlocked pretty fast, but it may slow her down a few seconds. I'll take all the time I can get.

I look left. The man is running toward me. His shadow is a giant, growing behind him on the lobby wall.

I dip my chin, angle the lamp, and blow out the flame, plunging us into absolute blackness.

⌒

It's like when Buffalo Bill cuts the lights, Cam would say. His night vision goggles track Clarice's terrified expression as she waves her gun around. In a flash, before the light went out, I could see the man who tied me up. It's just a glimpse, but enough of a look to know: he was the one in the video feed, not Cam.

He's not a carbon copy of my late husband—he's taller, with broader shoulders, and his eyes seemed more narrow set in the second that I saw them—but he looks close enough for us to have believed it was Cam at the angle in the video. His hair is the same thick dirty-blond, cut the same way, so it lands over his temples. His jaw and chin are identical.

Now the soles of his shoe skid. A piece of glass crunches.

My heart thumps so hard I sense he can hear it.

He pants somewhere nearby.

He's not a ghost. He's real enough to have tied my hands and locked Quinn away. Quite real enough to have a girlfriend with whom he's robbing the Pinecrest Estate. There's so much adrenaline surging through me, my head swims. Two minutes ago, he'd had me tied to a chair. Now, I've evened the playing field a bit. I can't see anything, but neither can they. But I know this house and picture every square foot. I've known it since I was a teenager.

Who's the ghost now?

I know I should keep quiet, but I can't stop myself. The words leave my mouth before I can contain them: "Who are you?"

His shoes squeak as he turns toward my voice.

My fists clench. "Did you *know* Cam?"

"You..." His shoe squeaks again. "You haven't figured it out? He and I do favor each other."

Favor each other.

I think back to what he told me in the office. He knew my name, knew Rick, knew that I knew the combination to the safe. He didn't mean for me to see his face, but he knows I did.

But he didn't know about the camera. Rick hid it well.

I hear him fumble around as I try to slow my breathing. Without lamplight, darkness presses like we're swimming in it. I keep my breath shallow, a soft sound that might be an echo from anywhere.

I hear Audrey knock into something inside the office, trying to find her way to the door.

"Mom?" Quinn's voice carries from upstairs.

My head turns. I want so desperately to answer.

I was right about where we were in the estate. If I've done nothing else, I've managed to throw him off. I move to the wall and set the lamp gently on the floor. I don't want either of them finding it until Quinn and I get out of here.

"Colin!" Audrey shouts, afraid.

"So, you're Colin."

Silence.

"Are you...related?"

The summer of Breathless, *did you ever see a little boy?*

His feet shuffle, but he doesn't answer. His shoe squeaks, then squeaks again. He's closer now. I picture his hands extended in front of him.

"You know Rick Plummer?" I ask.

The night he woke, startled by a ghost. *"I saw something. At first, I thought it was Cam."*

Then, it hits me.

"You're Rick's son."

As soon as the words leave my mouth, I know they're true. I can't figure out how it's possible—too much is happening at once—but I know. They look similar enough that the sides of their faces look nearly identical in grainy footage.

Even his voice *favors.*

Feelings wash over me. My breathing accelerates to near panic.

"Listen, stop this right now. I don't know what you think you're doing, but it doesn't have to be like this. I can help you find Rick."

I hear a floorboard creak.

"Your...mother? She knew Rick? Cam didn't know anything about you. *I* didn't know anything."

Another squeak, even closer this time.

The earlier conversation with Rick flashes back to me. I put two pieces of information together, fit them into my memory of being here, on the set, twenty-five years ago. "Your mother is a woman named June? Is that right? *How much does Rick know? About you?*"

"Rick had his chance to know about me."

He's less than ten feet away.

"You were here last summer, right? Rick said he woke up one night and saw you. What were you looking for? He said nothing was missing."

No answer.

"Cam saw you, too," I say, then close my mouth.

"Cam learned a little too fast, didn't he? I just wanted to borrow his keys...at first."

Everything clicks into place so forcefully I'm dizzied. Colin didn't know Cam would be working here last summer, so when he broke in, Cam was surprised. I don't exactly know what happened next, but I know now that Cam didn't take the boat out alone.

I open my mouth again, but no sound comes out. My stomach aches as if I've been punched. *Oh, Cam, I didn't want to let you off the phone that night.* I move as I'm talking. "You dumped him in the bay, didn't you? You son of a bitch! He found out about you, saw you, so you killed him."

I hear another step and slide in the opposite direction.

That's when it occurs to me: he and Audrey have been breaking into this place for over a year. He knows it as well as I do.

Audrey knocks into the wall, the counter, something, then in the office, something crashes. He hears her mumbling, cursing to herself.

I hear a brushing sound as Colin feels along the wall, and my jaw tightens. I can't play his game. I need to be smart. I'm talking to a man who has killed three people already, at least. Do I think he's going to let Quinn and me walk out of here?

I force myself upright and draw in a breath. The room stops spinning momentarily. My fingertips find the thick, rounded edge of the banister. I can make my way up easily, but it's going to take time to find the right door, unlock it, and get her out the fire escape. Once I start up the stairs, Colin will know which way I've gone. He'll track me by the sound. Fast.

I wonder: could we stay like this until the first daylight? I start guessing at the hour when I hear him shift again.

He's even closer than I realized.

"This is going to go so much faster if you play nice, Lexi. We can't stand here forever. Actually, let me rephrase that. *You* can't stand here forever. You'll give yourself away, eventually. I've been waiting for a long time. I'm good at it."

Don't answer, I think. *Don't say a word now.* Maybe he'll doubt and second guess himself, start to wonder if I've slipped out.

The floor creaks.

I step, then he does.

It's only a matter of time till he orients himself, finds his way.

Can he tell I'm on the stairs?

"You can end this any time you want. It has to be exhausting."

More brushing. He's getting closer.

"You listening, Lexi?"

The thought chirps in my head: *I can make something crash, too.*

I lean down and, with both hands, lift off the glass cover of the oil lamp. Already, it's cooled. I heft the weight in my hand, estimating the distance to the other side of the lobby.

I stretch my leg, shaking more circulation into it. Once I start, I'm going to have to be fast.

When I throw the glass cover, I take off up the stairs before it shatters loudly against the opposite wall. I've done two things, misdirected him with the sound and scattered broken glass everywhere.

Good. I hope he steps all over it.

I've probably bought myself sixty seconds.

Maybe less.

I yank myself up on the heavy banister, taking the steps two at a time while he calls out.

The stairs are slick under my shoes, nearly making me fall twice. I adjust my gait when I reach the hallway at the top. I picture the antique furniture, the creepy mirror halfway down the hall, the oil painting above the fire exit. There's just as little light as on the first floor, and I knock into an end table before I find my footing. My fingertips scrape the edge of a doorframe, and I reach to my right, locating the other side of the hall.

At least I understand where I'm going.

I call out to her. "Quinn!" It comes out as a kind of stage whisper. I don't want to make it any easier for them to find their way up to me.

"Mom, I'm in here!" It's so dark I literally can't see my hand extended in front of my face as I step forward. I pass the first door on the left, then the second.

Downstairs, I hear them. Audrey's found her way to the office door while Colin's voice is firm like he's scolding a dog: "Calm *down*. Breathe, okay? Go in the..."

I don't hear the rest of what he says.

"Keep talking," I call down the hall. "I'll come to your voice."

"Um, okay. I'm in a bedroom. The door's locked," Quinn says. "It's...oh, it's the last bedroom on the left side!"

I know which exactly. I looked in it this morning. I picture the plain white bedspread, the four-poster bed frame, and the brass nameplate beside the grooved doorframe. It's where Cam slept the summer *Breathless* was filmed.

Ibis.

"Hang on, Quinn."

My shoulder aches from where it hit the ground when Audrey tricked me. I slip on a damp patch of the hardwood but catch myself. I can picture her on the other side of the door. Her hands pressed flat against the dark wood. I'm just three or four steps from the door when I hear her.

"Mom, they locked the door."

There's terror in her voice.

I reach into my pocket for the keys. "I know, sweetie." I slip on another puddle, and I lose my grip, sending the keys clattering onto the floor. It's like a bad dream where you get close to what you want but mess it up right at the end, a nightmare about helplessness. I bend down and swipe my hand around, the wet wood vast as I search.

"Mom, hurry!"

My heart pounds in my head.

I'm right outside the bedroom door.

"Mom?"

"I'm coming, baby. Hold on."

The edge of my pinkie nudges the keys, and I reach farther, grasping them tightly. My hand searches around the ring for the key I need—the blue one—then I stop.

I hear a sound from downstairs.

I see the distinct color brightening and understand what's happened exactly.

"Oh, *hell.*"

⤳

They've lit a marine flare.

I hear it before seeing the light: a sharp pop, then a hiss. More of a fizz, really. It's been more than two decades since I've seen one, but I recognize the sound immediately. It's what happens after an emergency when you're on the water when there are no options left. It's the last resort. You just say your prayers that no gas has leaked into the bilge.

The entire lobby downstairs turns flamingo pink. I can already smell the bitter phosphorous.

My stomach sinks; my whole body is turning heavy. I was so close to getting Quinn out. I even glance over my shoulder at the fire escape we would have run down. It's only going to burn for sixty seconds but burns as bright as about five thousand of the lamps I broke.

If only I'd had ten more seconds.

I stare in the direction of the stairwell for a full second. My jaw opens as two shadows rise on the lobby's back wall. "Lexi? Any luck with that lock?" Colin's voice fills the hall as they climb the stairs. The angle of the shadows changes with each step they take.

"Mom, what's happening?"

I need more time, just a few seconds more. But there's no way to find the blue key and run out the fire escape. They're just too close now.

"Quinn, I'm going to push the keys under the door."

"Mom?"

"Look under the door. Ready?"

"Okay." I hear a thump, and then I see the tips of her fingers wiggling in the growing light. I push the keys toward them. Quinn's thumb and index finger grasp through the keyring, but the key chain catches as she pulls, once, twice.

The space between the bottom of the door and the floor is too small.

"The keyring is stuck. Can it come off?"

I glance toward the stairs, the shadows steadily rising. "Baby, I'm sorry."

"Mom, please, you have to get me out of here."

She beats on the bottom of the door.

I want to scream, at them, at this insanity.

"They're coming," I tell her. "What about the window?"

"I tried. It's painted shut. Even if I broke it, the fall is too far."

She's right. From that height, a fall could easily break her leg. I glance again at the fire exit. "Quinn, listen. Work on that lock. That's the only way. When you get it open, go left down this hall. Okay? Go out through the fire escape at the end. Do *not* go down the stairs. Understand?"

Colin calls: "Oh, Lexi..."

"*Understand?*" I ask.

"Yes. Mom? I'm so sorry. I shouldn't have lied. I shouldn't have made us come down here. I'm *so* sorry, Mom."

"It's okay. Everything's going to be okay. But you have to stay quiet now," I whisper, just as the top of Colin's head emerges into the hall. "I'll keep them distracted."

Them. Colin, my, what? Half-brother? Quinn's uncle? I'm not ready to begin thinking through the implications. I palm the keys before slipping them into the back pocket of my jeans. I don't know how I'll use them, but they're like an ace I've been dealt that I want to hold on to desperately. They increase our chances of survival. I have to get back upstairs, but until I do, I need to keep whatever tools I have to open the bedroom door.

Audrey climbs behind Colin, the pink light reddening everything as they approach, so bright I squint and shield my eyes. She looks at me harshly, with narrowed eyes, as if angry at how I caught her off guard.

We're a little more even, I suppose.

She's the one holding the flare, I notice. Colin has something in his hand, too.

A gun.

My gaze flies everywhere, like my eyes themselves don't want to look directly at it. The pink light reflects off the greasy black metal, and I step toward them, angling myself in front of the door as if I'm somehow blocking their path. I want them away from the bedroom, from her. I've been around horror movies all my adult life. I've seen more made-up blood and guts than one person ever should. I've caught and cleaned fish with an efficiency that scared adult men, but guns make my stomach turn.

My heart pounds, but I start past them, as one of the students at the high school might, as if to say, *I'm caught, fine, let's just begin my detention now.*

"You hadn't thought your escape all the way through, I guess," Colin says.

I catch a glance at Audrey in the roseate light. Her bottom lip is swollen and bears a dark vertical line where I split it. Her eyes are narrow and flash a kind of smug disgust. "You chipped one of my teeth, bitch," she spits.

Another one, I think.

We go down the stairs. Audrey's hand is warm and firm on my shoulder like she means to keep me from slipping away. I don't mind. Let them follow me away from Quinn.

Just communicating with her has settled me in some tiny measure. She knows what she has to do. I think of the days after Cam died, when she and I huddled in her bed, the lavender paint on her walls blurry from my tears. I'd wanted to shield her from my feelings, but didn't, entirely. She supported me, too. Seeing her be strong made me strong. "We can do this, Mom," she'd said. "We can get through this. We can get through anything. I know we can."

Now, what's happening tonight is our *anything*.

The flare's light makes taking the steps much easier on the way down. When we hit the lobby, I see the broken glass from the lantern I smashed. In the corner beside it, I see Dustin's boot, again, and the body it's attached to. I recognize his uniform from earlier, his clipped blond hair. He's laid out flat as if he'd dove for the door to the parlor but simply not made it. He was so young. He must have known the risks when he signed up to become a police officer, but could he have understood this might happen? I grip at my stomach, feeling like I might throw up again. It takes everything I have not to sob and yell, but I have to hold it in. I have to work on the safe—it will give Quinn more time.

Behind me, Colin has noticed the direction I'm looking. He intuits what I'm seeing, how seeing Dustin's body has slowed my pace. He nudges me with the gun barrel. "Keep walking."

I try to refocus my eyes on the door to the office. But the reality that they don't mean to let me, or her, ever get away from here settles in.

I force my head straight, my gaze forward, but on the way into the office, I see something that I'd missed before I ran up the stairs.

I hadn't seen them earlier because of the dark, but I catch just a quick glimpse before the marine flare goes out in Colin's hand.

Beside the last door on the right are six more plastic jugs of lamp oil.

———

They're clear with white caps, a gallon each. I happen to know from power outages when I was a kid. Except they're not here to keep lamps lit.

Their purpose is to torch this place.

The thought makes me bite down so hard I have to force myself to think.

We're halfway across the lobby when we stop. "Wait," Audrey hisses. She opens the door, and a sliver of lamplight follows her into the room, the shape of a knife on the tile floor.

"There's someone fucking *here*." She stammers as if to disperse hard news. The energy between her and Colin changes. I imagine his expression shifting behind me. "I think it's another *cop*."

"Impossible," he says.

Audrey wrings her hands before cutting an accusatory glance my way. Despite everything, I'm tempted to respond with a shrug as if we are conspirators, each trying to play a part in this robbery. But I know it's not that way.

I had to believe that Quinn would find her way out of that bedroom, but I knew there was very little chance I'd get out of the Pinecrest alive.

At least until ten seconds ago.

The twists to this plot we're living in just keep coming.

"Don't look at me," I tell Audrey. "I'm not the one who's been using my cell phone."

She juts her head toward the door. From the angle she's standing, she can't see the lobby directly, which means the cop can't see her, but she can't see the cop very well either. She gives Colin a glance. I try reading the look in her eyes. They're something like, *This is getting worse by the minute.*

She grabs my shoulder, then pokes her head between the door and its frame. "Go," she insists. "You have to go talk to him."

"*Me?*"

"Find out what he wants, then make him go away."

I hear rapping on the outside door, firm taps in a cheerful rhythm.

"What do you want me to tell him? I don't know what he wants."
I'm playing dumb, but we all know this is an opportunity.

Metal presses against the base of my skull. A gun at your head is
its own kind of language. The suddenness takes my breath away as
the pressure makes me lurch forward. I glance at the wall and imagine
parts of me splattered where shadows play in the flickering flame. The
possibility of how quickly everything could be over brings a wave of
nausea from my stomach.

Audrey leans close enough that I can smell the coconut in her
skin lotion. She wrings her hands. She talks to me like she's trying to
convince herself, but also like she's had too much caffeine: "Say it's
your family's place, and you're helping out. Tell him you're fine. He's
probably just checking on everyone."

"I'll do my best," I say.

"Just get him to *leave*. You won't like what happens if you don't."

Colin nudges me again with the gun. "Some ways of dying are
fast, like falling from a second story. But other ways can take a very
long time and can be extremely painful."

The knocks come again.

I wipe my palms over my jeans.

"Move," Colin says. He hands me one of the lamps to carry. I'm
tempted to throw it back at him, to run, but the gun is level with my ribs,
and I know I wouldn't make it far. I hadn't understood the feeling of *hate*
until now, but it heats my blood. It's so strong that if it was just me here,
I might end this night, right now. I might try for the door or reach for the
gun and see if I might take one or both of them out of this world with me.

But Quinn is upstairs, and this cop doesn't deserve to have his
life risked because I'm coming apart. I want to call up the stairs to ask
how it's coming with the lock. I wonder if she found anything to use
in the room, something metal in one of the drawers.

I shuffle into the short hallway, stepping around a framed photo that must have dropped off the wall during the storm. A few more steps, and I can almost see the side door, my shadow cutting into the tangerine lamplight.

A voice calls from the outside door: "Anyone home?"

I stop.

My heartbeat switches from pounding to jackhammering.

I recognize the voice immediately.

This, I realize, I did not see coming.

I'm not about to talk to a cop—someone with training, a firearm—someone who could call for help.

I'm about to talk to Luke.

I don't understand how, but I'm sure of it. My mind spins through the calculus of this new reality, but there's so much I don't understand. I'm not sure where to begin. I touch my stomach. He came because of what I told him, which put him in danger.

More than he could ever know.

When Audrey instructed me to get him to leave, she didn't know how much I'd agree. I can't tell him what's happening, *and* I can't make Colin and Audrey aware I know him. They may not be able to see directly, but they'll be able to hear every word I say. I want Luke gone as fast as possible.

Unless there's some way he...

I make my way to the door with dreamlike slowness.

He wears a police uniform and is shining a flashlight through the glass. The sight takes a second to absorb but explains why Audrey thought a cop had shown up. The end of Luke's and my conversation flashes back: I encourage Luke to go out to get his mind off the pregnancy. Me suggesting he go to a party, that he find a costume.

A costume? he'd asked.

It's Halloween, after all.

The flashlight beam finds me in the low light, and I see his eyes through the glass, somehow sad and hopeful at the same time. *Oh, Luke, how is this happening?* I turn the lock on the door handle and pull it open.

My gaze flicks up toward the eaves, where the camera Rick installed months earlier surely continues to run, recording everything.

The realization hits before we speak: Luke and I will be actors, now, starring in our own personal horror film. Except he doesn't know that yet. I swallow the irony and step delicately back around what used to be the check-in desk when the place was a hotel and give my head the slightest shake, willing my eyes to project fear.

I learned about movies from Cam and Rick.

Communicating subtly, I learned as a librarian.

I purse my lips and speak with my eyes, trying to telegraph this thought: *Something is wrong here. Please, please get it. The people behind me still think you're a cop. And them thinking that may be your and Quinn's only chance to get out of here.*

Luke opens his mouth, but I feign surprise that he's come, trying to make my voice as wooden as possible while not stumbling over my words. There's so much I want to say, but what comes out of my mouth is: "Hi, *Officer,* I was just in the back... What can I do for you tonight?"

His eyes refocus, some understanding washing across his features.

He gets it. Gets *something.* I don't know how, but he does.

Relief fills my lungs.

Luke coughs into his fist, blinks a few times. His chin dips, and when it rises, the side of his mouth becomes a smile. "Good evening, miss. I'm Officer, um, Landis, from the Islamorada Police Department. The light from your lamp there"—he points—"was visible from the street. Just stopping in and see how you're faring. Power's not on here? It looked like it's coming back on."

I can't say the lights are off because the place is being robbed, and I don't dare glance over my shoulder.

My gaze stays fixed on his eyes while my hand searches the desktop for a pen. I need to bullshit with him, keep him talking. "Things are, well, you know... Power is still spotty, I guess. I've got these lamps burning so I can see a few feet in front of my face." I force a clipped laugh. The tension in the room makes the air thick and warm.

I can feel them listening.

I ask, "How are things on the rest of the island?"

"Quiet, for sure. Almost creepy, I guess. No trick or treaters out this year, obviously. Probably the worst storm in two decades."

Am I imagining it, or is he speaking in a slightly southern accent? Luke, a ham?

"Ha, yeah, I guess. No time for kids to be strolling around. Everyone will maybe have to wait till next year."

He makes a slight movement with his chin, lifts his eyes toward the hallway, then returns them to my gaze.

I angle my body, so my back blocks the view of my hand from the hallway to the office and extend two fingers with my left hand.

There are two of them, I'm saying.

I wink at his belt, hoping he'll flash a gun.

He swivels his hips slightly, shows only a nightstick, then turns the other way to show a pair of handcuffs. "Yeah," he says. "You wouldn't believe some of the damage."

My fingertips sweep back and forth until they land on what I'd been looking for: a plastic, round cylinder with a sharp point. I turn the pen and cough as I click it open, then shuffle my hand around again, searching for something, anything, to write on.

His eyes track my movement, and he bends to retrieve a magazine that's blown onto the floor. He lays it on the desktop.

Southern Living.

Of course.

I shift the magazine in front of me. Writing a message is a risk, but I have to take it. Keep talking, the roll of my eyes tells him. The paper's edge slices into the pad of my index finger, but I hardly wince.

I write at an unnatural angle, my wrist too near my body. The effect is like writing left-handed while Luke rambles: "Tide's in quite a place tonight, the dark is making everything harder, for sure..."

I scribble:

A COP IS DEAD
QUINN UPSTAIRS GET HER OUT
FIRE ESCAPE
BLUE KEY

Luke continues his monologue, looks up and away, saying: "...Fishermen wait at those narrows for the tide to go out and then let the fish come to them. Catfish, sometimes, but sometimes grouper or sea bass . ."

"Sea bass?" I ask, reaching into my pocket, setting the keys beside what I've written.

He glances down. "Sure," he says. "I could take you sometime if you'd like?"

This is an especially nice touch.

I shrug as my fingertip taps the page, a blue vein pulsing on the top of my hand. "I don't know, I'm just down here for a while helping my family, and there's so much to do. But, really, thanks for stopping in."

He looks at the page quickly, then gives another short nod. "No problem at all. Well, if you're sure you don't need help with anything?"

His voice trembles slightly.

Hold it together, please.

"Not tonight," I say. "Just straightening up."

"Then guess I'll get back to the mess out there." He makes like he's tipping a cap before stepping out the door.

I wink, my voice becoming recklessly authentic. "Be careful," I tell him.

He smiles and closes the door firmly, then clicks on his flashlight and starts toward the road, the soles of his shoes slapping the stone steps along the path.

Only acting I've done since *Breathless.*

The best scene of my life.

I face the hallway, where my captors wait in the dark.

~

I've just learned that I was wrong about Luke lacking imagination. If I weren't so afraid, I'd smirk right now. I don't know *how* we just pulled off our little improv scene, but we did.

He was a natural.

But we can thank the academy and the foreign press later. Now I have to create as much distraction as possible and pray he finds his way up the fire escape.

One scene has ended for me, but another is just about to begin. I smell the lamp oil burning as I near the office. Back here, the air is still and feels thick with their anticipation. I need to remember my character and my lines. Colin and Audrey assumed I'd be acting, but Luke and I were acting *on top* of acting. Now, I have to transform back into someone who didn't know the man she'd been talking to. Someone that was *only* frightened and nervous that I wouldn't carry it off.

Audrey greets me at the office door. "He's gone?" she asks.

I brush past her, casually, like we're friends now. "Yeah, it was like you said, he saw the light from the road and is checking in with whoever is on the island."

Audrey glances in the direction of Dustin's body, her eyes seeming to calculate what police showing up means for her and Colin's plan. They mean to be in and out of here, leaving no connection between them and the Pinecrest. "So much for keeping the power off to not attract attention," she says to him. "Lamps are more subtle, right?"

Colin glares at her, the revolver beside him on the desk. He stands and picks up a lamp, then sets it on the floor beneath the wall safe. It casts an upward shadow, the dial a long, gray oval. "Okay, let's get this done," he tells me, then turns to Audrey. "Check to make sure the cop is really gone. Leave the other lamp here."

They stare at each other for a second before he says, "Go."

Audrey looks at me suspiciously before disappearing into the pitch-dark hallway. The tension between them makes me wonder how well they know each other, whether they're starting a new life together or using each other temporarily. But they trust each other, clearly; they know that at this point, one wrong step on either of their parts would land them both in jail.

Her footsteps quietly vanish on the damp hardwood. Colin leans behind me on my left, close enough to see my hands as I examine the safe. Part of me wants to study his face, to explore the features I thought belonged to Cam. There is so much I'd wish to ask him in a different world.

But here we are.

I wonder if Luke can find his way around the estate and up to the *Ibis* room and if he can manage that without being detected by Audrey.

Time. If he's going to have any chance, he needs a little time.

The safe's dial is grooved like the edge of a quarter and feels tacky from the humidity.

I'm completely sure I can open it, but Colin will know I'm stalling if I move too slowly. Rick could easily have changed the combination when he installed the cameras. He told me earlier he'd called the police that he thought he might have been robbed. Except *nothing was missing*, he'd said.

"Like I said, I've never done this before," I say.

Colin's silence is commanding.

I turn the dial randomly the first time, right, left, right, then pull on the lever, which doesn't budge. Of course. Could there be something valuable inside this thing? Maybe he and Audrey know more than they're letting on.

"Not that one," I say. "Sorry."

"Hurry," he says.

It's been two, maybe three minutes. I try to picture where Luke might be as I start another intentionally wrong combination.

"Why Marla?" I ask. "Because she wanted to stop the movie from being made? It wasn't Rick that nearly ran her off the road, was it? It was you. Those borrowed keys came in handy because you had one to the truck? Then, you left the box cutter on the seat to set up Rick since you didn't get to finish Marla right away."

"Just open the safe, Lexi," Colin barks. The way he's lived has jaded him, but in that instant, he sounds young, as if a kid in high school.

Not just young, *nervous*. I can feel him glaring at me from behind.

"You could talk to him, you know," I say. "I could help. We go to him now. He would want to know what you've been through. Rick would want to know..."

Colin picks the gun off the table and presses it to my neck. The rounded edge of the metal is cool against my skin. "Don't say his name one more time. I won't tell you again. Shut up and open the safe."

The interaction with Luke left me buzzed off too much confidence, but the feel of metal reminds me of the stakes. My legs wobble as if I've just been shoved to the very edge of a cliff.

Right here, right now, I could die.

Just like Dustin and Marla, and Cam.

"You're lucky I haven't taken you on a ride to the bay already. Too bad the tide's already out."

I spin the dial. Left, right, left.

I pull the lever.

It doesn't budge. I pray he can't tell I'm bluffing, buying time.

"He changed it, maybe. I don't know."

"You better hope not."

"I don't..."

Audrey appears. "I think he's gone."

"Good," Colin says. He makes a rolling movement with the gun. "Lexi. Open."

My hand shakes as I turn the dial through the numbers of Quinn's birthday: left, right, left. *Please.*

I pull the lever and feel the mechanism release. The safe door opens with a pop that sounds like a soda can's tab coming off.

Audrey claps her hands once. "Bingo."

The safe door swings slowly open.

⌒

There's just enough light for me to see a fraction of what's inside. I don't know what they are expecting, but there's only paper: a few neat, clipped stacks on top of a few manila envelopes.

"Move," Colin says, pushing past. "Stand in that corner, there."

The shadows look like the end of *The Blair Witch Project.* I do stand there but face outward, watching Colin withdraw the paper. Being aware that I'm no use to them now makes me shiver. His eagerness to examine the safe's contents was probably keeping me alive. Colin raises the lamp and peers inside to ensure he hasn't missed anything, then sets the stacks on the desktop and pulls up a chair.

Behind him, Audrey leans in, chewing her pinkie nail.

How much time has passed? Three more minutes, maybe. I fold my hands in front of my waist like I'm praying as his eyes move back and forth over the pages, his lips twitching as he focuses.

"Is that it?" Audrey whispers.

He doesn't answer.

Take your time, I think, half of me wondering what the hell he could be reading, the other half unable to care.

She leans forward like she means to ask again when he finally says, "Yeah."

The desk chair screeches as he pushes back. He grabs one of the lamps and strides purposefully down the hall. He never leaves earshot, but for a moment, it's just Audrey and me alone in the office. She avoids my gaze. I sense that's because of their plan for me. If it weren't for what was happening with Quinn and Luke, I'd be too terrified to think at all.

Colin reappears, and the lamp he's holding cuts a semicircle of light into the room. He won't look at me, now, either. Sweat beads at his temple, the front of his dark hair damp. He's holding the metal trashcan that was behind the front desk.

He sets down the lamp, lifts the glass cover, and touches the paper he'd been reading to the flame until it catches fire. The paper burning is yellower than the lamplight, and the sharp scent of the smoke burns my nostrils. He twists his wrist to accelerate the spread—happening so fast that, for a second, I think it will catch onto the walls—then drops the ashen paper into the trashcan, where the clamor of its landing seems softened by the flames. Audrey rests her hand on Colin's shoulder while he watches it smolder.

I imagine it blackening.

What *is* it? What would they want destroyed so quickly?

I wonder what will happen next when there's a loud, startling bang.

All three of our heads turn.

The sound came from beyond the lobby.

They have no idea what's happened, but I do.

Colin eyes me suspiciously. Without taking his gaze off me, he nudges the revolver across the desk toward Audrey. It heavily scrapes as she picks it up, her eyes uneasy.

"See what it is. Shoot whoever's there."

"No, look, you got what you wanted. You can't—" I lurch forward, but he steps in my way.

"*Go*," he says to her again, his hand closed into a fist.

She hesitates before grasping the handle of a lamp and leaving, the room dimming behind her.

I plead: "Listen, whatever happened before can be fixed. Just don't hurt her." I start again toward the door when he shoves me, hand to my chest, backward into the wall. No one's pushed me in two decades. If it weren't for the adrenaline in my blood, his physical power might have stunned me.

But I'll claw and bite him to get past. I don't care.

I need to get between Quinn and Audrey.

Adrenaline surges through my muscles, tensing them. My eyes search for the right angle to push past Colin and through the door.

Just as I take off, I hear Audrey scream.

Then a gunshot rings out.

Chapter NINETEEN

OCTOBER 31ST

The sound drains the hatred from Colin's eyes, like an angry mask being ripped off of a scared boy.

For one black instant, time freezes, and we're somewhere else: still in *Breathless*, maybe, or stumbling forward in the more recent past, all finding our way to this moment.

Maybe Rick is waking me up in the spare bedroom earlier that afternoon, saying,

It's just a movie. Everyone you saw, just actors having fun.

Marla is okay after all.

You can wake up, now—

Perhaps you're frustrated with me. That's a convention of horror. Perhaps you think I'm stupid to have run into this house tonight and that you would have done everything differently. But it was grief that made me start driving this morning. I couldn't take any more of it. Here I am with rope burns on my wrists, a baby inside me, praying Quinn and Luke got out alive.

I'm probably going to die in the next few minutes. You've heard that at the end, your life flashes before your eyes? After the gunshot, visions filled my brain, disjointed scenes from half-completed stories. In one, I'm a girl, skipping work at the marina, watching my future father-in-law make his film. I had a part in the movie, and I was killed on camera. Actors in costume, set assistants, and makeup artists taught me what was pretend and real.

Now, I'm a widow, thirty-eight years old, in another scene. My friends and I left this island years ago. Jessica is married now and has two kids of her own. Cassie is a news anchor on a regional TV station in Tampa. She got a measure of fame after all.

Cam was right: readers can be hard to please. But I can hardly tell what's real sometimes, myself.

Who knows what's just happened or how these psychopaths will try to get rid of us.

In this frozen moment, I think of the lamp oil jugs and know this estate may burn, and all I want is for Quinn and Luke to be safe. A gulf of silence washes over me in the wake of Audrey's scream. Colin grabs the lantern Audrey left and rushes away. Something's gone terribly wrong.

I follow at a distance, and my heart thumps as we sprint to the lobby, my eyes refocusing haphazardly in the shifting shadows. I smell the sharp scent of the oil burning as the amber shades grow and shrink with each swing of the lantern, crunching through the glass from the lantern cover I broke earlier.

Audrey lies on her back, eyes staring upward, blankly. A dark circle halos her head. Colin skids on his knees across the lobby floor. He cradles her head in his hands, his voice low, commanding her to speak, the tenderness between them evident enough for me to flash to wondering about their history, the depth of their connection. He may be a murderous monster, but not so villainous that he won't help his accomplice. He'd promised Audrey things. They'd created plans in the previous weeks, maybe months. She'd done her part and taken risks based on his assurances and on the future she wanted.

She'd trusted him.

But my gaze searches the space, tracing the trajectory of Audrey's fall and finding Luke's face, peering down between two slats of the balcony railing.

I run, taking the stairs two at a time, my shoes hardly seeming to touch down. Upstairs, the fire escape door stands open at the end of the hall. I imagine Quinn running out into the night.

Bang on the door until Rick's awake. Don't stop, baby. Go. Keep on, no matter what you hear happening behind you.

I pray the cottage still has power.

Luke lies beside the railing. In the lamplight, dark patches appear everywhere. I know what they are. I saw them years ago on docks after sharks were caught. So much blood is scattered, it's hard to comprehend. I don't know what I'm saying, but it's something like "oh my God" over and over.

As he rolls onto his back, I rush over and slip my hand beneath his head. He grasps at a patch of his uniform shirt that looks wet and glossy, black in the greasy light. Beside him is a large dark splotch on the floor. An ammonia smell reaches my nose. He's thrown up. I learned from a horror movie that it happens when someone is shot.

My heart feels gone. It feels like *ache*.

"We have to get you up, have to try to get out of here," I say, wiping his cheek with my sleeve.

The lamp wick is a twisting reflection in his dark eyes. His head shakes from the effort of keeping it off the floor as he says, "Quinn ran. The girl downstairs came just as we got to the back door, aiming the gun. I was trying to take it from her when it went off." His voice is weak but steady. He gestures behind him with his chin. "She stumbled, fell back as she pulled the trigger." He didn't see Audrey hit the lobby floor, I realize. He asks, "After she fell, did she…?"

"I don't know."

I look over the rail, where Colin leans over Audrey's body. I run to a bedroom and return with a pillowcase to press on his wound.

"I think the bullet went in and out. I felt it leave, I think."

"How did you even get down here? We have to get you to the hospital."

Luke sits up slightly, winces, exhales like he's whistling. "The roads are blocked off, so I took my boat. I fueled up and ran down the coast. The only trick was dodging the crab traps to not get one wound around my prop and keeping away from the Coast Guard. Their searchlights nearly hit me twice. I just wanted to get you and Quinn out."

I touch my hand to his chest. "What's this uniform?"

"You're the one…who suggested a costume," he says, smiling weakly. "I wanted to make sure if I were spotted, they'd assume I was police and let me go. You're really pregnant?" he asks.

The terrible timing just gets worse and worse, but I see us, Luke and me, our future. It's just a glimpse, a shining but a clear one, an arc bending over the agitated waves headed toward years to come.

I glance over the balcony, but I can't see Colin and Audrey now. I look at the fire escape, calculating the challenge of navigating the outside stairs in the dark.

I tug Luke's shirt. He sits up a little more.

"I know it hurts, but we've got to try to get down the back stairs. We've got to move, now."

It's then that I hear footsteps downstairs. Luke groans in my ear as I slide my neck under his arm, get my legs under me and try to stand.

"Lexi, I..."

"You've *got* to. There's no choice." If we can get into the dark, maybe we can get away. I know what it took for me to see anything on the way in. I can keep pressure on Luke's wound. We can wait for help, maybe find Rick, maybe flag down a car.

I straighten as Luke gets his legs under him, half supporting himself. His forehead brushes against mine, warm and wet like he's fevered. I angle us toward the rear exit.

Downstairs, the footsteps turn louder.

Closer now.

We move like two people tethered in a three-legged race. The hall's carpet runner feels quicksand-soft beneath my feet, seeming to drag us down.

We take another step. I can smell the warm, salt air blowing in through the open door.

Then, I hear a click.

It stops us, dead.

⌐

I don't have to turn to know it's a gun, less than ten feet away. Close enough that he could easily hit us. Light from Colin's lantern reaches forward in the hall, spilling past our feet and over our backs until our shadows land on the door we mean to exit. When I turn, Colin's face is distorted with emotion.

"You killed her," he says.

I realize in that instant he still believes Luke is a cop.

He raises the gun.

But there's a different light behind him now. Brighter than the lanterns.

I can already feel the warmth on my cheeks.

Downstairs, Colin has lit the place on fire.

When you're on a boat, fire is a worst-case scenario. Don taught me that from his time onboard an aircraft carrier. The protocol is this: Every sailor drops what they're doing and mobilizes to put it out—all hands on deck. Extinguish the flames. The mission detours and becomes extremely simple. Otherwise, everyone aboard risks either burning alive or drowning at sea.

This is worse.

The difference now is that this fire won't be extinguished.

Colin set it on purpose.

Just like the angry locals did to this place years ago.

Already, I can smell the smoke: it's pure pine, the gray sweetness of a teenage bonfire.

But it is growing rapidly now—out of control.

Colin's aim has an almost propulsive force. It seems to push Luke and me back from the hallway into a bedroom. The heave of Luke's breathing warms my neck.

I know where we've backed into immediately, which room, despite all the adrenaline and panic.

I know this room.

I was stabbed to death here, twenty-five years ago.

Except now there are no cameras, no emerald-green nightgown. No friends are waiting for me at the beach, and Colin isn't holding a spring-loaded hunting knife. As Mia Farrow screamed, *This isn't a dream.* *This is really happening.* Light from the fire enters the hall. I picture it spreading across the wood downstairs. I imagine the way the documents from the safe blackened. The whole estate will look like that soon.

Colin aims the gun, meaning to finish us.

"Don't!" I yell. "You don't have to!"

I think I might stumble backward, look up in terror, reach for the old telephone, just like I did when I was acting.

But like Casey, I still have the ferocity of a startled animal. I square my shoulders. I know how to fight. Maybe I learned not to give up right here in this room. I want to swing my fist and send Colin tumbling into the closet, where he'll break some of the wooden slats in his fall.

I have to save us, and somehow, I have to get us out of this room.

Colin closes his left eye. The gun leveled at us.

I step in front of Luke, just as the windows fill with blue flashing light.

A siren begins to wail.

⌒

I realize immediately what the police coming means.

Quinn made it.

To somewhere safe, most likely Rick's. She found someone with an operating phone and made the call.

The relief of knowing that nearly brings me to tears.

Colin rushes to the window, where the blue light flashes on his smooth cheeks and in his damp eyes. He almost pulls the trigger anyway, right then.

Almost kills us both.

I can feel his desire in the reluctant way he lowers his gun.

He's killed before.

Multiple times.

And he would have done it again—to two people willing to talk and give away his risky scheme—then burn everything and everyone behind him and disappear back into the ghostly night. But now he wonders if he's missed his opportunity, if the police are close enough to hear the gunshots, maybe even to see a muzzle flash through the broken windows. Colin wants us gone, but a clock is ticking.

He couldn't save Audrey.

But now's his only chance to save himself.

He blinks.

He might have made it out in the ambulance if he was already there. He looks over his shoulder, estimating the angle of the driveway to the main road. The space between his path to a vehicle and where the lights are coming from begins to close. Rapidly.

Now there's no way Colin would ever let us live.

His only hope is to run.

And we've seen him.

We'd tell everything.

He points the gun at Luke. "You, your car—"

"—boat," Luke says. "I drove a boat here."

"Gimme the keys." Colin practically lunges for Luke's pocket, but Luke angles his body away.

In that second, I realize the way out. Is that how plans come together? In instants?

Because I already know what I'm going to do. Colin gave me the idea.

A year ago, without knowing it.

I grab for his wrist. "You're going to drive yourself out in the bay? Find the channel in the dark? You won't make it past the harbor. There's no moon. You'll crack the hull in the rocks, and they'll follow the running lights right to you."

His eyes shift between Luke and me. Awareness washes over him. He's almost got it.

He'd had a thought about getting out on the boat but can't do it. He knows I'm right. *You may as well light another flare*, I almost say, *and show the police the way you're leaving. But without light, you'll end up circling the mangroves or stuck in the rocks, trying to find a path to open water.*

He knows he's trapped himself and stops pointing the gun at Luke. He does what I want him to.

He aims it directly at me.

"You'll drive us out," he says.

Done. I hide the glint of satisfaction in my eyes.

The place is surrounded and burning, and I'm the only one of the three of us who knows the waterways.

I turn Luke toward the back stairs and start to walk. "Then we're all three going."

If this were a game of chess, I would have just put him in check. Now, he has to move to not lose the game, and there's only one move he can make. I *am* his only chance out of here now. Colin's thinking like me, making up his plan as he goes along. He can't consider destroying any evidence he's left here or what his life would be like as a wanted fugitive, living on the run indefinitely.

Or maybe he has, I wonder in an instant. Maybe that's how he's lived his life up until this point.

His hesitation is just a stutter step. There's no time to think this through.

This is immediacy: run or face the police. Die or live.

The blue lights brighten.

～

"Fine," Colin says. "Hurry."

I pull the keys from Luke's pocket as we make our way down to the dock.

I know I wouldn't have the courage to try this if Quinn hadn't run. Because with Colin, I'm dealing with an unknown quantity: a person impulsive enough to be violent but planful and strategic. Except now, all his plans are ruined. I'd take my chances if it were just he and I, but I know what Colin wants: no witnesses. If we'd left Luke in the estate, Colin would have shot him, point-blank. I see the silhouette of Luke's boat tied against the dock. Just a ghost, really, an outline of a canopy and hull. Beside it is Rick's *Pursuit*, still suspended above the water, just secure enough to stay in place.

I touch my wrists.

"You're who tied up that boat before the storm, aren't you?" I ask.

He's looking over his shoulder as he answers, "So?"

There's no time to figure out why.

"Come on," Colin says, rushing us. Luke staggers through the grass. I can see the shadow of his boat rocking against the dock—Luke hadn't tied it off well, and the wind has picked up just slightly.

Luke winces as we climb on. He can barely raise his leg to get onto the bow. He bites his lip, stifling a yell from the pain but manages to get aboard, somehow. I'll have to cut the running lights and keep them off while I find our way out of the harbor, otherwise what I've told Colin will turn true: the police will follow the light directly to us. And I can't let that happen. I've talked a big game, but it won't be easy even for me, who knows these channels from rote memory. I can't let them find us...yet.

I sit Luke beside the wheel and start the engine. I kill the lights immediately and untie us as Colin stands at the bow, watching the lights approach the driveway. "Let's go, let's go," he says. He makes the same hurried, rolling motion with his hand that he did before. "We're headed south."

Key West, I think, where he can disappear into the mix. What was it Captain Tony said about the place? *Key West is an insane asylum. We're just too lazy to put up walls.* From there, Colin probably figures he could buy a ride even farther south, then wait a while until the investigation is over and everything calms down. Then he plans to reappear, Rick Plummer's heir.

He can still do it, I realize. His accomplice is dead, and he probably kept out of Quinn's view or could take care of her later. He plans on never letting Luke and me off this boat. Once we're in open water, he'll have no need for my guidance skills.

The salt smell of the bay carries in on the breeze. I can see the flames have spread through most of the downstairs through the non-boarded parts of the first-floor windows. The absolute darkness of fifteen minutes earlier seems like part of a dream. The fire gives off enough light that I can see the controls that aren't lit, the edge of the dock, the gleam of the silver steering wheel. The first channel green marker reflects the firelight a hundred feet out.

I shift the boat into reverse as Colin unties the bow and pushes us off with his foot. I help Luke onto the seat beside me and cut the wheel, backing us into the harbor. Colin keeps looking between the estate and us, and for good reason: more police vehicles have arrived. He knows he's taken the only possible way out. Any chance he'd had of driving off smoothly in the ambulance is gone. It was a clever escape strategy, but this makes for a suitable Plan B.

I shift gears and start toward the channel. Colin holds the gun beside him, and from the corner of my eye, I can see the barrel bobbing slightly from the waves.

I haven't been behind the wheel of a boat in years, but everything is the same: *trim* and *light* controls exactly what I expect. The growl of the engine and the slight smell of gas wafts over us. Luke uses this boat to guide, so the controls feel pleasantly broken in. I was right about the tide being out and about the darkness. If it weren't for the fire, I wouldn't be able to see twenty feet past the bow, but I can see where the edge of the waves hits the mangroves. The fire must be doing something else, too, I realize: masking the sound of the twin outboards on Luke's boat. Even running on idle, their rumble would be audible at this distance.

The water is low as we pass into the channel. I sense where the water laps against the marker's beams. The second Colin looks away, I lean to Luke and whisper, "I need your belt. And those handcuffs."

My eyes are on Colin making sure he can't hear, but the sound of my voice is swallowed by the engines and the lapping of the waves. Luke wobbles and nods, unsure of what I'm planning but too drained to question it. He winces as he reaches behind his back and undoes the cuffs, and holds them between his legs. Then he starts undoing the belt.

I know I'll have to time my next moves perfectly.

I pass the second marker on the left, a few feet away from our port side, then bear toward the next. There isn't much time now. I have maybe two, three minutes.

Colin moves to the other side of the bow, looking starboard, trying to see the bay.

He can't.

He doesn't know where we are, but I do.

If I didn't know this Key by heart, I'd be as lost, too. It doesn't matter what year it is. This place is inside me. Waves slap the hull with enough force that we rock up every few seconds. I cut the wheel subtly with each one.

I squeeze Luke's shoulder. The waves knocking must hurt, I know, because to stay upright, his stomach has to remain tense.

What's about to happen is going to hurt even worse.

"We'll be okay," I whisper to him.

Our eyes meet in the near-absolute dark. Only the orange of the distant flames reflect.

Behind us, the fire rises. I can see it's already spread to the second floor when I look back. I picture it all crackling, smoldering: the woodwork, the bedspreads, the open fireproof safe. I whisper again, "Just a little farther, okay?"

"Stop talking," Colin spits, pointing the gun at me as a reminder.

Cam, I know what happened now.

Is Colin planning to shoot us both? Just push us over the side? How far does he think we need to be away from shore before he executes that part of his half-plan?

We both know he needs me for at least another hundred yards.

I cut the wheel slightly on the next wave. I pluck the handcuffs from between Luke's knees when he looks away again. I lean behind him and latch one cuff around the seat's sidebar and the other through one of Luke's empty belt loops. I'm close enough to his cheek that I can feel the warmth of his feverish reaction to the gunshot.

Colin's seen me. He takes a step toward the stern. Gun pointed directly at me. "The hell are you doing?"

I lean forward and point to the next marker as we pass.

He turns to look as we glide past like ghosts.

When he does, I grab Luke's belt.

"Hang on," I tell him. Then, I hit the throttle suddenly enough that the jolt knocks Colin to his knees.

We're at twenty knots, thirty knots, forty...

Twin outboards, this boat can move.

I never thought I would recreate the worst boat accident I ever responded to.

Colin grasps hold of the rail, struggles upward, and stands. He waves the gun around wildly, then shoots, aimed upward, the muzzle flash like a star exploding in the dark, but when we hit another wave, his legs buckle.

The boat continues to accelerate. I look over and over at the shore, judging the angle against the tide. I want to hit head-on, so the hull tips as little as possible.

I drop to the seat and wrap Luke's belt around the seat's base, buckling it over my waist.

Luke grabs my hand.

Colin aims the gun at me.

I close my eyes.

⌁

The sandbar is exactly where I'd expected it to be when I closed my eyes. We hit it violently. The impact on the hull brings the bow forward and tips us slightly starboard. I couldn't have done it better if I'd practiced a hundred times. We dig straight into the ground, stopping like I'd yanked an emergency brake. I jolt forward, my jaw knocking against the console, sharp pain ripping through the side of my face, my neck. I feel Luke tense beside me and hear him shout from the pain, our hands wrapped together.

The engine props are whirling chaotically. Saltwater sprays up and around, and I can taste it on my tongue. I look over the bow, everything blurry in my watering eyes, tilted at a disorienting angle against the straight horizon.

Colin is gone now.

I know where he is, at least approximately: a hundred or so feet in front of us.

The angle the boat has stopped leans me against Luke. I undo his belt and fall forward, touching his face, his hair. "Are you okay?" I ask.

His eyes are open. He's blinking the salt out of them.

"I love you," I say. "I'm going to find a way to try to get help."

I climb to the bow, where I see a shape on the horizon. I wonder for just a second if it's Colin, moving, still holding a gun, when a searchlight appears, sweeping the surface of the water. Engines, much larger than this boat's, rumble deeply.

When the light sweeps again, it passes over the Coast Guard orange beneath it.

It will find us in a few seconds.

Later, it will find Colin floating, faceup in the shallow water.

EPILOGUE

ONE YEAR LATER

It's dusk, and Luke and I are in bed. I'm in the state of half dream, half thought, remembering the fire, just now, the orange flames from the estate rising over the choppy bay.

After Luke was loaded onto a Coast Guard boat, I clutched at my arms, standing knee-deep in the cool October water, watching the autumn colors reach the clouds as blue flashes spread over the ground.

I was happy to watch the estate burn, I admit.

Fire, the ultimate transformer.

Some days, my jaw still hurts from where I hit the boat rail. I can feel the repair when I run my tongue over my two new teeth, but if I look at them in the mirror, I can't see anything different about them.

Now a scream that could only be described as "bloodcurdling" rises from downstairs. In college, I read about how mothers can discern different varietals of their children's cries: frustration, anger, pain.

This one, I recognize immediately: it's hunger.

Luke stirs in the bed beside me, mumbles into his pillow, "I'll go. I'll go. Stay in the covers." He stands and stretches, his hair misshapen by the pillow he'd been resting on. The sky outside is burnt orange from the encroaching dusk.

I can't help but smile. "It's not time for me to be sleeping all day. I have to get up anyway."

Simon cries again, almost comically loud, his voice carrying over the hardwood floors of the house we moved into last February. Luke insisted on using a baby monitor, and the effect is something like hearing Simon in stereo. I'd assured Luke we wouldn't sleep through Simon waking up, but he has the overeager attentiveness of a first-time parent. "Coming, coming," he says in Simon's direction, scratching the back of his head. "He's been down for what? Like ten minutes?"

"Something like that." I reach over to turn the monitor's volume down and toss Luke his T-shirt, which he must have taken off before lying down. I catch a glimpse of his tan back as he trots down the stairs and the star-shaped scar from the bullet that went through his side. Above it, I know, is the corded line of scar tissue from the emergency surgery he underwent in Miami the day after the boat accident.

I sometimes lose track of what time it is and even what day of the week we're on.

Other times, I seem to misplace the year.

I'm a new mom again, eighteen years later. Love fills my heart in ways I would never have guessed were possible.

We'd fallen asleep, Luke and I, after putting Simon down for a nap that extended for how long? The green numbers on the clock at my bedside tell me it's nearly 7 p.m.

Quinn will be home soon, I think.

She elected to start college at the nearby state school but moved into a freshman dorm to have a traditional college experience. After the tumultuousness of the last two years, she wanted the security of staying near home, which I didn't discourage. And she wanted to be involved in Simon's life, which I love.

I slide my legs off the bed and stand. I stretch, too. The house is decorated in modern-newborn. Clothes are piled on end tables. *Some of them are folded.* Plush toys, many of which squeak, are strewn over pastel mats. Getting used to the new house, living with Luke and the baby has been an adjustment over the last year, to say the least. Sometimes, my head swims from all the change. And sometimes, I wonder how we all got here.

But mostly, I feel grateful that we're each fully intact.

We *survived.*

There's a sense of naturalness about what Luke and I have started, the feeling that we're in the right place at the right time, doing what we should be.

Cam, I know, would approve. I'm sure of it. He'd even refrain from making analogies to movie plots or discussing their lessons about life.

I try not to think about last October. I can't help but be reminded of it by the slightly cooler weather, the parade of kids in costumes, and the weather forecasts about hurricane trajectories. I'll probably never trust plotted courses tracking storms or their probability cones again.

I've put in my fair share of counseling sessions.

So has Luke. The gun was in his hands, after all, when it went off. In the flash that followed, he saw Audrey's expression when she started to fall.

Halloween itself looks different now, too. I still enjoy seeing kids dressed up, but I'm finished with violence and gore. If I never see another skeleton dangling from a tree or a decoration tombstone in a front yard, that's fine with me. Until people experience what we did, those adornments seem playful, like the campier parts of horror movies, approaching fear with a smile while keeping it safely at bay.

Soon, kids wearing costumes will arrive, with bags extended to collect their loot. I anticipate a number of Marvel superheroes this year: Spider-Man, Thor, Black Widow.

I'm ready.

Beside the front door is a wooden salad bowl I've filled with Luke's and my favorites: Snickers and Peanut M&Ms, respectively. I know I can take whatever we don't eat to the school library, where the kids there will devour it with the feverish and dreamy carelessness of teenagers.

I haven't seen ads for *Breathless* on television this year. Maybe a different horror movie has cycled into the rotation. Luke suspects that last year's events at the Pinecrest picked up enough media attention that the networks want a breather before featuring the film again.

Maybe he's right. Whatever the reason is, I'm happy for no unanticipated glimpses of my own terrified eyes and for not hearing a younger version of myself scream from a TV speaker across the room. It feels like the current carried it farther away like it went out on the tide.

Maybe that film has been seen enough, at least for now.

The film was part of our family story for a while, a beginning.

Then, it haunted us.

Now, it feels like a story we escaped.

I'm fine if I never see *Breathless* again.

People can stop a movie any time they like, pause a screen, stride out of a theater.

They like the sense of control over fear.

Not that Rick helped matters. Of course, he finished the sequel, albeit at a different location. In the final cut, he even left in Quinn's part as a cameo, which I didn't protest too vehemently. She watched it with her friends when it came out.

One film I'll never see.

As I descend the stairs, I hear the dishwasher change cycles. It's always running with a baby in the house. It's the same with the laundry. There's always so much to do. I haven't been this tired in a while, but I also know how quickly this time goes.

Next thing you know, your kid is in college.

My phone chirps on the kitchen counter, and I assume it's Quinn calling. Maybe she's stopped to pick up something to eat or got caught up in a conversation with one of her new friends. But when I turn it over, I see it's Rick. I smile despite myself. We're closer than we've ever been, but sometimes just as conflicted. He sold the land the Pinecrest was on, and as far as he knows, the new owners have no plans to rebuild.

"I thought I'd call to see how everyone is doing," he says. "Getting any sleep?"

I cradle the phone between my shoulder and ear as I navigate the kitchen island. "We just woke up, believe it or not. Simon's still figuring out the difference between day and night." I hear the jostling of road noise in the background, a car horn honking, and I ask: "Are you in the car?"

"I'm leaving Starke just now. I went up for a visit."

Colin will likely never leave prison. It's a relief to me, but I know better than to bring it up. Rick's not coy about visiting Colin, aware the topic isn't my favorite. Not that I can blame him for wanting to see his son, even if that son had planned to kill him, and us, too.

In the last year, Luke had helped me process how to think about Colin, patching together information we learned through the police investigation. "Before we crossed paths, Colin had spent two years in jail for aggravated larceny, where he learned how to scheme. He was full of resentment, cast aside by a father who wanted nothing to do with him. At least, that was what his mother had told him while he was growing up. Colin thought he was finally going to get what he deserved."

"I guess it makes sense that after Colin felt locked out of Rick's life for so long, he would find it pretty satisfying to destroy Rick's actual will," I said to Luke later.

"He knew you could open the safe because he'd been through Rick's text messages the night of the break-in. I guess he thought the timing was perfect," Luke said.

I thought back to all of Rick's messages after Cam had passed the previous year, him amending his will and where he would store it. He'd said he wanted to make sure Quinn and I were taken care of. He didn't trust lawyers, so there were no copies.

"The idea of inheriting Rick's wealth, the land, even the fancy boat was too tempting. When the hurricane changed directions, he knew it was his chance to make anything that went missing look like a burglary. He'd planned to try to steal the safe, to make it look like looting after the storm. When you came to the Keys, he figured you could just open it for him. That way, he would know the original will was destroyed." Luke had done some research. "In the state of Florida, when a person dies without a will, proof of paternity is enough to make a claim on their estate. The fewer other heirs, the better."

Still, I struggle to understand Rick's perspective. I struggle to understand how he can speak to someone who killed his *other* son. Colin's mother had told Rick that Colin was his son twenty-five years earlier, during the filming of *Breathless*. The day I took my part, he was rattled by the news. Why hadn't he believed June? At least enough to meet Colin? His decision not to believe June is something *he* has to live with now. The thought of who else Colin had been willing to kill had sent a chill through me: Rick, eventually.

But first: me.

And Quinn.

This is the man Rick visits in prison.

I don't judge Rick for visiting Colin, for trying to have a relationship now. Maybe Rick knows he isn't blameless, either. Maybe he knows he should have handled the relationship with Colin's mother differently.

Despite everything, Colin is Rick's only living child. I can't imagine what starting that relationship was like for Rick. For them both. I believe he didn't know about Colin. The Rick I know wouldn't have turned his back on one of his kids. Even after his and Cam's falling out, it was Cam that kept the distance between them.

Colin finally gets to know the father he thought had forsaken him. This was a son who had broken into his estate to collect a DNA sample to prove paternity. I can't help but wonder about what would have happened if he'd never killed Marla. Marla evidently told Dustin enough about spending the night inside the Sea Shell Café that he became suspicious. In a report that was found later, he noted that he'd "been to the Sea Shell numerous times over the years and never knew an employee named Audrey."

Her story about shutting down the production of Breathless 2 may not have been believable to Rick but concerned Audrey and Colin enough that they decided they needed to stop her from going forward. They knew that there would be far less for Colin to inherit if Rick sunk his own money into the film and it cratered. Audrey had invited Marla to the café to keep her on the island until Colin could get to her. Audrey drugged Marla's rum, then left her in her car to awake in the morning.

After seeing an ambulance in the estate's driveway, Dustin was curious enough to investigate. It was then that he met Colin, who took his life.

It aches to know that if Dustin hadn't gone to the estate, he would still be alive today.

Their deaths were so senseless.

On the phone, I ask Rick, "You're okay?"

"As well as can be expected. I want to be present for him, even if it's from a distance. He's taking a few college courses now." There's a pause in our conversation.

I hear the fatigue in his voice. I know Rick's conflicted about his relationship with Colin and that feeling drains him, particularly after visiting. Details about that night last year and Colin and Audrey's lives came out in the weeks afterward. Everything Audrey told me in the coffee shop that morning was true: She'd moved to the Keys from Cincinnati, met a man who was very protective of her, who was also a talented artist. They planned to move away together when they had enough money saved. When Colin told her the plan, she went along with it.

It was what cost her her life.

I'm still trying to process what Colin confessed to after being arrested. I was surprised he was so open when I read a transcript of his interview, but I figured he knew he would be in jail indefinitely. He must have figured: what would it hurt to tell the whole story? When I read the words on the page, I heard them in his voice from that night at the Pinecrest, the voice I first heard with my face covered. At that time, he and Audrey still thought they could get away under the cloak of the storm's chaos and the general insanity of the Keys.

He'd been on the set of *Breathless*, too.

Marla had seen him hiding, playing in the shadows.

"Do you remember seeing a little boy on the set?"

Of course, June had let him go there. She'd even encouraged his "mischief" out of spite. When the detective who debriefed me told me Colin had admitted to setting the boat fire that killed the actor, I grabbed the chair nearest me to keep from falling. I felt my eyes close briefly.

Not four people dead.

Five, including Audrey.

"Colin said on tape that he didn't know what would happen when he lit the bilge," the detective told me. "He'd been playing with fire for years. Then he went to juvie three years later for theft, and get this, for starting a fire that burned the field behind his school. He was remorseful about it if that means anything."

Of course, it meant something. It means everything. It means Colin had a conscience, at least at one point in his life. It means he was a scared little boy at the time of the explosion and was probably even more scared after. I imagine him running, running, running back to his mother, keeping the secret of what he'd done all those years. I hate how much pain and hurt he must have endured that brought him to plan what he had.

The thing I don't know, what I'm not sure if I'll ever know, is whether or not I can forgive him.

I don't think I can.

That explosion put a tightness in my chest—and many people's, too, I'm sure—that never quite loosened. There's a book in the school library about trauma called *The Body Keeps the Score* that I've been reading to help process what's happened.

I don't know if I'll ever find acceptance, but I'm gaining clarity, little by little.

My heart stored everything that happened at the Pinecrest.

Everything.

The detective told me, "Colin moved around after he finished high school, eventually made his way back to Miami where he went to EMT school, then came back to the Keys. His mother told him Rick wanted nothing to do with him, that he'd told her to stay away from him. He'd been planning to find a way to get to his father's estate for years."

I carry the phone with me through the hall, into Simon's bedroom, where the walls are grass green, and animal shapes are everywhere. A mobile with plush stars and rockets dangles over his crib—Luke coos to soothe our son.

I see headlights cut across the driveway from the window, then darken. I recognize Quinn's car. She steps out, and there's a soft creak as she closes the door. I hear the crunch of shell gravel under her shoes as she makes her way toward the front door.

I tell Rick, "Quinn's just getting here. Will you come visit us soon?"

I hear the front door open and picture her kicking off her sandals by the door. Quinn calls out to announce herself: "Hey guys, ready or not, here I come. I want to see my baby brother."

"That's a plan," Rick tells me. "Oh, one other thing before I let you go, I wanted to share a little news."

Quinn strides into the bedroom, taking Simon from Luke's arms and bouncing him on her hip. She's cut her hair shorter than it was this time last year and is wearing a sea-blue T-shirt with the logo of her college across the front.

Around us, the shadows deepen as the sun sets.

"News?" I ask.

"It's about Cam's book, the horror survival manual. You remember the film rights sold? I learned today that one of the studios is going forward with adapting it into a film."

I can't help but smile.

I can imagine the smile on Rick's face, the soft, gray stubble of his beard.

Cam would have been thrilled, I know, but he also would have rolled his eyes. He'd wanted to be a novelist, after all, and always wrestled with his life being separate from the movies Rick made.

But I know he would have enjoyed seeing what became of his book.

I tell Rick the news is wonderful, and it is.

It fills my heart in that instant.

And I think, just then: isn't that a perfect ending?

Reading Group Guide

1. Horror movies play a pivotal role in the story. Are you a horror movie fan? If so, what's your favorite and why?

2. In the prologue, the narrator mentions Rick's movies giving "a promise of fear." Why do you think people are drawn to horror as a genre and this promise of fear?

3. Imagine you were Quinn right before the hurricane was due to hit the Keys. How would you feel? Have you ever had to make a natural disaster plan? If you had to quickly evacuate, what three things would you bring with you?

4. What do you make of Lexi's connection with her husband, Cam? What role does he play over the course of the story?

5. If you had the opportunity, would you star in a horror movie like Lexi? What role would you want to play? How do you think you'd feel seeing yourself get killed on screen?

6. What do you make of Rick Plummer's methods for capturing his

actors' "true, authentic fear"? Do you think they are effective? Do you think they are warranted?

7. Why do you think the Pinecrest was chosen as the set of Rick's most famous horror movie? Would you like to spend a vacation there, even after knowing about the Pinecrest curse? What movie set would you love to visit?

8. What do you make of the relationship between Lexi and Marla Moretti? Do you think Marla was treated fairly by Rick and the other characters in the story?

9. Do you see any parallels between iconic horror tropes and *Always the First to Die*? Which can you name?

10. What do you make of Rick's relationships with his family members after the story comes to end?

A Conversation with the Author

This novel has such a gripping, slasher edge. What was your inspiration?

I have fond memories of watching the campy horror films of the '80s late at night on HBO, usually while clutching a pillow to my chest and then feeling delightfully nervous afterward while in a dark hallway or watching shadows outside my window. At that time, horror felt edgy enough to be intriguing while still being fun to watch. I've always been interested in filmmaking; in high school, I watched some of my friends actually make a movie. The result was never going to be nominated for an Academy Award, but the process of making it was incredible, as was the "world premiere" party when it was complete. My subconscious probably worked these elements together as I was brainstorming plot ideas for this book. I wanted the setting to be near where I grew up, so when I put everything together, *Always the First to Die* found its groove. Besides, Florida is the perfect place to make a horror movie.

Are you yourself a horror fan? What are your favorite horror movie recommendations?

One thing I learned while researching this book is that there are horror fans, and then there are *horror fans*. Truthfully, I enjoy the suspense elements of horror much more that the CGI effects. A college professor of mine was actually on the set of *The Texas Chainsaw Massacre* and screened the film for our class. Before dimming the lights, he warned everyone that the film was gruesome, but he assured us the cast and crew had a wonderful time on the set and sometimes cracked up seconds after the director said, "Cut." This idea stuck in my head for years and partially inspired the writing of this book. I remember the same professor saying that if used correctly, a shadow moving under a door could create tremendous suspense. His class really made me see movies—especially horror movies—as effective and evocative art.

You're based in Nashville, but the story is primarily set in the Florida Keys. Why that location?

Aside from having a tremendous natural beauty, Florida's regions are culturally unique. The Keys have a colorful mystique that drew me in as a kid growing up in Southwest Florida. They seemed like a place that tolerated and welcomed eccentric characters and where anything might happen. Tourist culture presents a lot of opportunities for a mystery writer, where visitors' coming and going creates ways for characters to disappear and maybe even reappear. More than a setting for this book, I think of the Keys as a dynamic character that moves the story forward. A friend who helped me while I was researching the book started her email to me by saying: "Any information below is either true or something I was told to be true by a drunk in a bar, which means, by Key West standards, it's factual."

There are so many great twists to this one! When you're writing a thriller, what does your process look like?

My writing process keeps changing. I start with an outline so I can keep the larger story in mind, but as I work, the plot inevitably gets refined. Finding time to write is easily the biggest challenge. Sometimes, I have to write whatever or wherever I can and take advantage of free moments. There was an evening a few years ago when I used the Notes app on my iPhone to write in the hallway of my daughter's middle school while she was cheerleading. Usually the best times for my writing are early in the morning or in the evenings, when my kids do their homework. On those nights, it's like we each find a quiet space to do our own "homework." I try to stay disciplined about getting *something* accomplished, even if it's a small step that day.

How did the story evolve over the course of your writing?

Evolve is the perfect word for how my stories develop. I'm asked a lot about whether I outline at the beginning of writing a book. I'm definitely a planner. I like having a sense of how each character's motivation and the plot points work together to drive everything forward. That said, the more time I spend with each character, the better I get to know them. Sometimes, those relationships deepen, and I realize they would approach situations differently than I'd first considered.

The length of a novel also distorts proportions of the story for me, too, because I can only work on a few pages at a time. Sometimes the parts seem disjointed or repetitive in ways that need to be fixed. Dialogue can be streamlined, and sometimes scenes can be combined in interesting ways.

Also, not all ideas translate onto the page. In the first draft of my second book, *Somewhere in the Dark*, the main character, Jessie Duval, is visited in her prison cell by the ghost of Waylon Jennings. I loved this part, but earlier beta readers thought it was just too far out there. As cool as I thought the idea was, I had to keep the bigger picture in mind and not let that scene become a distraction from the story.

With such a tight cast stranded on an island, there are so many fantastic character moments here. Which character was your favorite to write?

I probably relate most to Lexi's character because my kids are teenagers, and I know how driven I'd be to ensure their safety in an emergency. Rick's character was the most fun to write because he's so ambitious and has such a strong vision for what he's trying to create. It's fun to watch someone's relentless pursuit of their dream, and I understand being willing to have an unbalanced life to find out what your limits are.

Readers sometimes ask me what happened to the characters after the story ended. I think that's a good sign—they're attached enough that they want to know! I feel that way all the time as a psychologist—some patients stop therapy before a conflict is fully resolved, and I end up wondering what their next chapters were.

If you had an opportunity to be cast in a horror movie, would you take it? What role would you want to play?

Definitely. Without question. And I'd ask to play the villain. They always get the most memorable lines.

What's your biggest bit of advice for aspiring writers?

Don't get discouraged, try to stay positive, and find a group of other writers to talk with, even if you don't critique each other's work. Take feedback from editors seriously but not personally—they're trying to help. And keep writing—all first drafts have to do is exist. You can fix your mistakes later. In fact, "fixing" mistakes will ignite your imagination, and you'll see fresh opportunities to improve the story.

Be gracious. The people you encounter also have dreams and are working hard. Politeness and timeliness go an incredibly long way.

One of the most challenging parts is multitasking; some time is spent on writing, some on editing, and some on promotion. I enjoy focusing on the actual writing part, as I think most authors do, but a book's success takes more than that. You have to keep putting yourself out there.

Who are your author inspirations? Any books we should be adding to our reading lists?

Most of the books I read aren't in the mystery/thriller genre, which surprises some people. I'm a big fan of Sally Rooney's books. Same with Jonathan Franzen. I think they will both be taught in English classes years from now.

There are a lot of conventions in mysteries and thrillers, so I'm impressed when one tells a story in a fresh way without being confusing. Ruth Ware always hits the mark for me, as does Peter Swanson. Their books are exceptionally well-paced, and the writing is so clean.

When I'm in a reading rut, I turn to memoirs to get me out—the more salacious, the better. Rick Ross's is excellent.

What're you working on next?

I'm hard at work on a thriller set in a university psychology department where grad students run an experiment on deception and one ends up dead. I spent a lot of time in departmental offices and labs all through college and graduate school (I even acted as a confederate in a social psychology experiment as an undergrad), so the setting is fun to revisit. Psychological research has its own specialized language and equipment (one-way mirrors for observation) that can create some interesting dynamics. I'm hoping to stay true to academic culture and research procedures while telling a twisty, fast-paced story and promising fresh, authentic dark academia vibes.

Acknowledgments

A great many thanks to my family for their patience as I worked on this book. I truly could not have done it without each of you.

I'm deeply grateful to have worked with MJ Johnston. Your insights, suggestions, and diligent work on this book made it what it is. I cannot thank you enough.

Many thanks to my fantastic agent, Rachel Ekstrom Courage, for your support and thoughtful guidance on this journey.

Much gratitude to my friends whose names I borrowed for the story. The characters bear no resemblance to real life; you're each too gracious and wonderful to be imagined.

About the Author

© Jason Myers

R. J. Jacobs has practiced as a psychologist since 2003. He maintains a private practice in Nashville, focusing on a wide variety of clinical concerns. After completing a post-doctoral residency at Vanderbilt, he has taught Abnormal Psychology, presented at numerous conferences, and routinely performs PTSD evaluations for veterans. He's the author of *And Then You Were Gone* and *Somewhere in the Dark*, published by Crooked Lane. Find out more at rjjacobsauthor.com.